CRIMSON WINTER

GIDEON WOLF BOOK 3

ERNEST DEMPSEY

138 PUBLISHING

For my friend, Becky from the Brew Crew. Love you.

JOIN THE PACK

You'll get VIP member-only discounts on new releases and preorders, exclusive content, contests, giveaways, and updates on upcoming projects. It's all FREE.

Join here: http://bit.ly/3of3007

CRIMSON WINTER

As the light fades and evening calls,
    Winter's chill awakens.
    The shadows creep and darkness falls
    For righteous and forsaken.
    Over the river all must cross.
    The ferryman awaits.
    The hand I am and vengeance lost
    For those who tempt the fates.
    Beware the mist with watchful eyes.
    Pray tell your heart won't fail,
    That evil dwells not inside,
    And hear the winter's wails.

1

I should have known something like this would happen. One second, I'm driving a rental car down a country road toward Santa Rojo. The next, I'm being shot at by men in a black SUV.

The only certain thing in all of it was that there was no way I'd be getting my security deposit back.

Another bullet tore through the beat-up sedan's trunk and punctured the back seat. The thing was already barely hanging on by a thread. I half wondered if the rickety car was being held together with Bondo and unseen duct tape.

I swerved to the left into the empty lane just to make the target a little harder for the gunmen to hit.

These guys obviously didn't know who they were dealing with. Or maybe they did, and simply thought they could get lucky. After all, the only way to kill me was to take my head. And that wasn't going to happen with bullets.

There was no way to tell if these guys were cartel or the secret agency spooks I'd run into before.

More rounds struck the car. Two cracked the back window and pierced the windshield in front of me, sailing out into the air over the road ahead.

I ducked my head down out of sheer human instinct, momentarily forgetting, as I frequently did lately, that bullets would do nothing to me. I'd even just had the thought seconds prior as to how impervious I was to such an assault, but still I'd ducked.

I jerked the wheel back to the right and into the proper lane and looked back in the rearview mirror again. One of the gunmen hung out the passenger side of the SUV with what looked like an AR-15. Another shooter leaned out the window behind the driver with a similar weapon in his hands.

From the looks of them—even from this distance—I surmised these men weren't with any of the cartels in the area, though it was still a possibility. These guys looked like they were from Europe. Or somewhere else in the world. Definitely not locals. My last visit to Mexico had pitted me against a powerful drug cartel run by the infamous, and now dead, Vicente Carrillo.

The man had executed my wife right before my eyes in a hotel room in Guadalajara after enlightening me as to her infidelities. It was because of him that I now found myself in the bizarre and strange reality that had thrust itself upon me. I'd been given no choice in the matter, and resisting this enormous responsibility seemed like it was out of the question.

Would I have preferred to go on living my ordinary life as an archaeologist and researcher, assuming that everything in my marriage was fine? It was difficult to say. Ignorance, after all, can be bliss, but not in hindsight. When looking back, it always feels like a nightmare.

It was possible these gunmen were the remnant of Carrillo's organization, out for blood—revenge for what I'd done to their boss and their business. I doubted that. While the revenge factor was certainly possible with Carrillo alive, these cartel types were just as prone to assassinating the ones above them in the hierarchy simply to get their shot at the top spot.

I considered that mindset and the governing structure of cartels, the way underlings tried to climb the ladder, similar to Ancient Rome and the political games that littered their history.

Another round blew off the driver's side mirror on the door, leaving it a mangled mess of broken glass and plastic dangling from the doorframe. Every subsequent bullet that struck the car only pissed me off more. And I found myself stuck in the odd position of trying to decide between fight or flight.

I wouldn't run because I was afraid. Nothing really scared me much anymore—one of the perks of being nearly immortal. For the moment, the flight idea didn't seem to be working out. And I didn't know where I would run to. I knew I was only about fifteen minutes from Santa Rojo. I certainly didn't want these guys to follow me there. Santa Rojo had only just entered what was probably its first peaceful stretch of time in the last few decades—or so I hoped.

After being tormented for so long by Carrillo's cartel, and others, the last thing I wanted to do was bring more trouble to the innocent villagers of that town—assuming there'd been no trouble in recent weeks.

I hadn't heard anything out of Vero, though I'd messaged her to let her know I was returning. She'd replied with a smiley face and said she couldn't wait to see me. Her text stirred something in my chest that I hadn't felt in a long time—actually, for more than a decade.

Any semblance of passion had left my marriage long ago, so far back that I almost didn't recognize it when I sensed it in my heart. That strange, exciting feeling of possibility, the unknown, and the chance for something beautiful and grand seemed like a friend I'd not seen in ages, and it took effort to recognize it.

I glanced back at the SUV again, trying to figure out what to do while I suppressed the urge in my mind to transform into the beast. Once that happened, the car interior would be ruined, although with all the bullet holes in the seats, windshield, and dash, I don't know why I was even worried about it at that point. There was no chance I'd get my deposit back—that much I knew.

Then again, I had opted for full insurance through my company back home, so they would cover at least a portion of the bill. The silliness of thinking about car insurance and deposits while in a high-speed shootout didn't miss my attention, and I smirked.

Then I refocused.

If I could get these guys off the road before we reached Santa Rojo, that would be optimal.

More questions filtered through the web of thoughts as I continued to wonder who these guys were. If they weren't cartel, who were they? I hadn't noticed them at the airport or at the rental car place, but I knew they must have followed me from there, or somewhere close to the terminal.

I hadn't seen them behind me until a minute before they started shooting. They'd roared up behind me, seemingly out of nowhere. Along the winding road to Santa Rojo, rolling hills and twists and turns wrapped in dense forests offered pursuers such as these ample places to hide. So, I didn't beat myself up too much for not noticing them before.

Another bullet hit the trunk, zipped through the back seat, and through the rear of the driver's seat—striking me in the back.

I winced in pain as the round stopped somewhere in my torso. Getting shot hurt every time. There was no diminishing law of returns when it came to that. Taking a bullet wasn't something you got used to like lifting more weights. It sucked, to say the least.

I knew within seconds my superhuman body would purge the metal and heal itself. I grunted more in anger than at the pain.

"You don't happen to know who these guys are, do you?" I said out loud.

The voice in my head didn't respond. It had accompanied me since discovering the medallion in the jungle, here in Mexico, but when it spoke seemed random at best.

"You only say something when it's not helpful," I complained.

"I didn't know you knowing who they were was so critical," the calm, eerie voice replied.

No one else could hear it, which caused me a sliver of concern that I was part monster, part schizophrenic. It sounded as if there was a person sitting next to me and was as real as anything else in my perceptual reality.

"Well, it is," I replied. "You could at least give me a hint."

"I would suggest you eliminate them before you reach the village."

I rolled my eyes.

"Yeah, no kidding. Thanks for the advice, Captain Obvious."

More bullets peppered the car. I figured I'd already lost both taillights, and it was only a matter of time until they struck the tires. I always wondered why tires weren't a primary target in a car chase, although the only ones I'd ever seen were on television or in movies.

I pondered the science behind that once, wondering if bullets would pierce a tire that was moving so fast or if they would simply bounce off. I'd never taken the time to research the topic in depth, partly because I never thought I would find myself in a high-speed car chase. As an archaeologist, the most excitement I was accustomed to was finding shards of a broken bowl buried in a few hundred or thousands of years' worth of dirt.

Occasionally we would find utensils, tools, or even degraded weapons that had eroded over time. Rarely, we would discover gold or silver items, a few coins here and there, and even less frequently stumble upon valuables such as jewels, ceremonial items, or a treasure trove buried with a wealthy person or royal from history. In the case of marine archaeology, such things were more common in shipwrecks, which was what people seemed to love to see in the headlines —though common only meant once a decade most of the time.

But most of the life of an archaeologist was pretty boring to an outside observer. Personally, I enjoyed it. Hours spent under a canopy, brushing away layers of earth to find traces of the past was calming to me. It was methodical, and relaxing. It gave me a sense of purpose, and I felt exhilarated no matter what we found, whether it was a spoon made of wood or a spear crafted from gold.

Nothing, however, like a car chase, or an attack of any kind usually happened. In fact, it never happened to me or any of my peers—that I knew of—whether in the field or conducting research in a lab. I wondered if I would ever get accustomed to this life, this new path that had been thrust upon me by the fates. I was burdened with an ancient responsibility that I didn't fully understand, but that I knew couldn't be passed off to anyone else.

But I longed for companionship on this journey—more than just the voice in my head. I wanted someone who could understand what I was going through, what I was experiencing, feeling, hearing, seeing. And the only way that could happen was if I found another guardian, and the second medallion.

"You're right about that," the voice said.

I chuckled as I swerved back toward the left and slammed on the brakes.

"Which part?" I asked.

"All of it. You must find the other six before the forces of evil do."

"Easier said than done," I spat through clenched teeth as the car tilted forward, the inertia pushing ahead against the brakes.

The driver in the SUV behind me reacted too slowly and shot by me—his tires squealing in protest in the attempt to slow down. But it was too late.

Now I was behind them. No longer the hunted but the hunter.

My intention was to chase behind them like I had seen on a few cop shows, using a maneuver to touch the back quarter panel of the SUV with the front of my car and send it spinning out of control.

Instead, they merely stopped outright only fifteen to twenty yards ahead of me. The doors of the SUV flung open and four men spilled out, each wearing black suits with black ties over white button-up shirts.

The outfits were hardly practical in a tactical sense, I thought. And suits advertised the likelihood that the gunmen were government agents of some kind. Based on what little I knew about the United States Department of Defense, I doubted they were CIA. And they certainly weren't Mexican *federales*. The latter would have been equipped with Kevlar vests and random street clothes—a company jacket with yellow letters, perhaps.

For a split second, I figured the gunmen would order me to get out of the car. But as I shifted the transmission into park, they instead opened fire—shredding the windshield and hood with round after round.

The bullets tore through my flesh, each one with the sting of a few dozen wasps, burning and cutting through nerve endings.

My body shook with every hit until the men's magazines ran dry. They continued toward me, ejecting their empty magazines and replacing them with full ones strapped to their sides, partially hidden by the suit jackets.

Now I was really pissed. And since the car was already destroyed, I figured a little more damage didn't matter.

The men kept pressing toward me as the swirling red mist I'd come to know so well spun and twisted around them.

The strange fog told me who was wicked, my nemeses, and my responsibility to eliminate. The crimson mist was the judge and I the executioner. I could only trust that it, and the voice, didn't make mistakes.

I'd questioned it the first time I laid eyes on it, but it hadn't steered me wrong so far. In my past life, I had never experienced a desire to kill anyone. But now, I felt an innate, burning drive that begged me to purge this world of evil. That internal push conflicted against who I believed myself to be as a person—a historian, researcher, and humble man who preferred to live a quiet, peaceful life.

Resigned that the option for flight was long gone, I knew fighting was the only choice left. I closed my eyes and commanded the medallion with my thoughts and a whisper.

"Okay. Do it."

2

M y body swelled in an instant, muscles doubling, then quadrupling in size. My skeleton grew just as rapidly. Fur emerged through my skin, covering every inch of my morphing form as the monster awakened.

I kicked open the door of the car as the transformation finished, and I set foot...er, paw, out onto the pavement. What had been a clear, sunny day had rapidly turned.

I towered over the sedan now, standing easily seven feet tall.

To my surprise, the men in the suits didn't wet themselves, at least not that I could tell. Instead, they reloaded their weapons like a professional hit squad and opened fire once more.

"Fools," the voice said to me. "Kill them and move on. We have work to do."

But something didn't sit right with me, and it wasn't the fact that these goons were trying to blast me into next week.

They'd shot dozens, if not hundreds, of rounds through the car, many of which pierced my body. If they'd seen that, and known the bullets would do nothing but anger me, why did they continue in this exercise of futility? A band of local outlaws or cartel henchmen might react that way, convinced that if they could just put enough bullets into the creature, it would be compelled to die. But these gunmen were pros.

I noticed more magazines strapped to their waists as they continued the barrage.

These guys brought a lot of ammo, I thought. *Almost like they knew it would take a ton of it to bring me down...or....*

The strange consciousness that accompanied the spirit had the epiphany at the same moment I did.

"It's a trick," the voice snapped.

"Yeah, and I see the punchline."

In the SUV, a lone gunman remained behind the driver's-side door with a long rifle propped in the wedge between the car frame and doorframe.

I wasn't much of a gun guy, but I knew what a typical hunting or sniper rifle looked like, and this thing didn't fit either of those descriptions.

It was long like a .50 cal, and had been fitted with a powerful scope, but instead of a magazine on the bottom, it was attached to the top on the right side at an angle.

My senses tingled, and I realized one of two things—either that shooter was using explosive rounds, or tranquilizers.

The other men continued to fire, but retreated back a step as I shielded my face with my thick, right forearm.

"He's going to fire," the voice warned. Through the hazy gun smoke, I saw the sniper twist the weapon slightly.

I dove hard to the left, rolling into the ditch as a loud boom thundered over the popping sounds from the smaller firearms.

An explosion sent a concussion wave through the air just over my head, rippling across the cornstalks to my left.

"Explosive rounds," I muttered.

"Figure that out all by yourself?"

"Not helping."

The wounds all over my body healed themselves, pushing every last bullet out of my furry flesh within seconds.

I heard the men up on the road shouting, just out of sight. I knew they'd be on me again in a moment. Looking to the left again, as the tall stalks of corn righted themselves and stopped their wavy motion, an idea came to me.

"Oh, you are clever," the voice said.

I ignored it and bounded into the field like a cat on all fours.

More shouts followed, along with the loud popping of gunshots, but without a clear target, the bullets missed on all sides—the only damage delivered to corn stalks as the rounds broke through them as though they were made of paper.

I sped between the rows of corn, keeping the bulk of my form low until I'd run nearly a hundred yards. I slowed to a halt and paused, catching my breath as I listened for the sounds of gunfire.

I was out of range now, and they would have to pursue on foot into the field, which was exactly what I wanted.

My ears twitched as the sound of shouts faded into hurried but wary footsteps. The men were in the field now. Here, their visibility would be reduced to the row ahead of them, with little peripheral sight beyond twenty feet.

I sniffed the air, tilting my snout upward until I sensed something. I bared my teeth in a satisfied grin. The amplified sense of smell served me well, particularly in situations like this. I detected the first of the four gunmen to my right, then closed my eyes and used my ears to pick up the others.

One straight ahead, just to the left of the first, then two more farther left.

The men moved in a line, fanned out in hopes of catching me with a wide net. They would have been better served to stick together in a group. At least that way their combined firepower could keep me back—for a finite amount of time. Funny thing about dying, what a person will do to stave it off for a few more precious seconds of light.

These goons had made their choice. Whoever they were, whoever they worked for, couldn't have been the good guys.

"Unless they believe they're the good guys," the voice said.

"Again. Not helping," I hissed. "And besides, the mist doesn't lie. Not that I know of."

"That is correct."

I darted to the right through a row of corn and into the next gap. They went on forever, or so it seemed. I knew they ended abruptly at the edge of the forest a few hundred yards away, and while the idea of luring these hired killers into the jungle where I could end them and leave their bodies to rot appealed to me, I decided against it.

"Rather toy with them here, huh?" the voice teased.

It had grown bolder as the days and weeks passed. While still random for the most part, the power contained in the medallion spoke more often than it had at first—both a blessing and a curse, though I'd say that split was closer to sixty-forty on the blessing side.

"You had an ancestor that once thought that way," it said. "Thousands of years ago."

Glad to hear I'm not the only one, I thought and slipped through another row of corn.

The men pursuing me had stopped shouting, and I continued pushing around them on their left flank.

They may have seen some corn stalks shudder as I passed between them, but I doubted it. The gunmen were venturing into the field with limited vision, and I'd moved far enough away that they couldn't track me easily.

When I was fifty yards to the right of the row I'd started in, I paused and listened.

I heard the footsteps of the nearest assailant, and closed my eyes to pinpoint his exact location with what I could only describe as a sort of radar-like tracking sense.

The sound intensified, and I detected exactly where the killer was. I waited, allowing him to get parallel to where I crouched before I carefully eased through a row in his direction.

The only threat that concerned me was the sniper at the truck with the explosive rounds. That guy could still cause problems, even at this range—if he got lucky.

"I agree," the voice said. "You should eliminate him first."

I rolled my eyes. "No," I sneered. "The immediate threat is here in the field."

The voice said no more, allowing me to keep going through the next row, and the next.

Pressing ahead, I passed through another row, and another until I sensed the target creeping toward where I'd been just moments before.

I saw glimpses of movement through the corn stalks. The first gunman was only two rows away.

I readied myself to charge, bending my knees for maximum spring. That's when I heard the gun report from the sniper rifle up on the road.

My supernatural reflexes were the only thing that kept me from being blown to pieces, which I had no desire to experience. I leaped through the air and over the corn row ahead of me just as the explosive round from the sniper struck the ground where I'd been crouching, and erupted in a flash of fire.

I sailed over the second row, spying the gunman below as I way overshot the target. "Crap."

The shooter didn't see me, instead snapping his head to the left where the explosion had come from. He whirled with his gun pointed in that direction just as I landed behind the corn to his back.

"I told you you should have taken out the sniper," the voice gloated.

Yeah, yeah.

Then I lunged forward through the stalks, breaking them under my weight as though they were mere twigs.

The gunman heard the sound, but his reaction was too late as he spun around to defend himself. The red mist swirled around him, pulsing with a crimson light as if it anticipated the kill. The man never got off a shot.

I growled as I opened my maw and tore into his neck. He tried to scream, but only a pathetic, gurgle-filled yelp escaped.

Blood flowed into my mouth—a taste I still didn't enjoy—but the mere touch of it to my tongue sent a powerful pulse of energy through me.

The man dropped his gun on the ground—his strength fading

rapidly. Then I released his neck, grabbed him by the legs, and spun like an Olympic hammer thrower. I let go at the perfect point in the arc, and watched the killer fly through the air, spinning and toppling forty yards before disappearing with a crunch behind the endless rows of corn.

Based on the trajectory and velocity, I figured he landed somewhere close to one of the other guys, if not between them.

"You're toying with them," the voice said. Its tone was not an approving one.

I ignored it and jumped back through the row that I'd landed behind before, and not a moment too soon. The sniper had adjusted, and fired again. The round ruptured into a ball of flame accompanied by an explosive blast.

"No more screwing around," I said.

"Probably wise."

I leaped again, sensing the next of my targets only thirty feet away. This time, though, I didn't jump high like before. That made things too easy for the sniper, who could spot me in the air and adjust his sight depending on where I landed. It was unclear if he could get a clear view through the corn stalks, but I figured keeping low would make things more difficult until I turned my attention to him.

I landed a few feet to the right of the next gunman, who'd already turned my way on hearing the sound of the explosive round. He may have seen his comrade fly over his head, but I didn't bother to ask.

He turned his gun and fired. The rattle of the muzzle ejecting rounds in quick succession filled the air, but the bullets missed as he tried to correct his aim amid a full-blown panic.

I grabbed the wrist that was cradling the underbarrel and forced the gun back on him. The resistance he offered felt like that of a child trying to keep from being tickled, and the barrel turned easily.

He yelled, but it was too late. I felt his trigger finger snap from the awkward angle and the suddenness of the gun twisting, and he couldn't stop the stream of rounds pouring out of the muzzle.

His voice cut short when the bullets cut through his throat.

He fell to his knees as the red mist danced around him before spiraling into his gaping mouth as he died.

Shouts from my left—where the other two hunters were—echoed to where I stood. Even if the sniper hadn't seen me, he would have noticed the corn bending and swaying as I passed through.

With that in mind, I charged forward again. The stalks and vibrant green leaves smacked against my face. I disregarded the irritation, only tightening my eyelids as I hit them to protect my eyes.

I saw the last two men up ahead, one standing slightly staggered behind the other. Their black suits stood out between the gaps in the corn rows. Both men aimed their weapons in my direction. I crushed another row of corn, leaving only two rows between me and them.

They opened fire, wearing expressions of fear and determination even as they retreated a step, then another.

Bullets cut through the stalks, most of them missing me. One ripped through my right arm. Another hit me in the chest.

I growled at the pain and jumped straight ahead, covering the distance in a blinking second. As I flew through the air, beating down the last row of corn, I spread my arms out wide like a furry chupacabra bird and hit both men with a powerful clothesline.

Their bodies pounded into the ground. Their heads smacked against the hard earth, sending them both into the concussion protocol—if they were to survive.

"Which they aren't," the voice said.

"No."

I reached my left paw up to the one on the left, my long, clawed fingers wrapping around his neck. I did the same to the one on the right and squeezed both.

The men's eyes swelled as if they might pop out of their skulls. I sensed trouble, so made quick work of both by twisting their heads back, popping their necks in a single, muted click.

With both of them dealt with, I left them for the mist to consume and dove through the next row before turning right and breaking toward the road.

The corn stalks flew by in a blur as I easily surpassed forty miles per hour. A gunshot rang out across the field. I dipped to the right. The round blew up the dirt near where I'd been a second before. I kept going, my eyes locked on the road now and the SUV parked along the side.

Through the leaves and corn atop the stalks, I saw the sniper shifting, trying to get a clear shot. He adjusted his aim again, and this time before he could fire, I surged back to the left. The round didn't even come close to hitting me when it exploded in the soil.

Within seconds, I reached the edge of the field and scrambled up the side of the ditch. The sniper leaned over the hood of the SUV, apparently under the impression I was still down in the cornfield.

I watched him watching the field, suddenly jittery as he couldn't spy where I'd gone. It was almost cute. Almost. He was, after all, trying to kill me. For a few seconds, I considered how to play it.

"Seriously? Just kill him."

I will. Make no mistake. But I need answers first.

3

I thought I heard the voice sigh. Of course, it could have just been the wind blowing across the road as dense, charcoal storm clouds churned overhead.

I stepped up to the back of the SUV and positioned my paw-hands under the bumper. The red fog around the sniper danced around him much the same way the clouds above whipped around in a vortex of ominous rhythm.

An ancient power coursed through me as I lifted the back of the truck as though the vehicle were made of cardboard. I exhaled with the slightest growl as I flipped the SUV's back end up into the air.

The shooter reacted in slow motion, turning his head to look at the windshield and the roof of the vehicle as it dramatically tipped up before gravity started pulling it down toward him.

He instinctively put up his right forearm, letting the rifle fall to the ground at his feet. Unfortunately, he also fell back onto his rear as the top of the SUV collapsed down onto his legs.

I wasn't certain, but I thought I heard bones crunching under its weight.

Within a second, the man howled in pain, screaming bloody murder.

I leaned around to the left and saw him lying there, squirming and writhing as if the erratic movements would somehow pry his legs free from the vehicle pinning them to the asphalt.

For a few breaths, I stared at the man with the shaved head as he kept tugging, desperately attempting to pull his legs out.

I grinned at him, baring the fangs that hung down over my lower gums. "What's your plan once you get your legs out from under that?" I asked in a gravel tone.

He twisted his head to the left, then drew a pistol at his side, aimed the firearm at me, and shot.

I wasn't a fan of being hit by bullets, but this time I decided to let the bad guy have it. I stood there allowing every single round from the magazine—the ones that were on target—hit my body until the sound of clicking signaled he was out.

I inhaled deeply, then let the breath out—allowing my body to purge the bullets. The rounds fell to the ground, metal clicks accompanying them as they hit the pavement at my feet.

Terror rippled through his unbelieving eyes. For a few seconds, he kept the pistol extended toward me as if he might manifest one last round in the chamber that could deal the final death blow.

Then resignation flashed in the whites of his eyes, and his arm fell limp to the ground as acceptance of the inevitable settled in his mind.

I stalked toward him, slowly, methodically, like a murderer in a predictable horror film. There was no escape. He knew that now.

I suspect the man figured I would simply kill him straightaway, perhaps by ripping off his head or stomping his skull into goo. But I had questions that begged for answers.

When I reached the man, I stopped short, letting the claws on my feet graze his shoulder. The subtle action sent a ripple of fear through the man, expressed by a shudder from the waist up.

"Who are you?" I demanded.

The man shook his head dramatically. "You can go to hell, demon spawn."

I frowned at the response, then bent my knees and crouched

down low, lowering my nose so he could feel my breath against his skin.

"That isn't a nice thing to say," I answered in a beastly deep baritone. The man's Italian accent hadn't escaped me through his impeccable English.

"You will burn forever, monster."

I leaned closer and loosened the tie around his neck. Ignoring his unfounded threats, I dragged a claw across his face. The red mist around him slowed its circular movement, as if it knew I wasn't going to give it another victim yet.

"First of all," I drawled, "I don't believe in a place called hell. Second, I am no demon spawn."

"You're a child of the devil himself," the man spat, crossing himself in the process.

The action and his continued words slathered in archaic beliefs told me one thing: This guy was a religious fanatic. That didn't tell me the entire story, though.

I sighed and put my right foot down onto his chest. The weight sucked the wind out of the man's lungs, and his face bulged with the effort of trying to breathe.

"Now, who sent you?"

He shook his head. "I won't tell you anything, monster. You may as well kill me now. My salvation is assured."

I puzzled over the response. Growing up in a church, I'd heard that sort of thing before, though not from my denomination. We were taught that salvation could be lost, and that there was no such thing as hell. It seemed most church organizations had a different take on everything. Oddly, mine had left out any knowledge about the seven medallions of power, including the one around my neck that had bestowed me with incredible abilities—and trouble.

That sort of mythology had probably been forgotten, or burned from any records that may have once existed.

"It was," the voice confirmed.

I considered the information for a second, then bobbed my head. "Makes sense."

My captive scowled in confusion. "What?"

"Oh, nothing," I replied. "Now, you were about to tell me who you work for. And before you say no, keep in mind that even though I'm sure you're never going to walk again, there are still plenty of ways I can make you hurt—for a very, very long time."

"There is nothing you can do to make me tell you any—"

I pushed harder on his chest, cutting off his words in midsentence.

He gasped, clawing fanatically at the enormous furry foot pinning him to the road.

I looked casually in both directions, hoping no other vehicles would come by soon. I preferred that none of the locals happen on this scene first. Then again, most of the villagers from Santa Rojo didn't get out of the little pueblo often—not that I'd noticed, though I'd only spent minimal time there. The bigger concern was a cop showing up while I still had my foot on this guy's ribcage.

I needed to know who they were, and why they were trying to kill me.

The sniper's face changed color, and I eased my foot up a little so the man could catch his breath.

He sucked in air deeply, rapidly, filling his lungs again with the sweet warmth of life. Once he'd calmed his breathing a little, I leaned close again.

"I'm not going to even bother asking why you were trying to kill me. Okay? You clearly have some kind of religious vendetta against me. But what I want to know is, why? I'm not the bad guy here. Quite the opposite." I noted the fog hanging around us, almost unmoving now. "I know who the bad guys are, though. And I'm getting a few hints that you're one of them. Just like all your dead pals in the field down there."

His eyebrows tightened together as he tried to decipher what I meant. Then his eyes fell to the medallion around my neck.

The shimmering metallic amulet, carved in the shape of a wolf's head, seemed to almost give off its own radiant, scarlet light.

The gunman remained fixated on it, as if mesmerized by the amulet dangling over him.

I looked down at it and lifted it with my paw-like fingers, holding it out to him.

"So, it's this you're after," I realized. "Not me. What do you know about this?"

The rapt wonder left the sniper's eyes, and he took on a gloating look. "You are not righteous enough to wear that. The Medallions of Power should have never been given to the sinners. Pagans. Witches. Devil worshippers."

I twisted my head slightly, mocking him with my glare. "I've never worshipped a devil. And I'm certainly not a witch or a pagan...not last I checked."

"You are all the same. Your houses will burn. And the medallions will be in the hands of the righteous."

I pulled my foot off of his chest and let him bask in the temporary relief as I considered his words. This guy wasn't going to give up the goods, no matter what I did to him. Freaks like him were addicted to suffering for what they believed to be a just cause, no matter how misplaced their motives and actions.

The irony of considering the guy a freak wasn't lost on me.

I breathed in a deep inhale, then blew it out of my mouth. "So, you know about the medallions. And whoever you work for knows too."

The man said nothing, which only served to confirm my assessment.

"Well, if you're not going to tell me, I guess there's no point in me keeping you alive any longer." I glanced down at the roof of the SUV still pinning his legs to the asphalt. Then I looked up to the sky. Thunder boomed in the distance, and the clouds began to sprinkle rain down on us.

"I guess I could leave you here for some Good Samaritan to come help. They'd call the police, the ambulance, all that. But, by the time they all got here, you might be dead from your injuries. Of course, doing it that way will cause you a lot of suffering."

"Spare me your offer of a quick death. I have no fear of suffering."

"No, I suppose you don't." I shook my head as I remembered hearing stories about fanatics from a certain sect of the Catholic Church that would punish themselves in unusual and painful ways to purge sin from their minds and bodies. "But I have to ask." I paused for a second, waiting until I knew I had his undivided attention. "Is it the guy in the lab coat? Is that who you work for?"

The bewilderment in the man's eyes told me the answer was no. *Hmm.*

"Is that the best you've got?" the voice in my head asked.

"No. Now, if you don't mind, I'm interrogating this guy."

The sniper looked more confused for a moment, then narrowed his eyelids to slits. "You converse with the devil himself. I knew it."

Exasperated, I exhaled and shook my head. "No. It's not the devil, which tells me you don't know that much about this thing." I let the medallion slip through my paw-like fingers. It fell to my chest, and I cracked my neck to the right before I continued the line of questioning.

"If you don't know who the man in the lab coat is, that eliminates him. And despite the suits, which made me initially think you could be with the agency that's after me, I'm not so sure about that either."

Once more, the man's body language answered the question for him.

"No, that's not it," I went on.

That means there could be another player in the game.

"Figured that out all by yourself?" the voice teased.

"You know, your English is getting better," I commented.

"I didn't say anything," the captive whined, more befuddled than ever.

"I wasn't talking to you. Oh, sorry. Since you're not going to help me, I might as well let you go."

He shook his head. "You wouldn't be so foolish."

I shrugged. "No. Probably not. Besides, I do what the mist tells me." I leaned in close to him again, letting him see the reflection of the swirling fog in my eyes. The mist churned faster again, the crimson light pulsing in faster and faster rhythm.

The sniper felt a fear unlike anything he'd ever experienced in his life. It drained the color from his face.

"Do you play football?" I asked. "Not soccer. American football."

The man didn't answer, instead watching me with curious trepidation as I took three steps back, then one to the side.

"I never really got to play much when I was young, but I love to watch the game. Always fascinates me how kickers miss so many kicks. You know? Seems like they just have to practice that all day, do nothing else, and yet there are so many inconsistent ones in the pros. Weird, right?"

The sniper swallowed, his head beginning to tremble as he started to see where this was going.

"Of course, it's easy for me to say. I've never had the pressure of kicking a fifty-yarder to win the big game. But I like to think I could manage. It's all in the technique."

I took the first step toward him. Then the second. With the third, I planted my left foot on the pavement and swung my right foot as hard as I could at the man's head.

I felt the impact, a little resistance, and then watched as the makeshift football tore from his body and sailed down the road, and off into the ditch.

I craned my neck to the side. "Huh. Wide, right."

4

I looked in both directions once again, still amazed at the fact no other cars had shown up on the scene. I was extremely thankful. I closed my eyes and with a single thought, initiated the transformation back into my human form.

The metamorphosis took less than ten seconds.

I hurried back to my destroyed rental car and reached into the passenger side to retrieve my backpack, which had remarkably been undamaged during the firefight. I guessed it was low enough to the ground that most of the bullets had gone over it.

I slung the bag over my shoulders, then started jogging at a slow but steady pace toward Santa Rojo.

Two minutes after leaving the wreckage on the road, I heard a car coming from just beyond the clearing.

"Great," I complained.

I couldn't see the vehicle yet. It was hidden in the dense jungle about a half mile ahead, but it wouldn't be much longer.

I ducked over the edge of the ditch once more, dropping down about six feet, and then waded into the cornfield.

Corn was one of those staple things I could eat all the time, but at the moment I didn't want to see any form of it for at least a week.

I parted the first row, entered the gap between, then continued ahead, repeating the same process as I moved away from the carnage on the road and closer to the forest. Whoever was in the approaching car would find the wrecked vehicles, but the bodies were already gone—consumed by the red mist that always felt eager to cover my tracks.

I heard the car pass behind my position, and knew it would be slowing down as it arrived on the scene of what, at first, the driver probably thought to be a bizarre accident. *If they think it's weird now, wait until they find no one around.*

The thought amused me as I continued marching toward the jungle. I looked back occasionally, just to make sure no one had spotted me, but within minutes of leaving the road, I'd put enough distance between myself and any potential witnesses that they wouldn't notice.

I felt relief spill into my chest as I neared the jungle's edge. Under normal circumstances in my previous life, I probably would have been terrified to enter such a place as a mere human.

Dangerous wildlife occupied these woods, not to mention dangerous people like those in the cartels. But with the power I wielded, I feared little anymore. Except....

"Watch your step," the voice interrupted my thoughts.

"What?" I set my foot down in the jungle, leaving the clearing behind, and suddenly felt the world spin around me.

For a second, I felt as if I was falling, rapidly tumbling through a black void. Then I opened my eyes and found myself in a vaguely familiar place.

I blinked several times.

A fire crackled from somewhere nearby, and I smelled fresh bread baking, along with some pungent odors I couldn't identify but felt oddly familiar.

I knew I was lying down, apparently on a floor. I felt the smooth wooden floorboards under me, polished from ages of feet passing over them. A dim, flickering light to my left signaled the source of the fire I'd heard upon...awakening? I wasn't really sure I'd fallen asleep, or passed out, or what. But as my vision cleared, so did my surroundings.

"Welcome back, Gideon," an eerily familiar voice said, piercing the darkened room.

I sat up, suddenly alert. I kept my palms to the floor in case I lost my sense of balance, but surprisingly that didn't happen.

"You," I said, a little colder than intended.

"Yes, me," the shaman said from the humble kitchen in the corner.

I turned my head both directions to make sure I wasn't hallucinating—which I'm pretty sure I was. It was the only logical explanation for a medicine man's hut that appeared and disappeared in different locations.

"You're not hallucinating," my host reassured. "Did you think that was what happened the first time we spoke?"

I inhaled through my nostrils and sighed as I slowly got to my feet. Again, I felt surprise at there being no wobbly feeling in my head. Usually, after the simple act of waking from a night of sleep, I needed to steady myself for a minute before getting out of bed.

"No, I suppose not," I admitted. "Although, to be honest, I'm not sure what that was."

The man smiled back at me. His dark, leathery skin stretched across his face with the act, spraying crow's feet out from the corners of his eyes. I didn't know if his shaven head was part of some ancient rite of passage, or why he sported the tattoos of animals on his shoulders and chest. But I was pretty sure the beads on his wrists and the necklaces of various stones dangling from his neck had some kind of spiritual significance.

"And stop reading my thoughts," I added with a half grin.

The shaman replied in kind. He leaned against a counter made from a tree planed into a flat surface and propped up by legs made from thick branches. Leather breeches covered his legs, held up by a leather strap that passed for a belt. Moccasins laced up to his shins completed the outfit.

"I only see what you allow me to see, Gideon," he explained.

"You're a man who has little to hide, an open book for the world to read."

I snorted, muting the derision in my thoughts as much as possible, and stepped toward the fire, stopping at the base of the stone hearth. A huge iron pot that some might have called a cauldron hung over the fire. A savory brown liquid brewed within, bubbling slowly and filling the air with the scent of cooked red meat and onions.

"Fresh garlic is the secret," my mysterious host said. "It brings out all the other flavors."

"I agree. Always been a fan. Although I don't think I've actually ever made a stew. If that's what this is."

He nodded. "It is. Nothing unusual. It's a beef stew."

"Ah. Well, it smells great."

I didn't know where the small talk was leading, but a small part of me hoped it would end up with me eating a bowl of what the shaman was cooking.

"Of course you can," the host said with a smile. "Help yourself. I've already set out a bowl for you."

"I really shouldn't. I need to get going."

"Because of what happened on the road to Santa Rojo?"

I had to admit, I liked how direct the guy was. Although it did creep me out a little that he knew about the attack on the road. It made me wonder what else he'd seen in my life.

"No need to worry," he comforted. "I am only made aware of certain incidents."

That response brought on a whole new set of questions, but I decided to let them drift away like clouds in the sky of my mind.

"Thanks, I think. But I should leave. I don't want this to spill over into Santa Rojo."

"Vero will be fine," he said. "We are between the dimensions here. Time neither passes nor fades, neither accelerates nor stops."

"That's... comforting?"

The shaman laughed, which didn't make me feel better about the situation.

"You've been here before, Gideon." He pulled away from the

counter and sauntered across the room. "I don't understand what the problem is. This place exists beyond the three-dimensional plane you call reality. It's like a weigh station."

"What's being weighed? My soul?"

The shaman laughed again and shook his head. He picked up the two bowls and shifted over to where I stood, then handed me one. "No. There is no judgment in this place."

"No wonder you like it here." I eyed the man as he stepped over to the cauldron and plucked a ladle from a hook on the right side of the hearth.

He scooped a cup full of the stew, then a second, filling the bowl nearly to the brim before passing the ladle to me.

"Thanks." I accepted it and shuffled close to the warm fire. I helped myself to a couple of scoops and turned to find him already sitting at the table, breaking a chunk of bread from a fresh-baked loaf. The crust cracked as he tore the piece, and the aromas danced in my nostrils, mingling with the scent of the hot stew.

"Come. Sit."

I obeyed and sat down at a table that, much like the counter, appeared to have been made from an enormous tree cut thin to create the surface, and just like the counter it was propped up on legs made from thick tree limbs.

I set the bowl on the table and slid onto the bench, also made from a similar wood. I closed my eyes and said a quick prayer of gratitude, then opened them to see the shaman smiling across the table at me as he chewed his food.

"What?" I wondered.

"Always good to give thanks for the little things, Gideon. Those little moments of appreciation are seeds that grow into great wonders."

I bobbed my head. "I like that." Then I picked up a wooden spoon next to the bowl and stuffed it into the stew, shoveling a mouthful between my lips.

The salty, meaty flavors burst across my taste buds. I guessed the shaman could tell.

"Good, huh?" he asked.

I chewed for a minute, then swallowed before answering. "It's terrific."

"Way better than you expected from a medicine man in a creepy hut with a cauldron in the hearth, huh?"

I felt a flutter of guilt. "Well, yeah."

The man burst out laughing. He wagged his spoon in the air at me as if making a point. "Here's what's really going to bake your noodle. Is any of this real or not?"

I had just shoved another spoonful into my mouth and paused in mid-chew. Then I resumed slowly to test whether the food actually was real or not.

"Is it?" I asked, my mouth still half full.

"What *is* real?"

I swallowed the stew and reached across the table to the loaf sitting in the center. I tore a piece off and then broke that one in half before holding up the smaller chunk to my nose. "Well, if it isn't real, it's one heck of a show. This smells incredible."

"Our senses are only perceptions of the world around us. But that's another lesson for another time. You didn't come here to learn about ancient esoteric truths about the universe."

I dipped the bread into the stew and took a bite. "Why did I come here?" I arched my right eyebrow as I inspected his outfit. "And do you always just walk around without a shirt on?"

The shaman folded his hands on the table and stiffened his spine. "I find clothes restrictive. They are unnecessary in the realm where I dwell. We are bathed in light there. But for the human construct you know as reality, I take on this form. I can change if you prefer."

"No, it's fine." I didn't know what he might do next. Change into a horse? A serpent? A crocodile? "So, why am I here?"

"I could ask you the same question, Gideon. You're the one who stumbled into my abode."

"Yeah, but it's not like I went looking for you. Not that I'd even know how to do that. This isn't where your house was last time."

"Eh, close enough. But you're assuming I am local."

"Local?"

"Again, the local-versus-non-local consciousness concepts can wait for another time, Gideon. You came here because you have questions."

I had to think for a moment and used another piece of bread to give me a chance to gather my thoughts. I chewed for a long twenty seconds. It wasn't that I didn't have questions. I had too many. So, I went with the first one on the top of my mind.

"Who were the men that tried to kill me just now?"

The shaman peered at me for a few seconds, then lowered his gaze to the bowl in front of him and spooned more stew into his mouth. As he chewed, he broke off another piece of the warm bread and bit into it.

"What?" I asked. "What's wrong with asking that question?"

After the host was done chewing, he reached over for a wooden cup with water in it, picked it up, and washed down the food with a long sip. He set the cup back down and looked back to me again.

"Some answers cannot be given, Gideon."

"Why not? I'm supposed to eliminate the wicked. And those guys had red mist all over them. Whoever sent them must be just as bad. Right?"

"The men you killed were evil, yes. No question about it. The mist is never wrong. It is an objective judge, ruling purely on the contents of one's heart. However, it is not the only mystical force at work in your reality."

I noticed how he phrased it as *my reality* and not one he and I shared, but I kept that thought to myself and let him keep going.

"There are always two sides in all things," he explained. "And within those alignments are hierarchies just like in a corporate structure, or even in your line of work. Someone reports to someone higher up, and so on."

He was losing me at this point, but I gave him the benefit of the doubt and kept my mouth shut, except for stuffing more food in, which may or may not have been real. Either way, it tasted good, and I'd suddenly developed quite the appetite.

"The dark forces, the ones that are the most powerful, do everything they can to conceal truth from those who walk in the light."

"The light?" I'd suppressed my voice until then but had to ask.

"In the universe are beings of darkness and light. Those who walk in the light protect the way of balance, love, justice, and peace. The beings of darkness seek to consume mankind, absorbing their consciousnesses over time. Initially, this begins with simple distractions but is always focused on purely material things. Through materialism, these beings twist the thoughts of humanity, locking their attention on things rather than balance. In ancient traditions, the greatest of the dark beings was known as Ahriman. In ancient Judaic traditions, he was simply known as the adversary."

The statement sank deep into my gut.

"Like, the devil?"

"Some would say that, yes."

I don't know what I'd expected him to say to my question, but the bluntness of the answer hit me with the weight of a bag of bricks.

"The dark ones conceal truth from beings like me, as well as from the oracles, and others. They are far more powerful. We are able to see those we help, and can guide them through many obstacles, but our vision is veiled by those of greater power. So, you will largely be on your own in this investigation... until the answers are revealed directly to you through your own searching."

I'd heard of the angelic hierarchy before: the Cherubim, Seraphim, Archangels, and others. Much of that knowledge had been stripped away over time, either deliberately or by sheer lack of interest or irrelevance.

"So, whoever these guys are... they're being protected?"

"In a manner of speaking, yes," he half confirmed. The shaman reached to his right and picked up the cup of liquid again. I thought it was water. Mine certainly was, but his seemed to have a greenish tint to it. He noticed my interest. "Matcha," he said. "With a little ayahuasca."

His casual confession to the hallucinogenic compound in his tea caught me off guard. "Wait, like the psychedelic?"

"Of course," he said, taking a sip as if it were of no consequence.

"But doesn't that make you see things? Not to mention it's the precursor to the journey through the hallucinations."

He laughed at that. "None of this is real, Gideon. All is merely perception. But no, a being such as I does not suffer from the physical issues that occur before someone like you crosses over to the other side during a... trip, as you would call it."

He took a gulp of the tea and set the cup back down.

"The world just keeps getting stranger," I muttered.

"The universe is a strange and incredible place. Someday you will see it all. For now, you must return to Santa Rojo. Someone waits for you there. She has been awaiting your return since you left."

"Vero."

"She is a good woman, and will make a fine companion on your journey."

I shook my head at the notion. "Two weeks ago, I was married, making a speech in front of dignitaries in Guadalajara for the archaeological discoveries we'd made. I thought my life was pretty normal."

"All of that changed quickly, didn't it?"

I nodded, my thoughts drifting as I stared down at the half-eaten bowl of stew.

"When life changes, we must adapt with it. Whether the changes are swift or slow, we must also match the tempo of whatever comes our way."

I lifted my eyes to meet his gaze, questioning the words. "Are you saying I'm to just forget the years of marriage, the good times I had with Amy, the life I had before, at the drop of a hat?"

He merely shrugged. "I am not saying you have to do anything. But your past does not define your present moment, or your future. Only what we do now, in this flashing second, counts. You can try to hold on to memories, nostalgia, dreams of what you thought once was. But those things are gone. There is only now. And right now, there is a young woman who is endeared to you. You would be unwise not to at least see what that potential has to offer."

I sighed, letting my spoon fall to the rim of the bowl. I stiffened my spine, letting it crack a few times as I twisted left and right. "Being with me is dangerous now," I said. "I can't put her in that position."

"And yet you must. You are to take her with you on this journey."

"What do you mean? To Greece?"

He inclined his head but paused before saying anything. The shaman peered at me over the bottoms of his eyelids. The fire flickered higher in the hearth, splashing bright orange light across the room.

"Your mission is twofold. Protect the innocent, and find the other six medallions. And with them, the guardians they belong to."

I frowned, processing what he said. "Are you telling me that Vero is a guardian? Wouldn't she need to be Greek or something?"

"Wouldn't you need to be Mexican to be the chupacabra?"

"Fair point."

"As the guardian families moved around the world, things changed. Your family, your guardian house, lived in many areas of the world over the millennia."

"So, you're telling me that Vero is the guardian I'm looking for? The one who will bear the Artemis Medallion?"

He grinned. It was a toothy, mischief-filled expression. I was surprised at how white his teeth were for a shaman. Then again, I supposed he wasn't really human at this point. He was something else, an intermediary being between realms or dimensions.

"I'm not saying she is or isn't. That is not my job. But I can tell you to keep an open mind."

The flames in the hearth swelled to the point they lashed the top of the cauldron hanging over the logs. I heard the stew bubbling vigorously and for a second considered warning my host that he might burn his soup.

Then, suddenly, the fire disappeared, and everything went black.

5

The first thing I noticed after plunging into darkness was the breath going in and out of my nostrils, filling my lungs, then expelling with every exhale.

I lazily opened my eyes, gravity pulling on them with every drowsy second. I heard animals next—birds, squirrels, and something I thought might be a monkey but wasn't really sure. Mexican wildlife was not my specialty.

Light snuck in through the slits of my eyelids. My vision quickly adjusted as I fully opened my eyes and rolled my head around to survey my surroundings.

I was in the jungle, but not close to the edge where the untamed, lush vegetation met the neat rows of the cornfield. I sat up quickly, still looking around. I didn't see the cornfield anywhere, and I wondered how far I'd gone during or after the hallucination. It was as if the shaman had picked me up in a spaceship made to look like a hut and dropped me off somewhere else.

Did he put ayahuasca in my drink too? The thought seemed absurd, but how was I to know? I'd never touched the stuff before.

"You're within a mile of the village," the voice said to me, sounding almost amused. "And no, you didn't have any of his special tea. I would say you don't need it."

I exhaled again, this time with a sigh that let out any concerns I might have had.

"And why is that?" I asked, standing up and dusting myself off from the loose collection of leaves and dirt on my pants.

"Indigenous peoples, and those who seek such journeys, do so to either face demons from their past or to meet guides from beyond this plane."

I continued looking around, uncertain which way I should go. I heard the distant sound of car engines and figured that was as good a direction as any. I trudged ahead through the undergrowth, parting huge green leaves in my path. I watched for spiders and snakes, though now I figured those things couldn't really harm me as they could in my past.

"Guides?" I asked the voice. "You mean like spirit guides?"

"Yes."

"Okay, then."

"You doubt such things?"

I pulled back a particularly huge leaf and found a narrow path cutting through the forest toward where I'd heard the sound. "I used to think I had an open mind," I replied. "But the last few weeks have shown me that was not the case. Now? There is little I doubt anymore."

The voice remained silent, and I found the quiet of the jungle a welcome change after the fight on the road, the ethereal visit from the shaman, and the brief conversation with a being that only existed in my head.

The sounds of the village grew louder until I saw the outlines of buildings—homes, shops, vehicles moving—and heard music. I recognized the rooftop of the church, and for a second I wondered what day it was.

The voice said nothing, probably because I remembered it was Monday before he could speak up.

I stepped out of the jungle and secured the backpack on my

shoulders as I marched ahead toward the row of buildings on the main street where Vero's cantina occupied a spot near the end on the left-hand side.

I stuck to the back of the buildings to avoid people noticing me. The villagers of Santa Rojo loved me, which was cool and weird at the same time. Their town, after all, was named after the Red Saint—the chupacabra who had purged evil from it.

I reached an alley jutting off an adjacent street to the main one, and continued through the shadows, keeping a watchful eye on the doors and windows of the buildings until I made it to the next stretch of asphalt. A coffee shop to the left spewed a wondrous aroma of fresh brew and pastries into the air. Two older men sat on the cracked sidewalk playing chess, each with a cup of black coffee next to their right hands.

They didn't seem to pay me any mind, and I casually but quickly crossed the street, looking both ways as I moved.

Once there, I walked by a seamstress shop on my left and continued down the back street behind the row of shops toward the cantina's back entrance.

I kept thinking about the men who'd attacked me on the road earlier. I hadn't checked my watch before it all began, but based on the sun's position in the sky, I was fairly certain little time had passed between my visit with the shaman and when I awoke... or whatever.

Every little sound startled me as I walked.

The back street ran along the edge of more forest, though several old homes stood just fifty yards away through the trees and undergrowth. The thin patch of jungle was basically just a buffer between the pueblo and the dwellings.

I recalled the interrogation of the sniper, seeing the man's arrogant face in my mind's eye as I questioned him. He'd given no answers, except that whoever they worked for wasn't the man in the white lab coat I'd seen in my vision, or dream. I didn't know what to call it.

That sort of thing had happened before, when I'd used the red mist to actually kill a guy in an interrogation room—one of Carrillo's henchmen. The two spooks questioning him had freaked out at the man's abrupt demise, unable to see the fog as it choked the life from him.

This time, the vision had been passive—an observation. The lab coat guy was hunting me; of that I was certain, but just like the men on the road, I didn't know who he worked for.

As for the more recent of my victims, one distinguishing trait about them—based purely on the way the sniper spoke—was that they were some kind of religious zealots. Did they work for a religious organization?

"You can speak up whenever, voice," I said.

The voice didn't reply.

"You know, I don't think you have to worry about someone calling us out for cheating on this one. If you can tell me who they were, that'll speed things up. We can take out the bad guys, restore peace to the innocent, and go on living our lives... er, my life."

"It isn't that simple, Gideon," it replied. "And no, I don't know who is chasing you. If I knew, I would tell you. Unfortunately, my power is restricted to the medallion around your neck. I serve only as an extra sensory perception for you. I cannot control where your mind goes."

That was a funny thing to say. *Cannot control where my mind goes?*

"Did I stutter?"

"No," I sighed. "But you're definitely getting the hang of American sass. That's for sure."

As I approached the back of the cantina, I wondered what he'd meant. There'd been a clue in the words, some kind of hint. He couldn't control where my mind went, but I could. Did that mean I could... Then it hit me. "Remote viewing," I whispered as I paused in the parking lot. A red Mercedes sedan sat in the gravel. I brushed my hand across the hood upon hearing the crackle of the engine cooling.

"Still warm," I said. "We're not done with this conversation."

The voice didn't answer.

Irritated but feeling like I'd found a fragment of an answer, I continued until I reached the back door to Vero's bar. Like the Mercedes, it was painted scarlet.

My senses remained on high alert. *Was this more trouble?* I'd seen enough for one day, and I hoped that no one was causing any for Vero.

I quietly pulled open the back door, relieved that the hinges didn't creak, and entered the back hallway of the cantina. Once inside, I eased the door shut until the daylight was again purged from the interior.

The two single-person bathroom doors on the left hung open, as did the tiny manager's office door to the right. Vero's computer and a pile of paperwork sat on top of the old, metal desk I felt certain she'd picked up at a school auction in the 1950s.

The darkness of the interior contrasted with the outside world like every bar I'd been to in my life. Sometimes I wondered why bar owners kept the lighting in places like this so dim. Maybe it was to help customers forget the stresses of life that awaited outside. Or perhaps it was as simple as covering up filth or signs of an infestation that they could clean up later before a health inspector came by. I wasn't sure if Santa Rojo even had a health inspector. It was a small village of only a few thousand people at most.

More likely, it was to keep people descending into the hole that they'd fallen into so they'd keep asking for one more drink. Vero's place only seemed dark here in the back; it seemed as if it had been designed to get people back to the front, where the bar and dining area were situated with ample light through the clear windows along the outer walls.

She didn't view patrons as only money. They were friends and neighbors, and her place was one where the townspeople could gather to celebrate, grieve, or simply hang out with friends.

I heard a pair of voices at the end of the hallway, coming from the bar area. I easily recognized one of the voices. Vero's smooth, melodic tone blended with her Mexican Spanish sounded like Mozart in my ears.

From what I gathered, she was politely telling a customer that she would have to pass on an offer, though I didn't have any frame of reference. So, I didn't know what kind of offer she was talking about.

Then I heard a man's voice echoing through the corridor, and I slowed my pace just before I reached the corner.

"Don't be a fool, Vero. I'm offering double what this place is worth." The man's tone was gruff and haughty, the kind of voice that came from a life of expecting everything on a silver platter.

"Yes, and I appreciate the offer, but the cantina is not for sale."

The stranger inhaled loud enough for me to hear him around the corner. It was the sound of exasperation, of a person who was used to always getting what they wanted in life and was now being turned down by, of all people, a small-bar proprietor.

"That is unfortunate," he said. "Frankly, I don't understand what your attachment is to this place. You have few customers. None right now." I imagined him looking around at the empty tables and stools I figured filled the room. "And you barely make enough money to pay all the bills every month. If something were to happen, you may not be able to sustain the business anymore. And then what would you do? I won't come around with an offer like this again. So, be smart. Take the money, Vero. It is a very generous offer."

She remained firm in her response as I listened closely, standing near the wall just out of sight.

"Thank you, Señor Gonzalez. I truly appreciate the offer and your concern for my well-being." She laid the sarcasm on thick like salsa on a tortilla. "But I've been through worse. This cantina is all I have. On top of that, I'm not sure why someone like you would want to spend so much money on a business that won't make that amount in five years. It makes me wonder what your motive could be."

I couldn't help but smile at the response, and nearly laughed out loud. She was saying exactly what I was thinking. Vero was smart. Even if her business wasn't doing great, she had a good head on her shoulders and could see through a con like a seasoned grifter.

"Very well," Gonzalez replied. "I hope for your sake things go better. But if they don't, rest assured that this place will be mine, and for a much cheaper price than I offered."

"Noted," she said. "Now, would you like another drink?"

Again, I nearly burst out laughing.

"No, I think I've had enough of what you have to offer. Unless—"

I decided the conversation had gone far enough. It was easy to see where he might take things next—alone in a cantina with a beautiful young woman. It wasn't jealousy that drove me to step out from the shadows. Rather, I just didn't want him to do anything that might harm her.

Of course, I knew Vero could take care of herself. She was far from a damsel in distress, and I could think of no one better to be granted one of the Medallions of Power, as the shaman had suggested.

I stepped around the corner, revealing myself to both of them. The rest of the cantina was devoid of other customers, as I suspected.

Gonzalez was a rotund man—I guessed in his late forties or early fifties—a few inches shorter than me, wearing a beige suit with a black button-up shirt wrapped around his bulging belly. Too many of the buttons at the top were undone, revealing way more thick chest-hair than I would have liked to see. The only thing this guy was missing was a shiny gold chain and medallion around his neck.

"Medallion," the voice in my head said. "Now that's both funny and ironic."

I rolled my eyes at the sound I knew only I could hear and continued to the end of the bar, where Vero stood.

The man's gut tested the strength of the shirt's bottom buttons, as well as the belt holding up his pants. He wore brown alligator loafers with no socks—a stylistic choice that seemed both impractical and weird whenever I saw it.

"I hope I'm not interrupting anything," I said, deliberately doing just that—interrupting.

Seeing Vero's face light up as she rounded toward me caused my heart to do that little fluttering thing it hadn't done in years until I met her. Now, whenever I thought about her, it seemed like that happened to some degree.

She wore a white tank top and blue jeans with rips and holes fashionably torn into them over the knees, and smaller ones over the thighs.

"Gideon! I didn't know you would be here so soon," she exclaimed. Vero took one step toward me, flung up her arms wide, and wrapped them around me.

She squeezed me hard, letting her right hand slide down to the small of my back. The hug caught me off guard, but I embraced her just as firmly and felt a warm sensation wash over me.

I turned my eyes to Gonzalez and noted the jealousy in his gaze. That wasn't the only thing I witnessed. The familiar red mist danced around his ankles, spiraling up his legs and wrapping around his torso.

The ancient power called to me to end the guy, but I resisted. I didn't know anything about him, and now certainly wasn't the time. And her cantina wasn't the place.

Showing up to see the woman I'd been thinking about nonstop since I met her only to murder some dude in her bar didn't seem like a good way to reunite.

"I would have been here sooner, but I was delayed. There was a big accident on the road coming into Santa Rojo."

"An accident? That's so rare around here. Not many cars drive on that road."

"I know," I agreed. "I thought it was strange."

I looked to her obviously unwanted guest with a curious gaze, pretending I hadn't heard any of their previous conversation. "Who's your friend?" I asked.

The man didn't look pleased that I'd arrived when I had, which only confirmed my suspicions about his insidious intentions. He stood close to her, though not as much now that I held her in my arms.

I released her, and she stepped back to the bar, pulling back a strand of black hair behind her left ear.

Glad I stepped in when I did, I thought.

"You could always kill him, you know," the voice in my head reminded. "The mist doesn't lie."

I'm not going to kill the guy. Not right now, anyway.

"Your choice."

"And you are?" I asked the man, ignoring the voice.

"This is Señor Eduardo Gonzalez," Vero answered for him.

I moved closer toward the man, extending my hand to greet him. He hesitated but apparently didn't want to seem too standoffish, despite the suspicion oozing from his eyes as he stared at me.

He quickly erased the annoyed expression and slapped a polite mask on. "A pleasure, I'm sure. And you are?"

"Gideon Wolf," I said. "How do you two know each other?"

"Vero is a business owner," he explained. "I buy businesses like hers. I came here to make an offer on her lovely cantina." He made a show of looking around the room as if admiring it. "But she has refused, despite it being an incredibly generous sum of money."

"Don't want to sell the old watering hole, huh?" I asked her.

Vero squinted her eyes at me and shook her head. "It's not for sale."

"So you said," Gonzalez remarked. "But everything, and everyone, has their price, my dear. My offer stands until the end of the week. After that, you're on your own." He looked at her as he spoke, letting his gaze linger on her a few seconds after the words stopped dripping from his lips.

Then he turned his focus on me. "Perhaps you can talk a little sense into your friend. She would be wise to accept my offer."

I shrugged at the comment. "I don't know. She's a stubborn one. But I have a feeling good things are in store for her."

He puzzled over the comment and then excused himself. "I must be going. Business to attend to elsewhere."

I wanted to tell him not to let the door hit him in the tail on the way out, but I resisted.

"Pleasure meeting you," Gonzalez said as he passed by on his way to the back door.

"I'm sure it was," I replied coolly, watching him go. He only paused at my derisive remark, then continued beyond the corner, disappearing from sight. I kept watching the hallway until I heard the back door swing open then close loudly with a thud.

6

"I guess that's his red Mercedes in the back, huh," I said.

She blew air through her lips as if a huge weight had been lifted from her shoulders.

"Yeah," Vero confirmed. "I can't stand that guy. The nerve to come in here and try to take my cantina away from me. I don't care how big the offer is. I'm not selling this place. The people of Santa Rojo love coming in here."

"I get it," I said, even though I'd never personally owned a business before. "It's important to you. And to your friends here in town."

She nodded, planting her hands on her hips for a few seconds as she stared into my eyes. "I'm... sorry... for hugging you like that," she offered, stumbling awkwardly over the words.

"Why? I liked it." I felt my cheeks burn at the confession. "I'm glad to see you." I felt an urge to step close, pull her to me and kiss her, but I denied that desire. I felt like it was what she wanted, but everything was happening so fast. Too fast. I needed to give it time to make sure I wasn't just grasping at withered vines like a monkey falling from the jungle canopy.

I'd never been much of a risk taker. And my career in archaeology only stiffened that inner resolve to avoid fate's whimsical swipes at me.

That kind of mentality had, however, probably kept me from some great experiences in life, though I didn't dwell on that much. I'd played it safe since I could remember, and until the frightful events unfolded in Guadalajara when the cartel sent my life into a tailspin, it had worked out okay.

Now, though, that old self seemed less resilient, less willing to take charge and tell me to stick to my guns, play the odds, don't take any chances. All I could think about as I stood a footstep way from Vero was how much I wanted to squeeze her tight again.

I swam in her perfume—a scent of flowers and honey, I guessed. I didn't know how such things were made, or even what botanicals were used. But I liked hers. It was a sweet, tempting, relaxing scent that I could have inhaled for a hundred years without going nose-blind.

"What?" she asked, crossing her arms over her chest.

Crap.

"Busted," the voice said.

Shut up.

"Earlier you wanted me to talk more. Now you want me to be quiet. Make up your mind, Guardian."

I ignored him. "Nothing. I was just admiring the perfume you have on. It's lovely."

She grinned at the compliment, then turned, stepping behind the counter to a row of tequila lining a shelf behind the bar.

She picked out a particularly beautiful ceramic bottle painted white with swirling blue wreaths rising toward the top, where a silver topper plugged the spout. A matching silver emblem of an agave leaf adorned the front of the container, set in an indented oval.

Vero spun around and set the bottle on the counter as I shifted to the side and stood close to the bar opposite of her. I leaned forward, resting my elbows on the surface while she produced two clear shot glasses, setting one down in front of me and one closer to her.

She popped the topper off the bottle with a familiar thump that cork makes when pulled out of a wine bottle. Then she tipped the container toward my glass first, filling it halfway before doing the same with hers. She replaced the lid on the bottle, then set it off to the side before raising her glass toward me.

"Welcome back, Gideon," she said in Spanish.

"Salúd," I replied, and raised my glass to hers with a clink.

She smiled sheepishly again, but there was also a hint of something else in her eyes. Desire, perhaps?

I didn't stay fixated on it and instead lifted the glass to my lips and poured the golden liquid into my mouth. I swallowed quickly, noting that this particular brand burned significantly less than the cheap swill I'd been forced to consume when in college. I looked at the empty glass, impressed, as she finished her shot.

"This is excellent," I remarked.

"It's the best," she said and reached for the bottle again.

"So, it's that kind of party, huh?" I asked.

She rolled her shoulders. "I probably won't have any more customers for a while, and my shift ends soon."

"You got someone else running the place?"

"As a matter of fact, I do. Miguel has done a great job helping out, which frees me up to get some time off."

She took off the bottle's topper again, this time setting it aside. Vero held the bottle over my glass with inquisition in her eyes. "To the future," she said, pouring another.

This time, I didn't pound the shot like before—instead sipping it slowly as a good tequila should be.

I stared into her eyes for a long moment. How many seconds passed, I had no idea. I just knew I never wanted to leave those chocolate pools.

"So, what happened when you went home?" she asked.

I had the cup to my mouth when she spoke, and the question nearly caused me to spit out the precious liquid. Fortunately, I had enough self-control to press my lips together and cover them with my left fist.

I choked down the liquid, which burns significantly more when you're not anticipating a shot.

I coughed for a second to clear my thoughts, which put an oddly delighted expression on Vero's face.

She giggled at my abrupt misfortune. "You okay there, hoss?"

I coughed one last time while bobbing my head like an idiot. "Yeah. Just... a loaded question. That's all."

"I guess so," she said, chasing the comment with another sip.

I exhaled, finally getting my resilience back, and set the glass down on the counter. "Turns out things weren't so good back on the old home front."

"Oh? What happened?" She looked genuinely concerned.

I tried to blow it off like it was no big deal as I answered. "Well, let's see. My ex-father-in-law tried to kill me. And I had to take down a megachurch pastor who'd been filtering sex trafficking and drug money through his organization. Other than that, not much. Wanted to catch a Predators game, but I just didn't have time."

I thought the last part about hockey might disarm her concern, but it bounced off her like a pebble on a tank.

"Your father-in-law tried to kill you?"

"Ex," I corrected. "And yes. He shot me. Point blank. Of course, he didn't know what I am now." I averted my gaze, looking off through one of the windows to the left. It didn't matter which one. I just needed to look away for a second. My mind kept wandering to the way she looked. The black choker around her neck with silver skull and crossbones dangling from it distracted me. I couldn't deny I wanted her. It had been so long since I'd—*No. I have to stay focused.*

"Anyway," I rerouted back on course, "I let him think he'd succeeded. He left me there for dead."

"You could have killed him," she said, her words fading into oblivion.

"I know. The mist told me to. I ignored it."

She perked up at the statement.

I sensed the question brimming in her eyes and cut her off at the pass. "I don't know why I didn't do it. He told me that I was the one who was supposed to die here in Mexico. That it should have been me. Who was I to argue with that."

Vero's concern darkened her face. "No, Gideon. Don't talk like that." She reached across the bar with her free hand and stroked my right cheek. I closed my eyes at her touch. It felt like soft flower petals brushing against my skin. Affection had been so absent in my life for the last few years that I'd nearly forgotten what it was like.

"It's okay," I refuted. "Really. It just surprised me. The confession. The betrayal. His attempt at murdering me. All of it was a shock."

"I can't imagine," she breathed and slowly withdrew her hand.

"It's okay. Apparently, that family's loathing of me was a top-down kind of operation." I snickered at the deprecating humor.

"You don't blame yourself, do you? Because Gideon, this is not your fault. None of it is. Well, except for maybe poor judgment when it comes to your choice of a spouse."

I smiled at the humor. "Yeah. I definitely had that in the past." I looked down at the counter again, eyeing the half-empty shot glass. "Amy and I grew apart over the years. It happens pretty often from what I understand. And while I don't blame myself, I also know that for most of our marriage I'd been dedicated to my work, and maybe not as dedicated to the marriage."

"That goes both ways, Gideon."

"I know. And you're right. But I think, deep down, I married her because it was convenient. Two archaeologists intertwined by their passion for scraping away layers of dirt with old tools to find older tools people used long ago."

She laughed. "That's funny."

"Yeah. I know. But we were always more roommates than anything else." I couldn't believe how much I was dumping on this woman, and for a second I thought maybe I should hold something back in case I pushed her away and ruined any shot I might have at anything remotely amazing.

"I appreciate you opening up about all this," Vero said. "It's good to talk about stuff. Get things off your chest."

I inhaled through my nose and held my breath for a second, as if about to jump off a cliff with no hang glider, no parachute—just a leaky bucket full of courage in one hand and my heart in the other.

"I need to ask you something. And I think I know what you'll say, and that's okay. No is fine. You have a business to run and—"

"What, Gideon?" she demanded with a seductive grin.

Another inhale bought me a precious couple of seconds. "I am going to Greece," I said. "To the island of Delos. And I want you to come with me."

Her warm expression turned perplexed. "Greece? Like, on a vacation?"

"Sort of. Not really." I tightened the backpack on my shoulders. The contents within were more valuable than anything I'd ever found on a dig, or anyone else had found for that matter. The Kevlar lining had kept the documents safe. Fortunately, the men who attacked me on the road hadn't used grenades.

"I was attacked earlier today on the road. That accident I told you about before... that was for your other guest's benefit. It was no accident. Someone tried to kill me."

Concern washed over her again. "I'm glad you're okay," she gasped as she grabbed my arm in concern. "What happened?"

"Five men in an SUV hit me with everything they had. One of them was using explosive sniper rounds. I didn't even know those things existed. They're gone now. The mist took them. But I don't know if they'll be back, or if they know where I was going. I want you to come with me. You'll be safer that way. And there's something else."

"Gideon," Vero cut me off and placed her hand on top of mine on the counter. Her touch felt hot, and tender. "I would love to come with you, but I have to stay here. I can't just leave my cantina, even with the help I've brought on. I truly would love to go on a vacation like that with you. Greece sounds lovely, and I've always wanted to visit there. I don't know why, but I feel almost called to go there at some point in my life. It just can't be now."

I blinked away the rejection. I didn't know if I should tell her about my theory on why she felt like Greece was calling to her. To me, it couldn't have been clearer. With what the shaman had told me earlier, I knew she was meant to go there to receive the next medallion.

That was a heavy thought, and not one I was sure she was ready to hear just yet. And something else the medicine man said fluttered through my thoughts. He'd talked about two sides more than once—the struggle between good and evil. Did that mean there was an equal and opposite side to the mythical guardian houses? How could it be otherwise?

The question caused me to wonder if the houses of evil had ever obtained them, but I thought that answer to be pretty obvious. If that had ever happened, the world would have likely been ripped apart.

Or would it?

If the wicked were coming after me to take the medallion, perhaps the same happened the other way around at different points of history.

"You okay?" Vero asked, cutting through my thoughts like a sword through a watermelon. "I hope you aren't upset. It's just that—"

"I'm not upset at you, Vero. It's okay. Really." I decided to keep the real purpose behind the mission to Delos a secret for now. It was better that way. I'd go to Greece, recover the amulet, and bring it back to her. Then I'd tell her everything, including the part about her being one of the seven guardians.

"Are you sure?" she asked, refilling my glass as well as hers.

"I'm sure," I said with an easy grin. I ran my fingers through my hair, then motioned to the drink. "Are you trying to get me drunk?" I asked, changing the subject to something more comfortable.

She laughed. "Maybe. But I'm drinking too. But you look like you could use it more than me. Especially with what happened earlier. No wonder you're so talkative."

I pulled another sip from the glass and held it for a moment, pensively pondering the last few weeks. "Seems to be happening more and more lately," I muttered. "I don't want to put you or anyone here in the village in danger. Maybe it's best if I get moving."

Vero cocked her head to the right and gave me a look that she would a deranged animal. "You're not putting anyone in danger, Gideon."

I wasn't convinced. "If more people come after me, I wouldn't want anyone here to get hurt. Especially you."

The words touched her, and softened her face. "I'm not worried about that," she said. "After all, I have a monster on my side." She winked at me and downed the drink in one shot.

I hummed a short sound, then finished mine too.

"Miguel should be here any minute," she said, picking up a rag. She started wiping down the counter, then picked up the two glasses in one hand and set them in the sink. Her fluid motion bore witness to how many times she'd done this routine in the past. "When he gets here, we need to go see Myra."

"Oh?"

I'd expected that to some degree. No visit to Santa Rojo would be complete without popping in to see the village oracle. Of course, she was so much more than that.

"She said she has something for you. It sounds important."

"And I didn't get her anything."

Vero chuckled as the front door opened and sunlight spilled through across the old wooden floor.

A young man in his early twenties stepped in wearing a white T-shirt and faded blue jeans.

"Ah, Miguel. Right on time," Vero said. "I was just finishing up. Everything should be ready for the afternoon rush." The statement was laden with mischief.

He laughed at her and shook his head. "Afternoon rush. That's a good one." He walked by and nodded at me. "Welcome back, Gideon."

"Thanks," I said and watched him disappear down the hall, presumably to check in for his shift. When he was out of sight, I returned my focus to Vero. "So... Myra, huh?"

She smiled back at me, locking eyes with mine. "Yep."

7

Vero knocked on the red wooden door of the humble house Myra called home. The white walls showed their age with cracks stretching up from the ground and mysteriously stopping a few feet up. Other parts of the paint chipped and peeled from stress points where the foundation had settled, or from a lack of attention over the years.

The tin roof seemed to be in good condition. I didn't notice any holes where it could leak, though I wondered if that would even be an issue for someone of Myra's skills.

I wasn't sure if she had mystical abilities to the level of repairing her house, but I was quickly learning that pretty much anything was possible.

The doorknob turned, and a second later the door swung open revealing the older Mexican woman inside. She wore a welcoming smile to go with her long gray dress, a dark green shawl draped over her shoulders, and a pair of brown leather sandals. But despite all those details, it was her face, warm and wrinkled by her smiling mouth and eyes, that struck me the most.

"Gideon," she exclaimed. "I've been expecting you." She stared at me with an odd sort of admiration in her eyes. Then she quickly added, "And you as well, my dear," turning her focus to Vero. "Please. Please. Come in."

The second thing that hit me right after the kind welcome from Myra was the smell of food cooking somewhere in the little house.

What's with these mystics and always cooking something?

Despite having just eaten at the medicine man's ethereal hut earlier, I felt hungry, which only made me further question whether or not the meal he'd provided was real or not.

The smell of freshly made tortillas wafted over me, along with the scent of beef and onions.

Myra stepped back and allowed us to enter, closing the door behind as we passed. I glanced over my shoulder and noticed her looking out through the opening, as if wary someone else might try to enter. But when she turned around and looked up into my eyes, the woman didn't appear concerned.

"How was your trip?" she asked with a knowing twinkle in her eyes.

"Um, it was, okay, I guess. Saw some old friends in Nashville. And made a few new ones."

She nodded, unsurprised. "And?"

I felt like she already knew the story, though I wasn't sure how. The woman had insights unlike any ordinary human, and I couldn't help but feel like she had a crystal ball to see into the lives of others, particularly ones she was trying to help.

I thought maybe the voice would confirm or deny the notion, but it remained silent, as it seemed to do whenever I had pressing questions.

"And..." I paused, then glanced at Vero, who encouraged me with a single nod. "And I ran into a few other people."

I went on to tell her the story of what happened with Amy's father, and of the megachurch pastor who'd been running drugs and slaves through his operation.

"Yes, yes. I know all of that," she said to Vero's surprise. "Were you going to leave out the attack on the road earlier today?"

I puzzled over the question before answering. "How did you—"

"Oracle," she said simply. "We see things. Unfortunately, all we get to do is observe. We are not permitted to intervene through the visions. Did you find out who those men were?"

"No," I said, slightly dejected. "Although I tried."

"Yes. You did the right thing questioning the man with the rifle. I have to say, that was a little dark the way you ended him, what with the fútbol americano kick and all."

"You saw that too?" I tried not to sound amused, but it came through in my voice anyway.

She crossed her arms and arched her right eyebrow. "Mm-hmm. He had it coming, though."

"Yeah." I surveyed the room for a second. Beef sizzled in a skillet on the stove in the little kitchen to my left. "I didn't mean to interrupt your cooking. Don't want you to burn that."

She took a step toward me and put her hand on my right cheek, patting it gently. "Oh, you are sweet. I never burn anything."

Myra sidled by me and into the kitchen. She picked up a wooden spatula and stirred the meat. As she tossed and folded it, the crackling sizzle of the meat grew louder before waning into the steady, low volume from before.

"I think the men who attacked me work for some religious organization. But I couldn't get any answers out of them."

"Yes, I know." She stirred the beef slowly as she spoke. "Difficult to say with them. Or with any of the dark forces of this world. Always behind the veil, they operate."

She sounded like Yoda.

"So I've been told." Her head snapped toward me, eyes dark with concern.

"Who told you?"

Vero perked up at the question, also curious.

I looked from one to the other and back to Myra again. "Before I arrived in Santa Rojo, I..." The explanation faltered.

"You saw him again. Didn't you?" Myra asked. The question carried no accusation or judgment with it, merely curiosity. "The shaman."

I confirmed with a nod. There was no reason to lie or feel ashamed about it, even though it did make me feel crazy to admit it to anyone else.

"Yes. After the attack, my car was destroyed, so I had to come the rest of the way on foot. I wanted to avoid any unwanted attention on the road, so I cut through a cornfield and into the jungle. Shortly after I entered the forest, I woke up in his hut. I have to say, it's an unnerving thing to go from one place to another without any recollection of how it happened."

"I'm sure it is." Myra returned her focus to the skillet, still stirring and turning the beef. After another ten seconds, she turned off the stove and moved the pan to the right, placing it on a dark gray towel she'd folded and left there before I arrived.

Then she opened the oven and pulled out a baking sheet with a tall piece of aluminum foil set in the center. That smell of tortillas I'd noticed before grew stronger in an instant, and I realized she'd wrapped the tower of torts in the foil and put them in the oven to keep them warm before we arrived. And based on the size of them, there was no question she'd planned on feeding both of her guests.

She placed the baking sheet on the top of the stove, then turned to the white, weathered cabinet over the sink and pulled out a couple of wooden plates. She set those down on the counter opposite the stove where a bowl of fresh salsa sat next to a bowl of queso fresco.

"Help yourselves," she said. "Tacos for all."

I smiled at the offer. My stomach grumbled at the sight and smell of the food, again reiterating that whatever I'd eaten with the shaman previously wasn't real—despite how it felt and tasted.

"After you," I said to Vero, extending my hand.

She graciously accepted with a bashful smile and stepped past me. I followed her, picking up a plate, then moving over to the foil tower where she unwrapped the top and pulled out two steaming tortillas. The smell tickled my senses. Back in the States, I almost never got freshly made tortillas.

There was a Mexican joint where I used to eat fairly regularly that had a tortilla machine, and an old woman who would come in on the weekends to make them, but they hadn't done that in years. I found out, at one point, that the machine had broken down and the company that made it went out of business. Despite that, the owners of the restaurant kept it in place—I guessed in case someone happened to come along some time who knew how to fix it.

I didn't ask what happened to the woman who operated it, but assumed she'd moved away.

After Vero completed construction of her street tacos, I spooned beef onto both of the tortillas, then swiveled around and followed her to the salsa and cheese.

Myra watched us, pleased to be able to feed her guests. She struck me as the sort who took a great deal of pleasure in such a simple act. It reminded me of my mother and all the times she'd fed family and friends for lunch after church nearly every weekend, and always during the holidays.

We sat down at a wooden table near the edge of the humble living room and waited for Myra to fill her plate.

She made herself a couple of tacos and then joined us at the table. Three glasses of water were already waiting for us, which reiterated that she'd been expecting both of us.

"Would you like to bless the food, Gideon?" Myra asked.

The question caught me off guard, but I nodded. "Yes, sure." I said a quick blessing I always used when I was about to eat. When I finished, we dove into the tacos.

The savory flavor of the meat and onions, combined with the cilantro-infused salsa and creamy cheese, danced across my taste buds.

I grunted my approval as I took another bite. "These are so good, Myra. Thank you."

"You're welcome, *mi hijo*," she said, watching me with delight. She picked up one of her tacos and held it for a moment. "So, you are heading to Greece, I understand."

"Yes, ma'am."

Vero glanced at me as she chewed her food, waiting for me to elaborate.

I cleared my throat after swallowing and took a drink of water. I only now realized I still wore my backpack and slid my arms through it to set it down on the floor.

"I found new information in Nashville. Apparently, the man who was conning his church flock was looking for a medallion too."

"Ah." Myra's head slowly bobbed up and down before she took a bite of the taco in her hand. She set it back down as she chewed. A thoughtful look played in her eyes. "I was not aware of that part. Although I'm not surprised. The darkness veils its activities from those such as myself, and your mystical friend, as I'm sure he informed you."

"He did," I admitted. "Although I'm surprised neither one of you could see beyond whatever spell they wove. Especially him since... he doesn't seem to be bound by the laws of this world."

"Laws, as you know, can be broken, but some are much stronger than others. Especially when...." She let the words fade off into oblivion and shoved the taco into her mouth, breaking off a big bite.

I frowned at the abrupt ending to whatever she was about to say. "Especially when what?"

Vero obviously wanted to know too. She stared at our hostess with pleading in her eyes.

"I've said too much as it is," Myra explained. "You will come to understand in time."

I shook my head, growing tired of the mystical shell game. "He told me about Ahriman," I blurted.

The room seemed to darken at the mention of the name, and I thought I felt a draft of cool air spill over me.

Myra stopped chewing her taco for a second and merely stared down at the plate while still holding the last bite between her thumb and index finger. Then she continued chewing, set the piece of taco down on her plate, and dusted off her hands.

"Oh," she said. "So, the shaman mentioned the adversary."

For a few more seconds, she kept her eyes down. Then Myra slowly lifted them to meet mine, peering at me from under her eyelids.

"Yes."

"Then I don't understand the question. If you know who is behind all this, then what answers do you seek from me?"

"I don't know. I just know what he said. I guess I'm just looking for confirmation. Are we really in some kind of warfare against the devil or something?" Just saying it out loud made me feel like a crazy person. Then again, everything that had happened recently felt insane.

Vero's eyelids opened wide at the question. She held her breath, looking at me, then back to Myra as she awaited the answer.

"You have been approached by supernatural beings in the last few weeks, Gideon. You know this to be true."

She left the words to bounce around in my head as I searched for the answer to what she said. A collection of faces appeared, but the two most prominent were the agents from a government operation I'd never heard of before. "Division Three?" I asked, not sure if I should expect an answer.

Myra nodded. "And who do you think those agents are?"

"I haven't had much time to consider it, honestly," I said.

"But you remember their names."

It wasn't a question. But her statement did bring up another question in my mind. I wanted to ask how she knew about the two men, and how she knew I'd met them, but I was playing in a different sandbox than I had been my entire life. It felt disconcerting knowing that strangers, or those I barely knew, could see into my life, and I wasn't sure I wanted them to.

"It's okay, Gideon," she said, as if I'd spoken the concerns out loud. "I don't pry that way. The men you met with Division Three are Gabriel and Azrael, yes?"

I nodded.

"And do you recognize those names?"

"Not really. I mean, I remember they're Biblical names belonging to two angels. I just figured they grew up in super religious homes."

"Search your heart, Gideon. You know their true identities."

I did question that, and had done many times since meeting the two covert agents. They'd said their agency was more hands off, and multiple times they'd referred to themselves as watchers.

A flicker sparked in my mind. "Watchers," I muttered. Then another word bubbled to the surface as Myra and Vero kept their focus on me as I worked through the problem. "You're not saying they're Nephilim are you? Like actual angels?"

Myra's lips creased slightly while Vero merely sat in silent astonishment.

"No. They are not Nephilim. Angels, however...."

She didn't have to finish the sentence.

As the answer hit me, I realized it didn't feel foreign—as if I'd known all along. "Of course," I said. "But I don't understand. Why—"

"Don't they intercede directly?"

I nodded.

"Because direct intervention is prohibited. The forces on both sides are only permitted to influence. Free choice must never be tampered with."

"You mean free will?" Vero corrected.

"There is no such thing as free will," Myra answered. "Only free choice. We have infinite choices to make in this universe. But the will of all flows like a river. Choices can redirect its movement on either a large or small scale, but the flow never fully stops."

I felt like I was diving deep into a rabbit hole on this subject, and while I listened to what she said, my brain was still stuck on angelic beings actually existing and engaging with humans—particularly me.

"So," I said, still wrapping my head around the concept, "that means if there are good angels—"

"There are evil ones too. Yes. The forces of Ahriman, the dark one, the maker of shadows, the consumer of souls."

I retreated back to my self-defense mechanism of making a joke. "You make him sound so pleasant."

Myra didn't laugh, and a sort of darkness surrounded her eyes as she spoke. The lights in the room even seemed to dim. "He is the cause of all suffering. If those who seek his blessings discover the medallions before you can get them to the other guardians, the world will become a hellish place."

More than it already is?

I kept the thought to myself, although I wondered if she could pry into my thoughts like the shaman. But Myra wasn't like him. She was here, on this plane, and a very real person. I still wasn't sure what that guy was.

"You make it sound like we're all just pawns in a huge game," Vero said.

"Whether you're a pawn or a knight is up to you," Myra replied.

"That's pretty deep," I observed. "I like it."

She smiled at me the way my grandmother used to when I would walk into her house after school. Grandma would always offer me a couple of Oreos and that smile that told me no matter what was going on, everything would be okay.

"And since you've clearly taken on the mantle of the latter," Myra continued, "it's time you had a knight's armor."

"What?"

I looked to Vero as if she might know what the woman was talking about, but she simply lifted her shoulders and shook her head.

Myra stood and walked over to the corner of the room, where a black box sat atop an end table. An antique lamp with *calaveras*, or sugar skulls, adorning the shade glowed just above the little chest.

The movie *Seven* came to mind, and I so badly wanted to ask, "What's in the box?" in my best Brad Pitt impression.

Myra bent over slightly, then lifted the lid. A white light glowed from inside the container, and for a second I thought maybe there were some cool LEDs hidden within. That idea was shot down when she reached into the box and pulled out a shiny, metallic disc.

The hoop looked like it was made from titanium, and appeared roughly the size of the medallion around my neck.

Another peculiar thing I noticed was that the second she picked up the metal ring, my amulet started vibrating, and making a noise that I could only liken to a Tibetan singing bowl.

As she walked across the room with it in her hands, the vibrating strengthened, causing the medallion to hum against my chest.

I felt a strange energy pulsing through me, and I shifted nervously as Myra approached.

"What is that?" I asked.

"A gift," she answered. "The shaman gave you one of these to help you with the transformation."

"You mean with the clothes?"

"Yes. This is an upgrade."

The word sounded funny coming out of the woman's mouth. "What kind of upgrade?"

I spied the runes along the surface of the ring, carved into the metal and painted or burned black.

"What kind of an upgrade? That thing is making the medallion vibrate like crazy."

Myra blinked slowly, still smiling at me as she reached out the ring. The amulet around my neck elevated, rising out of my shirt. Then, as if by some powerful magnetism, the ring leaped from her fingers and clapped against the medallion. The white light burned brighter, pulsing as though it had its own heartbeat.

Then, as quickly as it began, the bizarre sounds ceased, the vibrations ended, and the medallion rested against my chest.

I looked down at it, lifting the thing with my left thumb. The ring had somehow become a part of the medallion, wrapping around the inner portion of the emblem I'd grown so accustomed to.

"What does it do?" I asked, raising my gaze to meet Myra's once more.

"The next time you summon the power, you will see."

8

Vero and I left Myra's without any more answers. Not that I could handle anything else on top of all I'd learned.

Angels were real, according to her. And they operated in secret agencies known as Division Three, and in the Sector, as I came to find out.

"Always be wary of them," Myra had warned prior to us taking our leave. "They are everywhere, always ready to strike and remove that thing from your neck."

She wasn't exactly filling me with a ton of confidence.

Based on what she'd said, the Sector used power-hungry, greedy, bloodthirsty humans as its agents to do the bidding of their dark leader, the one Myra called the consumer of souls.

"You okay?" Vero asked as we walked down the quiet street.

Night had fallen while we were in the older woman's home. I'd lost track of time, and until we left, I hadn't realized that a few hours had passed.

I once heard from a quantum physicist that time could change according to where you put your attention and emotion. He used an example of how he'd been on a bus going to see some ancient ruins in Egypt. The journey was supposed to take two hours from one point to the other, but when they arrived at the destination, only an hour had passed, which was impossible based on how fast the bus would have had to travel according to the current logic.

Yet there they were.

The physicist's theory was that because everyone on the bus was so focused on where they were going, what they would do when they arrived, and how excited they were to see this ancient place, their minds were already in that location—doing those things. And so, the quantum reality changed to match where their collective minds were.

I'd never really considered it a legitimate example—except for the fact that sixty people on a bus all experienced the same thing. Still, the rational mind always searches for that logical explanation of things, and to this day I've not come up with one that I could accept for the bizarre occurrence.

Then again, I was living a life that wadded up logic and reason and threw them into the Mariana Trench.

"That was an interesting conversation," Vero said. Her voice cut through the evening silence, and I realized we hadn't spoken for at least two minutes since leaving Myra's.

"Yeah," I agreed, but didn't know what else to add at the moment. My heart tugged at me, still begging me to somehow convince her to come with me to Delos. I didn't want to outright tell her that she was supposed to be a guardian, that the Medallion of Artemis was her birthright.

That was a lot to put on a person, to say the least. On top of the burden, I had no idea if that medallion's powers were different. Would she see the red mist too? Or was there some other specialty that came with each amulet?

"I guess you're going to have to find out," the voice in my head chirped.

You're a huge help, Xolotl. You know that?

"I do what I can."

The statement was slathered in truth and irony.

Instead of broaching the subject of Greece again, I decided to cross a different bridge. "You're sure it's okay for me to stay with you? I don't want to intrude."

"Don't be silly," she said. "I want you to stay with me."

The way she said it sounded more like a friendly invitation than romantic. That sentiment brought a sense of both relief and disappointment.

The truth was, if I was going to move on with my life—a life without my ex—I didn't need to rush it. I had to take my time, move slow. It wasn't like I didn't have something to do.

My new hobby was pretty intense.

"Hobby," the voice laughed in my head.

Well, I don't get paid for it.

"You think you should?"

That's not what I meant. I was agreeing.

"You seem pensive," Vero noticed, interrupting the insane conversation with the invasive persona in my mind.

I scratched the back of my head and looked down the empty street. Streetlights glowed along the sidewalks and at the intersection. A strand of cutouts in the shapes of colorful shoes hung from a string over the window of the *zapatería*. The sound of a child crying echoed through one of the windows and down the street. Violin music accompanied it from another home.

A warm breeze rustled my hair as we continued walking. I felt a nervousness I'd not sensed since I was in college. Or maybe even the first time I asked Amy out.

But Vero didn't want to take that step. It was obvious in her tone. So, the nerves quickly retreated to be replaced by conjecture brought on by insecurity.

"You okay?" she asked. "I said you seem pensive."

I realized I hadn't responded to her first statement.

"Oh, yeah. I'm fine."

"Smooth," the voice teased.

She looked at me across her shoulder and smiled, but her eyebrows lowered slightly, showing her concern. "You sure? It's okay, you know. If you need to open up about things."

"I know," I said, half lying. "I... I just—"

"Keep going, Romeo," Xolotl taunted.

I wanted him to shut up, but he had a mind of his own.

"You're disappointed I said no to Greece." She finished the thought for me, and while it wasn't entirely what was on my mind, it ventured into a subject that had been at the forefront.

I didn't try to deny it, but I wasn't the type to yoke someone with guilt. I'd learned a long time ago not to do that. Gaslighting never worked out in the long term, and it eventually unraveled in a way that revealed ugly insecurities.

"Yeah, but it's okay. I get it. Seriously, don't worry about it."

We kept walking toward the cantina.

Her house wasn't far from there, only a few minutes by car. I assumed I'd follow her there in my rental, except my rental was now a shelled husk of its former self. I realized that any emergency crews or cops on the scene of the "accident" would trace the vehicle back to me, which meant I'd be getting a call at some point in the next twenty-four hours. The thought nudged my gut with a pinch of anxiety, but I decided it could wait.

"You know, Gideon," Vero said, ending the silence again, "I do like you."

The statement caught me in the chest, then sent a warm feeling spilling through my entire body. I looked over at her and smiled, and noticed she was sending me the same expression.

"I like you too," I said. "But I'm just trying to be careful."

"I know. I am too."

She tore her gaze from me and looked ahead to the cantina a block away. "I've been hurt before," she went on.

"Who hasn't? Take a number," the voice in my head chirped.

"Shut up," I muttered.

"What?" Vero asked, looking at me with disgusted surprise.

"I said, yup. I figured you had been."

Her face twisted into a wry look of suspicion. "Oh really? And how do you know that?"

I didn't have to improvise with the question. It was one I'd considered for a while, and only now had the reason to voice it.

"You're a beautiful, smart, talented young woman. You'd do well anywhere in the world. Yet you choose to stay here in this village, isolated from the rest of the world."

"Maybe I just like quiet."

I snorted that explanation away. "Until recently, this place was anything but quiet. Maybe now that Carrillo is gone it's that way, but before, I don't think so. My guess is you were running from something."

She nodded absently; her mind lost in distant memories. "I had someone special. We were supposed to be married. Then he left, and never came back. All I got was a text message telling me he couldn't do it. A few weeks later, I found out he'd been seeing someone else behind my back, and had run off with her. Some model, apparently. For a while, I let the pain keep me locked up. I didn't do anything with my life, and my small savings were spent in a few months."

Vero chuckled. It was a regretful kind of sound, the kind people made when the power of hindsight told them plainly how foolish they'd been before.

"I did the usual things, stalking him on social media to see what he was up to—secretly hoping that he would come to his senses and return to me. I see now how stupid that was. What was I thinking?"

She shook her head in disgust.

I reached out my hand and touched her shoulder, shaking it gently. "Don't beat yourself up. We all make mistakes. Most of us have gone through something like that. We don't know how to handle that kind of rejection. There's no manual for it, only experience. We always look back and think we could have done better with the situation, but in the moment all we feel is pain, fear, loneliness, and regret."

She looked over at me, and I nearly tripped over a crack on the sidewalk. I caught myself, using her shoulder to balance, before I withdrew my hand with a laugh. I felt my cheeks burn from embarrassment.

"Don't tell me you're still feeling the tequila from before. That was hours ago."

I laughed. "No. Just clumsy. But I'm glad you think I'm a lightweight."

We didn't say anything else until we got to the car. Once inside, I put on my seat belt as she pulled out of the parking space and onto the back street behind the cantina.

"My point is, I know how you feel. You're not alone."

"I appreciate that, Gideon. And I know I'm not alone. That's one of the reasons I like being here. I've made friends here, and given people a place to gather."

"And having the cantina also gives you an outlet for socializing, I'm sure."

She nodded and turned down the next street.

"I appreciate the invitation to Greece," she said. "I really do. It sounds so exciting. And you're going there to find the next medallion?"

"Yeah," I said in a muted tone, still trying to mask my rejection. There was no way I could tell her she was supposed to be the next guardian, the one to bear the Artemis Medallion. A scheme arose in my imagination, and I visualized myself returning from Delos with the amulet. Then I would tell her. Then I would give it to her and fill her in on the conversation with the shaman, and the truth of who she really was.

But not now.

"That all sounds like a horrible idea," Xolotl said in my head. "You should just tell her now. She might say yes."

I sighed.

"What?" Vero asked, noticing the sound as she turned onto the road leading out of the village toward her house.

"Oh, nothing. I just have a lot of plans to make."

"So smooth," the voice cajoled.

I ignored it. "But I do need your help. I have everything I took from the office of a man named Vernon Wells. He was the megachurch pastor I..."

"Killed?" she finished.

"Yeah."

"You said he was doing horrific things. That's on him."

"I know. Still, it's weird to say it out loud. Anyway, he had a bunch of old maps, books, all sorts of things in his study. He was trying to find the Artemis Medallion."

"Do you think he got close?"

"No. I mean, I think he was close and didn't realize it. He was looking for it in the wrong place."

For some reason an old country song rang in my head. "Lookin' for Love in All the Wrong Places" it was called. It annoyed me, and I had to shake it off. Of course, Xolotl only encouraged it by repeating the lyrics over and over.

"I was hoping you could help me," I said, drowning out the off-key sounds ringing in my ears. "I need to pinpoint the exact location where the next hidden temple is. Once I know, I can go straight to it once I'm in Greece. Shouldn't be too difficult."

She smirked and looked over at me with an incredulous glint in her eyes. "You make it sound so easy."

I caught what she really meant. Nothing was ever that easy. Especially in this strange new role my life had taken on.

9

When we arrived at Vero's home, she flipped on the lights and showed me to the guest room, where a neatly made bed awaited me.

"This is great," I said, hoping she caught my appreciative tone.

"It isn't anything fancy," she replied. "But it's better than a hotel."

"Definitely."

She stood in the doorway with her hands on her hips, looking at me with distant, tired eyes.

"I don't want to keep you up too late," I hedged. "If you'd rather look at everything in the morning, it can wait until then."

She perked up and shook her head. "Are you kidding? You're letting me help you find an ancient, mystical hidden temple somewhere on a Greek island. If I can't go with you, the least I can do is this."

"If you're sure," I said with a grin.

She reached out and snagged the backpack on my shoulders. "Come on, mister. Let's open that thing up and see what we can find."

I followed her into the kitchen area where a little bistro table sat off to the side in what passed for a dining room.

We sat down and I placed the bag on the surface, unzipped it, and began removing the collection of things I'd found at the Wells mansion.

I'd gone to the trouble of sealing the maps and books in large plastic bags so they wouldn't be damaged by moisture or even the air while I traveled back to Mexico. I knew Wells hadn't taken similar care of the items, but that didn't give me permission to be just as careless.

"Wow," Vero gasped, looking over the maps and aged tomes as I spread them out on the table. "You weren't kidding."

I nodded and pointed to one of the maps, the one that featured the island of Delos. "This one here is very old."

"How old?"

"Several hundred years from the looks of it. You can tell a lot simply based on the material used."

I retrieved a pair of white gloves from my bag, slipped them on, and removed the map from the plastic bag. Delicately, I placed the map onto the table surface and spread it out until it lay flat.

"See?" I said, pointing at Delos. This is where I think the hidden temple is." I gently tapped my index finger on the spot.

"What makes you think it's there?" Vero asked. She leaned over and stared at the map. Standing so close, her perfume continued to tantalize my senses, pulling my attention in different directions—to places that wouldn't help me figure out this puzzle.

"Well," I said with a deep inhale and exhale, "there was a temple to Artemis on this island. While the main temple was in Ephesus, and that would be the obvious answer, everything I've seen up to this point makes me think the obvious answer isn't the correct one."

"It rarely ever is."

I felt a tingle in my cheeks when she said it. I'd used that line myself many times.

"Do you have a handheld mirror?" I asked.

She frowned at the question. "Why? Do I look that bad?"

I blushed and shook my head. "No. Far from it." For a split second, I regretted saying that although I didn't know why. "I just need to show you something with it."

"Okay... one second. I have one in my bathroom."

She walked out of the room and disappeared into the narrow hallway, leaving me in her modern, IKEA-furnished dining nook.

Somewhere outside, a dog howled in the night. I wondered if the beast belonged to someone or if it were feral.

"Can't it be both?" Xolotl asked.

"Seriously. Why do you only speak when I don't want you to?"

"That's not true, Gideon. And what a hurtful thing to say."

I rolled my eyes and clamped my lips together when I heard Vero's footfalls down the corridor.

She appeared around the corner a second later. "Did you say something?"

"I was just talking to the voice in my head that came with this thing," I admitted. "It can be very annoying sometimes."

She slowed down, looking at me like I should have a straitjacket on. "Does it talk all the time?"

"No. But it certainly does speak up when I would prefer a little silence."

"Aww, that hurts, Gideon," the voice said.

I sighed, noting the mirror in her right hand. "Oh, you found one. Bring it over here, and hold it over the corner of this map."

She did as told and walked over to the table, stepping even closer to me than before. I could feel the heat radiating off her body. The impulse to wrap my hand around her waist pulled on me like the gravity of a black hole.

"Now," I said, redirecting my thoughts, "you see that word there in the corner?"

"That's a word? Doesn't look like anything. Just some weird characters."

"Hold the mirror over it and look at the reflection."

"Okay..." She did as instructed, craning her head around at an angle so she could see into the mirror.

"Oh wow," she exclaimed. "You're right. It does say Delos. How did you know?"

"Just a hunch. I mean, to be fair, it's not like that's a complex cipher or anything. But it was hidden well enough that Vernon Wells missed it."

"You hope."

She was right. I couldn't know for certain if he had figured it out or not, but simply due to the fact that the man was still in Nashville at the time, and not on the Greek island, led me to that conclusion.

Now for the big finale.

I redirected her attention to the name of the man who the map belonged to. The fancy letters curved and flowed with a flourish. "See that name?" I asked, pointing at the signature.

"Yeah. So?"

"So?" Her ambivalence stabbed at my heart. "Do you know who that is?"

She peered closer at the name. "It looks like... Drake?"

"Yes," I exclaimed in exaggerated joy, throwing up both my hands. "Sir Francis Drake." I said the name like he was a professional athlete or celebrity I admired.

She looked at me with bewildered amusement.

"Is that supposed to mean something to me?" she asked.

I stared back at her, the blank look in my eyes displaying my disbelief for a long five seconds.

"Francis Drake," I explained, "is one of the most famous figures in nautical history, and one of the greatest sailors of all time. The guy operated in the 16th century, during a period of English history when they were challenging the Spanish Empire for control of resources and wealth around the world. Up until that point, the Spanish Armada had been the unquestioned power of the sea, which meant they could expand their borders around the world as they saw fit."

I paused and took a breath before continuing. "Sir Francis Drake was the biggest thorn in their side. He had such naval prowess and managed to escape so many impossible scenarios that many of the Spanish commanders and sailors believed he was dabbling in magic or witchcraft. Some even suggested he carried a witch on board with him, hidden in his quarters. The Spaniards even gave him the nickname "El Draque," or the Dragon. He was a scourge to the Spanish naval forces and seafarers, who were more superstitious than most, and were all too eager to believe that this man was supernatural himself, or using supernatural powers."

"Was he?" Vero asked sincerely. "Was he using some sort of magic?"

"For all my life since I first heard about this guy, I never thought that was a possibility, that he had some kind of secret, supernatural power on his side. I only learned about those Spanish rumors and superstitions when I studied Drake in college. But just like with anything else in a mystical or supernatural context, those notions are easily explained away or blown off by academics. But I always wondered how he was able to escape situations where he was outnumbered ten to one. Or how he sank so many enemy ships when he was so heavily outgunned."

I took a breath and continued. "There have been great naval commanders throughout the history of the world. Drake, for me, goes near the top of that list. Another like him was Hayreddin Barbarossa from the Ottoman Empire. He, too, got his start as a pirate and had similarly outlandish, inexplicable success against insurmountable odds. And just like with Drake, he was accused of using witchcraft or magic to achieve his victories."

I sniffled and took another breath. "I never gave that much credence until I found this." I shuffled a few of the other documents around on the table, careful not to move them too roughly and damage the contents.

"As a pirate, Drake tormented the Spanish for profit. Then, when the queen of England saw the potential that such a captain possessed for the future of her empire, she made a bold move. The queen created a new rank in their naval hierarchy—the privateers. These were pirates that were given paperwork that authorized them to sail without impediment from British ships. These privateers were basically legal pirates, given permission to seek and destroy Spanish merchant vessels, as well as Spanish naval ships. The more they plundered, the better, as far as the queen was concerned. It was a strategic and important move that helped shift the balance of power on the high seas that the Spaniards once controlled without rival."

Vero stared at me, soaking in every word like she was on the front row of a world history class. "You speak about such things with so much passion," she said, her voice dreamy and calm.

I shrugged, tilting my head to the side in an *aw shucks* kind of movement. "I love this stuff. I've always loved the mysteries of history, but also the history that we understand. Francis Drake lived an incredible life." I stopped talking for a second and weighed how I should word the next part.

Fortunately, Vero opened that box for me. "So, what does this Francis Drake have to do with you finding the next medallion on Delos?"

"I'm so glad you asked. I believe that Drake discovered the Artemis Medallion."

"Wait. You think this pirate that worked for the queen of England had one of the guardian medallions?"

She didn't sound like it was going to be an easy sell. "When you combined that with what we've learned in the last few weeks, the facts from the pages from history, it all lines up. He did things that the greatest naval commanders in the world couldn't understand. It wasn't like he had a technological advantage. The ships, while varying in certain ways such as size or maneuverability or speed or firepower capabilities, they shouldn't have been able to accomplish the many things they did. Keep in mind, we're talking about vessels that ran solely on wind power. Wind is a whimsical energy source, totally out of mankind's control. It blows one way then another. While there are ways to measure the currents and understand certain times of day in specific locations how it will move, those can change at the drop of a hat.

"Even if he had a slight tactical advantage, at least some of his adversaries should have been able to make adjustments in battle. You'd think someone would have. The argument against that might be that the Spanish training regimens differed from the English, and if they always played things by the book that would explain their lack of ability to compensate in the heat of battle. But it's hard to imagine a pirate—whose training was primarily done through experience learned on merchant vessels or under another pirate—would have such an advantage over seasoned commanders.

"As superstitious as they might have been, the Spaniards' explanation of Drake's ability could hold water in light of what's happened to me in the last few weeks."

She listened without judgment, and I could see she was willing to accept the theory, which led me to my last point.

I pulled one of the plastic bags out from the bottom of the loose stack and pointed at it, keeping the image inside the protective casing. "This is Francis Drake," I said.

She looked down at the portrait of the man, his face angled slightly toward the viewer as I'd seen in a million pictures such as this from throughout history. He wore a ruffled white collar with a crimson long-sleeve shirt. He seemed to peer back at us, as if questioning whether or not we had the authority to even gaze upon his likeness. For a second, the image felt alive even though it didn't move.

What caught Vero's eye, however, was the medallion hanging around Drake's neck. She leaned closer, holding her breath as the realization hit.

"Wow," she gasped. "Is that what I think it is?"

"Sure looks like it." I said. I gazed at the image with the same wonder I had when I first laid eyes on it. "How many people have looked at this same portrait over the centuries, staring at a supernatural truth right under their noses?"

She straightened up and crossed her arms over her chest, but kept her eyes on the image of Drake. Vero spoke as if mesmerized by a spell. "It's not surprising, really. Not if you think about it. The time that Drake came out of also bore the age of science and reasoning, a period in human history where the supernatural and spiritual sides of things were banished to the shadows of memory."

I marveled at the statement. She put it eloquently, but the words sparked something inside me.

"What did you say?"

She turned her eyes toward me. "You said he was alive during the 16th century. Based on what I know about that time in history, I said he came from a point in history where spiritual things were banished to the shadows of memory."

"Yes. That." I whirled away from her and paced over to the door, pivoted, then walked back to the table again. I thumbed my lower lip, biting down on the nail slightly as I thought. "The shadows," I said.

"What?"

I semi-ignored her, still stuck on the train of thought that now ran full speed through my mind. "Ahriman is the creator of shadows. He's the dark one. The consumer of souls. The time of human history that produced logic and reason, science based on matter or energy, rang in a new age for the destruction of anything that couldn't be explained or measured with instruments, or seen with the eye."

I shook my head in disgust, and ran fingers through my thick hair. "That was the beginning of 'I'll believe it when I see it.' Prior to that, things unseen were often accepted as truth. Since that time, everything has to be proven according to material sciences."

"What I've seen from you flies in the face of all that," Vero said. For moment, I lost myself in her eyes, as if she drew my essence from me and wrapped it in her embrace. I would have loved that moment to last a lifetime, but it only survived a few seconds.

"I really would love to go with you to Greece," she said, interrupting the awkward silence. "All of this sounds so... fascinating. Although you obviously don't need my help."

"I don't have all the answers, Vero. I could use your perspective on things. No doubt about that. And... I would just enjoy it more if you were with me."

I hoped I hadn't come on too strong. It sure felt like I did, but I'd said it and there was no delete button for spoken words.

"I know." She put on her best smile and blinked away the thought. "I'm sure I would enjoy it too."

I didn't press the issue anymore. I felt like I'd already made her feel guilty about it, and that was not my intention.

"When are you going to head to Greece?" she asked.

"I fly out tomorrow." I didn't tell her I had two tickets. I'd taken the liberty, and the chance, that she would come with me. Maybe that had been silly of me. And based on her answer, it was definitely a waste of money, but I could manage that.

"So soon?" She failed to hide the disappointment in her voice, if she tried at all.

"Yeah." I faltered. "I can see if I can change my flight to a few days from now if you like."

"No. I mean, you don't have to do that. I... would like you to stay longer. But you have bigger things going on than hanging out with me."

I felt myself move closer to her. That sugary scent of her perfume tickled my brain. My heart pounded in my chest. I felt the breath catch in my throat and tighten into a knot. I tried to choke it down, but drifting in her eyes, all I wanted to do was take that last step toward her and press her lips to mine.

The temptation to tell her nothing was more important than her hung on my lips, but I resisted, fighting it back with concerted mental effort.

"I'll be back soon. It'll be like I never left."

"Promise?"

I nodded. "Yeah. Now, do you have any more of that good tequila you were pouring before, or are nightcaps not allowed?"

She grinned at me as though a great weight had been taken off her shoulders. "Oh, nightcaps are definitely allowed, Dr. Wolf."

"Good. Make mine a double."

"Will do."

10

The smell of smoke woke me before anything else.

Even without being in monster form, the power of the chupacabra enhanced my senses beyond their normal range.

I sat up in the guest bed, rubbing the temples on both sides of my head to ease the hangover pounding them from within.

"How much tequila did I have?" I muttered. The room spun from sitting up too quickly, and for a second I felt like I was back in college all over again.

"What did you do to us?" Xolotl asked. His voice carried more reverb than usual, making it sound like he was talking to me from the other end of a long corridor.

I shook off the cobwebs and swung my feet over the edge of the bed. They dangled there for a second as I continued to struggle against the headache that wrapped around my skull, squeezing like a vise.

My nose twitched almost on its own, and I sniffed the air again. "Where is that smoke coming from?"

Then I heard the sirens in the distance.

They sounded far away, but based on my rough estimate of where

I was in Vero's house, it sounded like they were coming from the town.

Initially, I'd felt a dull panic snake through my mind at the smell of something burning, but I quickly realized how faint the scent was. Paired with the far-off sirens, I relaxed a little knowing that wherever the fire might be, it wasn't here in Vero's house.

Still, I decided to get up and check around just in case the vast amounts of reposado I'd consumed hadn't thrown off my senses.

I looked back in the bed and felt relieved that Vero wasn't there. "At least I didn't make that mistake," I said.

Getting hammered and sleeping with her would have been a bad idea, and could have easily ruined any possible chance I might have of something real with her in the future.

What was I saying? Future with Vero? I barely knew the woman. But the spark I felt, the gravity pulling my emotions toward her, those things were undeniable.

I opened the door to the bedroom and stepped out into the hall. Vero's door was closed on the other side. She hadn't smelled or heard anything. Not that I was surprised. Her human senses would have to be much closer to the source to detect those things.

I wandered down the corridor and into the living room. A clock on the wall in the kitchen ticked away the seconds. A fan blew in Vero's room, but other than the steady hum and the sounds of the clock, nothing else in the house made a peep.

After a quick glance back down the hall at her door, I walked over to the entrance and slipped into my shoes. At that moment, I became acutely aware I was in my underwear—a pair of black boxer briefs—and not in my own home. I figured I would be quick and silent enough to not rouse my host from her slumber. I'd be back in the guest bed before, if ever, she realized anything happened.

I unlocked the door and pulled it open. The cool, moist night air greeted me with a gentle embrace, tickling the skin on my arms and chest. The scent of smoke instantly grew stronger, as did the sounds of the sirens.

I stepped outside underneath a cloudless, starry night. The moon dulled the twinkling stars and planets with its radiating, pale glow. I eased the door shut behind me and walked a few more steps out away from the house before stopping to look east toward the town.

Something was going on there, but from this distance I couldn't see anything. A dense section of jungle separated Vero's home from the village, along with some rolling hills. I looked back at the home and briefly considered shifting into the beast and running into town to see what was going on.

Unfortunately, a light turned on inside the house and shone through the cracks in the window drapes.

I felt the energy drain from my body as I realized there was no way I'd be getting out of this one. Like the common nightmare where you show up to school in your underwear and everyone laughs at you, the sense of dread burned through my chest as I saw a shadow pass in front of one of the windows.

"Here we go," I muttered.

"You couldn't throw on a pair of pants?" the voice asked.

"You couldn't let me know she was waking up?"

"It's funnier this way."

I sighed, exasperated, and awaited my fate as I listened to Vero's feet pad across the floor. I heard her stop at the threshold. The door-knob turned. I pursed my lips, pressing them together tightly.

Then the door cracked open. At the last second, I had the bright idea to duck to the right behind a shrub.

"Couldn't think of that one beforehand, genius?" Xolotl asked.

You could have mentioned it too, you know.

"Again. Funnier this way."

I waited patiently as the light from inside the house spilled out onto the concrete pads that served as the walkway between the driveway and the entrance.

Through the foliage, I saw Vero look out into the night, sticking her head into the evening air. She looked both directions, then retreated back inside, closing the door behind her.

For a second, I felt a rush of relief. Then I heard the door lock.

I closed my eyes, grimacing at the mistake I'd made. By saving myself the embarrassment of being caught out here in my underwear, I'd also managed to lock myself out of the house.

"Pure genius," the voice teased.

My choices evaporated in an instant, and I knew the only thing I could do was go knock on the door. It was that or sleep out here in the cold. It wasn't *that* cold. I reasoned I'd slept in much colder weather while camping, but there was something harsh about not having a sleeping bag or a blanket. Or a pillow. Despite the powerful force I'd become, I was still baby soft.

I hesitantly walked over to the front door and paused, waiting with my fist in the air—debating whether I should do it or not.

I wondered many times before how the cowboys slept on the ground out on the open range, or how millions of people managed to sleep on nothing more than a blanket on the dirt with a rock for their pillow.

I imagined their backs must have been pretty jacked up.

"They were," the voice answered the unspoken question.

I ignored him and brought my fist close to the door. Then, suddenly, the deadbolt clicked, the knob turned, and the door swung open.

Vero stood there in the light, just a step away from me. She wore a pair of short, lightweight shorts and a tight T-shirt. I swallowed back the embarrassment with my hand still raised and did my best to keep my eyes locked onto hers despite the temptation to take in her night outfit in all its detail.

She crossed her arms and bit her lower lip. Unlike me, she took in the full sight, lowering her eyes all the way down to my toes, then back up again.

I dropped my hand and covered the front of my underwear a second too late.

"Have trouble sleeping?" she asked.

I choked on the answer and had to take a second to gather my thoughts. "I... um, heard a noise. And I smelled smoke. So, I decided to come out here and make sure it wasn't... you know, your house on fire."

She frowned and raised her right eyebrow at the explanation. "And you didn't think to put on some clothes?"

I sighed, fully defeated at this point.

"May I come inside?" I asked. My entire head burned from blushing.

She lowered her gaze and stepped aside, motioning me in.

"Thanks." I walked by and kept moving. "I'm just going to... put some clothes on."

Vero merely nodded as she closed the door and locked it again. "So, you're not going back to sleep?" she asked.

I disappeared into the guest room and switched on the light. I found my jeans where I'd left them draped over a chair in the corner. After I slipped into those, I threw on a gray T-shirt and a pair of black socks. Feeling like a soldier who'd just slipped into battle armor, I walked back out into the hall where I found her still standing by the door.

"I liked the other outfit," she said.

I felt the heat return to my cheeks. "Thanks. Um, yeah. Anyway, I woke up when I smelled smoke."

"You mentioned that." She still stood there at the entrance with her arms crossed.

She was flirting with me. At... I glanced at the clock on the wall... three o'clock in the morning. In her nightwear. After seeing me almost naked.

"Yeah. I did. So, I got up to check it out, but I didn't see anything outside."

"Maybe you just had a nightmare."

I shook my head. "No, something is going on in town. I heard sirens too."

Her frown darkened. "I didn't hear anything."

"My senses are enhanced. It's one of the perks, and curses, of wearing this thing." I pointed at the medallion.

"Oh. So, even when you're not in the... you know?"

"Monster form? Yeah."

She lowered her hands and padded over to the kitchen sink,

where she grabbed a glass from the cupboard and filled it with water. "What do you think is going on?"

"I don't know," I said. "But sirens, smoke, something in the village is on fire. I thought about going into town to check it out."

Vero started to raise the glass of water to her lips, then her eyes widened as if finally awoken from a long sleepwalking episode.

"You're right. We need to make sure everyone is okay."

She set the glass down and hurried past me into her bedroom.

"So, you're going with me?"

"Were you thinking of running into town?" she asked from somewhere in her room.

"It did occur to me."

"In your underwear?"

I exhaled. "No. I was going to come back in and put on clothes. I just didn't want to wake you up. Especially if it was nothing."

"So, you were just going to leave me here?"

"You live alone," I pointed out.

She reappeared a second later in the doorway. She wore a pair of torn jeans in place of the shorts from before. The T-shirt, however, remained the same.

"Come on," she said, a growing sense of urgency in her voice. "Let's check it out."

I saw the orange glow of the flames through the jungle trees before we reached the center of town. A towering pillar of smoke rolled into the night sky, blotting out a section of the stars.

Vero slowed down as we reached the outskirts of the village. Worry tugged at my heart, and I hoped none of the people I knew had been hurt in the fire.

As we neared the main street, my concern over the well-being of the townspeople dwindled. Off to the left, at the end of the back street behind Vero's cantina, huge flames lapped against the air, sucking in more oxygen for fuel.

"Oh. Vero."

She eased her foot down on the brake pedal, slowing to a

creeping roll. A policeman stood in the way, blocking off the alley. Vero lowered the window as she neared the cop.

"Sorry, Vero," the man said. "I can't let you back there."

"What happened?" she demanded, fear taking over her vocal cords.

"We don't know yet. But your cantina..." He stopped talking for a moment, and she decided to keep going. She stepped on the gas and drove around the corner as the cop warned her to wait, but she was having none of it.

"Vero," I said, looking over at her in the driver's seat. Worry filled her eyes, and it only got worse in the flashing red lights of the fire trucks parked along the street in front of her bar.

Roaring flames danced through the roof, leaping out from the windows, consuming the walls, the frames, everything.

"No," she whispered, choking back tears. "How?"

She parked the car haphazardly on the opposite side of the road, killed the engine, and flung open the door.

"Vero, wait," I urged.

But it was too late. Vero jumped out of the car and sprinted down the street. She was halfway there by the time I set foot on the asphalt.

"Wait!" I shouted again, but the caution fell on deaf ears.

She ran to the nearest cop, who stood around a loosely cordoned area to keep people out of harm's way.

She tried to run by the officer, but he stuck out his arm.

I caught up quick enough to hear her screaming in Spanish that it was her building burning.

The cop's face softened slightly, but he wouldn't let her closer. I stopped next to her, and even at a distance of nearly a hundred feet I could feel the intense heat rippling off of the building.

"You have to let me go," Vero demanded. The cop held on to her wrists, refusing to let her get closer.

Something loud crashed inside the cantina as the firefighters continued to douse the flames with their hoses.

At this point, the building was a total loss. The only thing the first responders could do now was keep it from spreading and damaging other parts of the town.

Vero struggled against the cop's grip until I finally put my arm around her. I gave him a look that said, "I'll take it from here."

He nodded and let her go, sadness written on his features.

"Hey. Hey. Easy. Take it easy."

She jerked and twisted, trying to free herself from me, but I wrapped my arms around her and squeezed her tight.

"It's okay. I'm just glad you weren't in there."

Sobbing took over, and the fight left her, replaced with utter despondence.

She put her head in my chest and cried. I felt the tears soak through the cotton to dampen my skin beneath. She shook as she kept watching the cantina burn. I knew what would come next.

Anger always lurked in the shadows behind grief, ready to jump in and make things right.

As luck would have it, standing about fifty feet away to my right was a prime suspect to be the recipient of her rage.

Gonzalez, I thought.

At first, he didn't see me standing there. Or if he had, he'd chosen to ignore me and Vero. His fleshy face reflected the bright orange glow of the fire as he stood there with his arms crossed, still wearing the same suit from earlier that day and a smug, oddly satisfied expression to go with it.

I couldn't ignore the red mist dancing around him, beckoning me to let it feast on him.

Not here. Not now.

"Why not?" Xolotl demanded. "You know he's the one who did this, don't you?"

You won't get an argument out of me on that.

"Then end him. Do it now. Make an example of him."

That's not how we do things here. Maybe a few hundred years ago, the last time you were around. But not now.

"The man burned your friend's bar—the woman you love. Just look at her. She's in shambles."

I will take Gonzalez when the time is right, I thought.

"The time is right, right now."

In front of all these people?

I continued staring at the man, glad that Vero had her back to him. Gonzalez must have felt the weight of my glare because he slowly turned his head toward me. His vapid, dark eyes met mine for a second, then he grinned devilishly. With a shrug, as if to say "tough luck," he turned back away from me and slowly ambled away, melding into the crowd.

The mist trailed after him, and then it too disappeared.

"Great. You let him go. I can't believe you just let him walk away like that. You know he's the one who did this."

Yeah. And I'm not letting him go. I'm giving him a head start. We have bigger issues to deal with right now. So, stay focused. Gonzalez is a small fish.

"I hope you're right."

Vero pulled away from me, her eyes still locked on her burning business. She wiped her cheeks with the back of her hand and sniffled. Choking back the tears, she shook her head. I could see she was trying to piece together an explanation of how this had happened, and why it had happened. I guessed her ideas didn't involve arson, or the first thing out of her lips would have been "Who do you think did this?"

Although if her mind took things that direction, the first—and probably only—conclusion would have been Gonzalez.

She sighed hard, and her hands fell to my chest. She planted her forehead just above them, looking down into my tear-soaked shirt. "What do I do now?" she wondered. "That cantina was all I had."

I shook my head and lifted her chin so she could meet my gaze. "That's not all you have," I corrected. "You have me."

Vero caught her breath and eased the crying, stemming the flow to a mere trickle. She searched my eyes, then nodded. "I guess there's nothing left for me to stick around for now. So, if you still want me to, I'll come with you to Greece."

11

Life, I'd noticed, had a funny way of making things happen. It wasn't always in my favor, but so far I'd managed to survive everything fate had thrown my way.

I didn't like the fact that Vero's cantina being destroyed in the middle of the night was the reason she was coming with me. I liked it even less that the man who did it wouldn't face justice—not for now, at least. I still had plans to pay Señor Gonzalez a little visit when all this was over.

But things happen for a reason. Or so I'd heard.

I used to get so sick of hearing that from pastors or parents or mentors who used that line as a crutch to try to help people through difficult times of loss or grief or depression.

There was no denying, however, that the villainous actions of Gonzalez had actually worked in favor of the greater good—which was bringing Vero with me to Greece. Besides, she could rebuild the cantina better than before. She claimed she had insurance that should cover the damage, so while in the short term things looked bleak, the future smelled like cupcakes and rainbows.

The captain's voice came over the airplane speakers, announcing they were making the final descent into Athens.

He performed the usual warning about tray tables and seatbacks being in their original positions and reminded everyone that the Fasten Seatbelt sign was still on.

Vero watched out the window as the plane drifted lower. The rocky hillsides and mountains of the Greek mainland spread out as far as she could see. She didn't know I noticed, but her breathing had slowed to almost nothing—shallow, rhythmic, full of wonder.

She turned around and faced me with excitement exploding from her eyes. "I can't believe I'm actually here," she said. "Thank you so much, Gideon."

I smiled back at her, genuinely happy I could take her mind off the mess back in Santa Rojo.

We'd left the next morning, flown into Atlanta, then caught the flight to Athens later that afternoon. She'd been inconsolable on the drive to the airport in Guadalajara, and the conversation had been minimal. But once we were on the plane to Atlanta, and I'd reminded her that the insurance company would handle all the details about the bar, she felt better.

Vero still offered resistance, of course, saying she needed to stay there to handle the paperwork, answer questions after the authorities finished their investigation, that sort of stuff. But the locals had actually encouraged her to go, and told her that with days of cleanup ahead for construction crews, she wouldn't be needed for at least a week.

And to be honest, after experiencing something like that, most people would need to get away for a while.

The plane wobbled a little as it neared the runway below.

Vero kept her eyes glued to the window, still watching the scenery whiz by—the trees, mountains, hills, and buildings all growing larger by the second.

The aircraft touched down with a heavy bump, a slight bounce, and then another bump as all the tires made contact with the tarmac. Vero rounded on me with a broad smile on her face.

Her eyes looked tired, with dark half circles hanging under them.

She'd slept a little on the flight here, but only after sheer exhaustion had wrestled her many thoughts away from her.

Vero fought through the fatigue, though. The excitement practically burst from her pores.

"Excited?" I asked as I took the phone out of my pocket and switched off the airplane mode.

"Yes." Her expression changed, and I sensed the gratitude radiating from it. "Gideon. I know I said I needed to stay in Mexico before. And if things were different, maybe that would still be true. But I am so glad I came with you. I can't thank you enough."

"Don't thank me yet," I replied.

She didn't seem to catch my meaning, and so I left it at that, allowing her to wonder for a moment as I pulled up the contact information for my friend Eliana.

"What's that supposed to mean?" Vero pressed, a flirtatious look in her eyes.

I glanced at her for a second, then shrugged. "I'm kidding. And you're very welcome. I'm glad you're here too."

Blowing it off seemed to strip away any fragment of concern she held, and she turned away from me again to look out the window at the passing airplanes parked at the terminal.

I tapped the screen on my phone and then typed out a quick message to my Athens contact.

A renowned researcher in the fields of Greek history and anthropology, Eliana was an invaluable contact—especially in light of my recent findings.

I'd messaged her before leaving Nashville to return to Mexico, and again before departing Guadalajara.

As always, Eliana was willing to help, and had even hooked us up with a short-term vacation rental in Athens for the night. Apparently, she rented the place out to visitors. She tried to give it to me for free, but I insisted on paying.

A battle I eventually lost.

I finished typing the message, which only consisted of a few words letting her know that we'd just landed.

I waited only thirty seconds before I got her reply telling me our cab would be waiting outside the terminal, and that it was already paid for.

Eliana lived more comfortably than many archaeologists I knew around the world. If not for Amy's family, I would have been in similar financial circumstances.

But things had recently turned around for me, particularly with the discovery in Mexico. I'd finally had my big breakthrough—speaking engagements lined up, talks of book deals.

And then everything hit the fan.

The stupid cliché I always heard people using finally caught up to me. "Life is what happens when you're busy making plans."

I still loathed that phrase, but now I hated it for two reasons.

Eliana hadn't made her money with archaeology, though. She'd never scored a book deal or been a guest speaker that commanded any sort of meaningful money. Her money, instead, came from the apartments she'd purchased and rented out.

She'd scooped up properties at deep discounts, renovated them, and started her real estate rental business, which now ran almost fully automated—freeing her up to spend more time on the research she loved, but in a lifestyle that she enjoyed.

"Eliana has a cab that's going to pick us up outside the airport," I informed Vero.

Her grin never faded. "That is so sweet of your friend. You said she's an archaeologist like you?"

"She's an archaeologist," I allowed. "But not like me."

I let her puzzle over the comment as the plane pulled up to the gate. The bridge extended toward the door at the front and sealed into place. Two seconds later she said, "Because you're..."

Vero leaned in close and shifted to a conspiratorial tone. "You know."

Her suggestion made me snort. A loud ding reverberated through the cabin, and a flight attendant announced that we could remove our seat belts.

Most of the people along the aisle immediately shot out of their seats and began opening overhead bins, rummaging through their things, and preparing to leave.

I'd never understood those people—in such a hurry to stand there and wait. I guess after a long flight it felt good to stretch your legs. I knew I sure needed it after the trip, but we were going nowhere fast until the door opened and people methodically made their way off the plane.

One by one, the rows ahead of us gradually emptied until it was our turn. I allowed the gray-haired man across from us in the center of the plane to grab his things and exit, along with the woman I presumed to be his wife. Then I stood and grabbed our carry-on bags —a black rucksack for me and Vero's blue roller bag.

We'd packed light for the trip, uncertain how long we'd be here, but I estimated that a few days' worth of clothes would suffice. And if not, we could always wash them or buy a couple more sets.

I let Vero lead the way off the plane, following her close as the people behind us pressed impatiently to disembark. Once in the terminal, the passengers spilled out into the open spaces like animals freed from their cages.

We made our way through the airport following the signs for ground transportation. Near the exits, several men waited with tablets displaying names on the screens. One man, a particularly tall Greek in a white button-up shirt and black slacks, held a device with the last name *Wolf* on it.

I walked up to him and smiled pleasantly. "Hi. I'm Gideon Wolf."

I extended my hand, and the man shook it as firmly as anyone ever had. His strong grip told of either a life of strength training, hard manual labor, or both. Based on the roughness of his skin, I figured both. People who spent their lives working indoors didn't have a grip like that. Not in my experience.

He grinned his appreciation at the way I shook his hand, then reached out to greet Vero. "My name is Yiannis. Your friend Eliana sent me. I will be taking you to the villa she rented you."

"Great," I said as he gently shook Vero's hand. He was surprised at the lack of daintiness in the way she shook back, and nodded his approval.

"May I take your bag?" the driver asked her.

"Of course. Thank you." She looked at me and giggled, impressed with the service. "No one has ever asked to take my bag before," she confessed. "Then again, I've never gone anywhere, so..."

Yiannis turned and finally stepped out into the warm, dry morning air of Greece. We followed him over to a parking area where several cabs sat in a haphazard line.

The lights beeped on one of the vehicles—a sedan made in the Czech Republic. He popped open the trunk and stuffed Vero's bag in, then quickly opened the back driver's-side passenger door for her. The big man deftly moved back around to the trunk as I slumped the rucksack off my shoulder and started to stow it.

"I'll take that, sir. No problem."

The man's movements were surprisingly agile. He moved around to the open driver's door and climbed in. But I hesitated for six heartbeats. Something felt off. I looked around the parking area, but all I saw were travelers milling about, loading into vehicles, waiting on their rides, or on their phones.

Thousands of words filled my head, twisting and churning like viscous black clouds in a hurricane. Beyond those sensations, one stood out above all. I twitched my head to the right, then left, feeling danger somewhere close. But my survey of the area produced no answers, no confirmation of where trouble might be lurking.

"Everything okay?" Vero asked from inside the car. She leaned toward the open door, looking up at me as I stood there in the open air.

My eyes darted back and forth.

I couldn't say there was no sign of trouble. Red mist surrounded some of the people within my view, but none of them seemed to be paying any attention to me.

Who are they? I asked in my mind.

"In this world, good and bad, right or wrong, positive and negative, these things are always represented. The mist doesn't merely show you who is bad. It tells you who is evil. The world is full of evil, Gideon."

What's the difference between just being bad and being evil?

"A good person can tell a lie, make a moral error in judgment, do the wrong thing for the right reason. A bad person can do the opposite, or is even able to change their life's path, just as a good person can go bad. But those who are evil... The wicked of this world seek only to consume at any cost. Just like the one who directs them."

Ahriman, I realized.

"You getting in, or you want to go on foot?" Vero interrupted.

The voice didn't say anything else. I guessed the conversation was over for the time being.

I scanned the crowds once more, then climbed into the sedan. As the driver shifted the sedan into drive, I kept looking out the window, hypnotized with uncertainty.

12

"First time in Greece?" Yiannis asked, oblivious to my anxiety. Not that he'd come close to understanding.

"Not mine," I said. "But it's hers." I forced myself into the distraction of polite conversation.

"Oh, welcome to Greece, then. I hope you enjoy it here."

"I'm sure I will," she said, looking out the window like an excited puppy.

He accelerated out onto the road so fast our heads bumped the headrests. I looked over at her and chuckled at the surprised look on her face.

The driver jerked the wheel to the left and merged into the next lane, cutting off another driver who didn't even bother to honk their horn.

"Sorry about that," Yiannis said. "Greeks are the second-worst drivers in the world."

Vero laughed at his confession. "Really?"

I'd heard the same thing before from my last cab driver here, so I guess at least some of them were kind enough to give the warning, but it made me wonder—who were the worst drivers? A few counties in North Georgia came to mind, but I doubted he'd ever been there.

"You will see many broken mirrors here in Athens. It's like this on the islands too. Roads are too narrow. And people are reckless. Find me a car in Greece without any scratches or dents on it, and I'll show you a car that was bought that day."

Vero and I shared a laugh over the comment, which I knew from experience not to be a joke.

"But we make up for it with great food and wine," Yiannis added quickly.

"I can attest to that," I said, looking over at her with a nod and a wink.

"Yes. And where you two are staying is very close to some excellent restaurants, bars, and good coffee shops."

"Three of my favorite things."

Vero grinned and shook with excitement. The travel fatigue hadn't set in yet, much less the jet lag I knew was coming in a few hours. We were several hours ahead of Mexico time where she came from, as well as central standard time in Nashville.

I had a feeling we were both going to need that coffee before we needed anything else.

"The coffee here is really good," I explained as Yiannis steered the car around a curve and then onto the highway. "It's strong and sweet."

"Like me," she chimed with a blushing grin.

"Yes. Like you."

The driver's eyes darted toward us in the mirror, and he raised a curious eyebrow. "So, how long have you two been together?"

"Oh, we aren't together," Vero corrected—a little too quickly for my feelings.

It hurt, even though I knew it shouldn't have. I was a married man two weeks ago. What was I thinking even coming here with this woman?

"Ah."

She looked over at me and caught the redness on my face, along with what must have looked like utter rejection. "I mean, we just met a few weeks ago," she added quickly. "But who knows what's going to happen?"

That seemed to appease the driver's curiosity, and it definitely made me feel better. Another comforting smile from her didn't hurt either.

She turned away again, looking out the window at the rocky hillsides that passed by. Within a few minutes, the scenery changed when Yiannis steered the car off the highway and onto a four-lane road. The open hillsides disappeared behind thick forests of pine and cypress trees, interspersed with homes, a garage here and there, or a roadside business popping up on either side.

Soon, more buildings crowded the road, with more and more streets branching off from it until the forest gave way to the massive, ancient city of Athens rising up from the valley floor.

Tall apartment buildings blocked out much of the landscape to the northeast. As we stopped for a red light at an intersection, Vero stared out her window at the Panathenaic Olympic Stadium. The fact her face was virtually glued to the glass told of her marveling over the old semi-oval structure.

When the light changed, Yiannis stepped on the gas again and continued down the street.

Once in the city, streets of tightly packed apartment buildings dominated the view. Most of them looked the same to me, which was a stark contrast in view to an area I considered to be a sacred place of culture, history, and natural wonders.

"So," Yiannis said, breaking the silence of the last few minutes, "what are you in town for?"

"We're here to do some research on some..." I hesitated for a second. "Ancient artifacts."

"Lots of those here."

He seemed to not catch my hesitation. "So, you ever play basketball?" I asked, diverting the conversation. "You look like you could play power forward."

The driver chuckled. "Yes. I played most of my life. A little professionally here in Greece, but nothing like what you have in America with the pro leagues there. Of course, here we all love the Greek Freak. He's pretty much the nation's favorite basketball player."

I didn't follow much pro basketball anymore. Not since Dominique Wilkins retired. When Jordan left the league for good, that sealed it for me. But I still had a faint grasp of who played where, and what was going on.

"Yeah, he's a good one," I replied. Other than that, I didn't really know what else to say. I'd maxed out my pro basketball wit on that one comment.

He seemed to be satisfied with it. "I still play every weekend. We have a group of guys that gets together. It's fun, but not like the days when I was competing."

"I can understand that. Good camaraderie on a team."

"I miss it. But life goes on."

"Very true," I agreed.

I watched the buildings blur by, the people walking along the sidewalks, the cars and motorcycles in the other lanes. Then we stopped again, went again, and repeated the process until the driver made a couple of turns that landed us in front of a four-story nondescript beige building.

He slammed the brakes as elegantly as he'd steered the car and accelerated—like a bull stuck in a subcompact—with a stick shift.

"This is the place," he announced as he unceremoniously swung his door open and stepped out.

From my experience here before, I knew that negotiating price of a ride plus tip was something that needed to be settled before getting in the car. But Eliana had taken care of all that, leaving any additional gratuity at my discretion.

Americans, on the international scope, are generous tippers, which can sometimes get strange looks when in another country where such generosity is not only uncommon but often viewed as either showing off, or wasteful.

Yiannis opened the door for Vero as I fished a fistful of euros out of my pocket and pulled a five from the stack.

The driver opened the trunk next and took out the lady's bag, handed it to her, then passed mine to me. I trade my five-euro bill for the bag, which he took with a grateful nod, barely pausing to take a look at the money.

"Thank you, Mr. Wolf. I appreciate it. But your friend already tipped me."

"I know. But you're not one of the second-worst drivers in the world. So, thanks."

The comment took a moment to root in the man's mind. I guess he wasn't accustomed to getting compliments. But when it finally dawned on him, a knowing grin creased his lips.

He nodded again, acknowledging the kind words. "Thank you. If you need a ride again while you're here, give me a call." He passed a business card to me with black letters on a simple white card stock.

"Thanks," I said. "I'll definitely do that should the need arise. Good to know a trustworthy driver in a different town."

"Most definitely," Vero added. "Nice to meet you, Yiannis. I have a feeling I'll see you again."

The big man got back in his car as we stepped up onto the relative safety of the sidewalk. The engine roared as much as a four cylinder can, and he disappeared around the corner onto the main street, I guessed to go get his next fare.

I took out my phone again and checked the message from Eliana. "Looks like we're on the top floor. That's pretty cool. We go in this door here." I pointed to the entrance of the apartment building. The glass door with two tall, skinny windows on either side allowed a view into a small lobby.

We walked up three steps, and I found Eliana's name on a panel with a series of buttons. I pushed on the button next to her name and inched away from it.

"Hello, Gideon. So glad you made it. Come on up. I will buzz you in."

A second later, a buzzer sounded inside the doorway, and then the lock clicked.

"Very nice," Vero said, looking impressed. "Where I come from, we don't have those kinds of doorbells."

It was cute how she called it a doorbell.

I pulled open the door and let her in, then followed her over to the lift just past the rows of black mailboxes occupying the wall.

After pressing the button, the elevator whirred beyond its doors. Ten seconds passed before it dinged and the doors opened.

We stepped inside, and I pressed the button for the top floor, then stood back and let the doors close again.

"So," Vero said, her voice echoing off the walls and marble floor, "what's the plan?"

The lift began rising.

"You mean like today? Or in general?"

She giggled. "When are we going to Delos? I assume we have to either fly or take a ferry there. How long will it take?"

"Oh yeah. Actually, Eliana took care of all that for us. She booked us ferry tickets and everything. Even a couple of hotel rooms there."

"Rooms?"

It would have taken a moron not to hear her emphasis on the plurality of the word.

"Yeah," I said, suddenly uneasy. "I... am just... you know, not making any assumptions or... trying to be respectful."

For a second, the look she gave me caused me to think I'd done or said something horribly wrong.

She saw my discomfort and shook her head. "No. No. It's okay. I appreciate your being respectful. You're... not like other men I've met. Most of them have always been after one thing. And they can't get it fast enough."

I peered into her eyes, and I wondered what else she might be thinking, but reading minds wasn't one of my powers. "I think you know I like you," I said, putting it all out on the line. "And I feel like you feel the same way about me. Am I wrong?"

She stumbled over the answer, and instead bit her lip before nodding. The gesture didn't exactly fill me with a ton of confidence, but I went on anyway.

"Like I've said before, this is a weird time for me. So, no pressure on my part if you don't feel the same. And no pressure means we have separate rooms."

"What about this apartment?" Vero asked. I thought I detected a hopeful tone in her voice.

I smiled as I answered. "Two bedroom. Two bath."

The elevator dinged, and the doors opened, ending the conversation at precisely the right moment.

We stepped out into the corridor and looked left toward the end of the hall. I spotted a woman with shoulder-length curly black hair standing in front of a pale wooden door. She wore a flowing white dress that reached down to her ankles. Two golden coins dangled from necklaces, just touching the bottom of the neckline on her dress.

She beamed back at me as I approached her.

"Gideon! It is so good to see you again." She extended her arms and embraced me, squeezing me tight. I hugged her back and then stepped aside so she could shake Vero's hand.

"Good to see you again, El. This is my friend Vero I told you about."

Our hostess smiled pleasantly and shook Vero's hand. "It is so nice to meet you," Eliana said. "Gideon has wonderful things to say about you."

Vero looked at me awkwardly. "I'm sure he exaggerates."

"No. Not Gideon. He's always been a pragmatic sort. Most archaeologists are, in my experience. It's the nature of our work."

Vero passed me a secretive glance, as if she might spill the beans about my alternate personality. Then the moment evaporated, and Eliana withdrew her hand.

"Please, come in. I just made some coffee for you. And I brought some cheese pies from the bakery at the corner. They're some of the best in Athens."

She turned and twisted the doorknob in the center of the door—a design I'd always thought intriguing. The door opened into a short hall with a closet to the left. We followed Eliana into a spacious living room with a kitchen attached to the left. The white cabinetry, the appliances, even the pendant lights hanging over the Swedish-style breakfast table, all looked modern and clean.

"There are two bedrooms, just as you requested," Eliana explained. "They are on opposite sides of that hall there." She pointed at an offshoot corridor that ran twenty feet along the exterior of the building. Then she waved her hand at the terrace visible through a sliding glass door. "The rooftop wraps around so you have plenty of space. And," she paused to add a playful smirk, "I think you'll enjoy the view."

She whirled around with a flourish, her flowing dress spinning dramatically in her body's wake.

Eliana slid the door open and stood aside for us to go have a look.

"Thank you," I said. I slipped the bag off my shoulders and set it down on the table as I slid past her and out into the warm air once more. This building was taller than most around it, and so offered sweeping views of the city, the mountains beyond, and the best of all —the Acropolis.

"This is awesome, El," I said. "Thank you so much."

Vero walked over to the far wall that faced the Acropolis. She put her hands on the railing and stared out over the city.

A pergola with fabric on the top offered shade just to the right of where she stood. A collection of black patio furniture with red cushions and pillows sat underneath it.

"I am sorry for what happened," Eliana said, sidling next to me. "About Amy."

"It's okay," I said. "That's nice of you to say. Really. But I know you never liked her."

It was no secret in our little collection of peers that Eliana held no fondness for my former wife. They'd been in serious arguments many times, and seemed they never agree on anything. Beyond that, Eliana didn't think Amy was a good person, and she'd said as much on a few occasions while imbibing too much white wine.

Eliana didn't appear to be taken aback by the comment. If I thought she would have, I probably wouldn't have said anything.

In her mid-forties, she'd learned long ago not to worry with what people thought, or if she'd offended anyone. That wasn't to say she was deliberately insensitive. Eliana was a kind person, and her distaste for Amy came more from a source of mistrust and simply trying to watch out for me.

She stiffened slightly, straightening her thin neck so the top of her head reached a half inch higher. Her sculpted face looked regal as she spoke. "My concerns are, and always have been, for you, my friend."

My eyes averted to Vero, who remained by the railing with her elbows on top of it. "I appreciate it, El." My mind wandered for a moment, taking me back through the years. I wondered how many times Amy had lied to me, how deep the betrayal rabbit hole truly went. Thinking about that stuff didn't help. That much was certain. It drained me, mentally and physically. Worst, it took my focus away from the present moment.

"I found out you were right about everything," I confessed, my voice just loud enough for her to hear over the breeze and the sounds of the street below. A central air conditioner hummed behind me somewhere.

"About what?"

I leaned closer. Even though Vero knew everything, I still didn't feel like rehashing it with her again.

"Amy had been cheating on me before... before she died. I have no idea for how long, or with how many men. I only know of one for sure."

Eliana scowled, glanced over at Vero, then returned her gaze to me. "I'm not going to ask with who. That's none of my business. I'm glad you weren't hurt in all of that mess. And I will not tell you I told you so. That would not be respectful of the dead." She looked back at Vero once more. "Tell me about her. It seems you're moving on rather quickly."

I shook my head at the assertion. "No. It's not like that."

"Oh? The way you look at her suggests otherwise, my friend."

"I don't know what to think. Or what to feel, El. I thought my life was in order two weeks ago. That everything was normal."

"What is normal, Gideon?" She lowered her head to give me that look down the bridge of her nose that my mother always gave me when I got caught doing something I wasn't supposed to.

"I wish I knew," I said honestly. "Things have been... definitely not normal ever since Amy died."

"I can imagine."

No. You really can't.

Eliana was a trusted friend. More than just a colleague, we'd known each other for the better part of ten years, having met on a dig site outside Thessaloniki. Even after I went on to focus on things in other parts of the world, we maintained contact, and occasionally saw each other at conferences or on vacation.

Things had always been tense between her and Amy, and it seemed Eliana's instincts had proved spot on.

"I like her, El," I admitted. "But it's so soon. I don't want to be one of those guys who jumps into a rebound deal with someone. She deserves better than that."

"And so do you."

"Thanks." My face heated with embarrassment. "And thank you for this incredible place. It's really amazing. I'm proud of how you're doing with all this. The anthropologist turned real estate mogul."

It was her turn to feel bashful. She turned her head away and looked out into the distance at nothing in particular. "Foreigners have been buying up property here in Greece the last few years. It's good in some ways, particularly for local businesses and tourism. But it forces native Greeks out of the city because the rent has been climbing. I figured I could make some money while maintaining a little Athenian integrity. You know, keeping some things locally owned."

"I can respect that," I nodded.

My eyes wandered over to Vero again, who turned just as I looked at her. The sun radiated off her face, and she soaked it up with a smile, leaning back against the railing while she inhaled deeply.

She tilted her head back, exposing the deeply tanned skin on her neck. For a second, I simply admired the view. She was beautiful. There was no debating that in my mind.

In a blink, however, the moment passed. I saw the glint from the scope from a rooftop a few buildings over about a block away.

"What the—"

13

In an instant, I summoned the monster within. But instead of shifting into the chupacabra, I forced all that power into my legs, and surged toward the unsuspecting Vero.

I virtually flew across the rooftop, covering the thirty-foot gap between us in a single second. The muted pop reached my ears as I slid into the rail next to Vero, using my right arm to shove her down below the wall.

The bullet pierced my back with terrible force, and erupted out of my torso just above my stomach.

I fell to my knees next to Vero as Eliana screamed in terror.

I hunched on all fours, summoning enough strength to order her to get inside. "Get in the apartment!" I shouted.

Panic froze her only for a breath. Then she scurried into the apartment as the mangled wound in my body healed itself.

I looked over at Vero, who crouched next to me.

"Are you hurt?" she asked, concern welling in her eyes.

"It's not a massage; I'll tell you that. But I'll be okay." I inspected the bloody wound and saw it was nearly fully healed. "Now, if you'll excuse me, I need to find out who is shooting at us."

I closed my eyes for a second and called on the power of the medallion with a single thought. *Unleash it.*

Instantly, my body mutated, transforming into the wolflike creature. But unlike before, this time it wasn't just the animal fur that covered my body. Shimmering armor the color of titanium unfolded from the medallion around my neck, and instantly wrapped around my torso.

A warrior's helmet grew around my head, and gauntlets on my wrists and hands. My thighs and feet received their own protective shells.

I looked down at the new gear as the transformation completed in under three seconds. "I guess this is the upgrade Myra talked about."

Vero looked impressed as she gazed at the sight with wide eyes. "Nice new digs."

I heard the muted pop again. This time, instead of a scorching pain, I felt the bullet ping harmlessly off my shoulder armor. The round splashed a spark across my face before falling harmlessly somewhere on the rooftop.

Vero stared up at me with disbelief oozing from her eyes. I smirked, which I can't imagine was in any way comforting coming from a monster, then I turned around and faced where the shot had come from.

My senses were fully empowered now, and I easily spotted the sniper exactly where I'd seen the scope glare a moment before.

He fired again. I saw the flash from the muzzle, heard the muffled report, and then felt something like an infant flicking my shoulder with its finger as the bullet struck my armor again.

"I gotta be honest," I said, looking down at the new protective gear, "Myra did good." Then I redirected my focus to the shooter again as he chambered another round. Even from this distance, I sensed the panic in him. "I'll be right back," I said.

Before Vero could say anything else or offer a protest, I vaulted over the railing and sailed across the street. I hit the floor of another penthouse and rolled to a stop just in front of a green Komodo grill.

Smoke spilled out of the iron cover on the top, and I knew

whoever was cooking would be out to check on whatever had just made the huge thud sound outside their apartment. The scent of roasted meat melded with smoking charcoal tantalized my senses even more than usual, begging the creature within to lift the lid and have a sample.

The shooter adjusted his aim and fired again. This round bounced off the metal helmet covering my face. I twisted my head in irritation, then pushed off the floor and jumped across the alley to the next building over. The sniper remained calm, though I sensed the fear in him.

"You're not going to let this one go, too, are you?" Xolotl asked in my head.

"Nope. Not this one," I growled. I ran forward toward the edge of the rooftop, then jumped again.

The shooter got off one last round that struck me right in the chest. I heard the .50-cal bullet hit my new armor, but barely even felt it. I landed on my feet on the next rooftop, a mere six feet away from the man with the gun.

He retreated backward, pulling on his rifle's bolt to chamber another round. His black windbreaker and matching pants must have been warm out here in the unabated sunshine.

I stalked toward him even as he stumbled back. "You only have one more in that magazine," I snarled, noting the size of it. "Not that it matters."

He tried to line up the weapon, squarely on my chest. The red mist whipped around the bald man in a fury. It danced along his shaven scalp, snaking its way down around his muscular neck and shoulders.

He twitched his trigger finger, and the suppressor muzzle popped with a puff of smoke.

The round struck me in the chest, right over the medallion. Again, sparks splashed off the impenetrable metal as the bullet flew off somewhere into the unknown.

I shook my head and surged toward him, grasping the long barrel with my right paw-like hand as he fell back onto his rump. I took the stock with my right hand and bent it in half like I'd seen superheroes do in television shows and movies from my youth.

"Oh," I remarked, tossing the useless weapon aside. "That's how they did that.'

I returned my gaze to the shooter as he scrambled backward, sliding away from me. He drew a pistol from his hip and opened fire.

I glowered down at the man as he kept scooting away from me while vainly emptying the pistol's magazine in less than five seconds. Every single round pinged off my armor, though one narrowly missed my right eye and sent a flash of sparks across my field of vision for a split second.

When his pistol's mag ran out and the clicking commenced, telling him he was completely screwed, I took a menacing step toward him, shaking my head.

"Seriously? If your .50-cal rounds can't pierce this, what makes you think that thing will do the trick?"

He rolled to the left and onto his feet. For a second, I thought he was going to run, which part of me would have enjoyed. When I took on the form of the chupacabra, I felt a primal urge to hunt. I didn't fully understand it, but figured it came with the fur... or suit, as it were now.

Instead of running, though, the guy primed himself to fight with his bare hands. He positioned himself at an angle and bounced loosely on the balls of his feet as if in the octagon, ready to take on an equal opponent.

I bared my teeth in a toothy grin, mocking him.

"You really want to do this?"

The man said nothing. He gritted his teeth and clenched his jaw. As he held out his left arm in front of the other in what I assumed to be some kind of martial arts stance, I noticed a tattoo on his wrist.

That's interesting, I thought.

"So, you want to do this the hard way, yeah?" I asked.

The man's eyelids narrowed to slits. He started moving around in a wild but controlled dance of movements I figured were meant to either intimidate an opponent or build up his own courage. In this case, it had to be both—and one of those wasn't going to happen. Maybe neither.

I sighed and waited until he finished his gyrations, then I reached out and grabbed him by the neck.

He couldn't even get one punch or kick away before his throat was squeezed in my grip. I lifted him off the ground and held him a few feet up, then moved over to the ledge as he kicked and squirmed. His shiny shoes clunked off the metal armor. He clawed at my furry paw-hand, desperately trying to free himself. Once he was over the ledge, however, me letting go was the last thing he wanted to happen.

"Now," I said as I held him over the street below, "who do you work for?"

All I got out of him was a bunch of grunting and more squirming. But as he grappled with my arm—the only thing separating him from a long drop and a sudden stop—the tattoo on his forearm grew more visible as the sleeve pulled back toward the elbow.

The black ink displayed a sword, the style that was used during the Crusades. The three-inch-long blade stabbed through a circle with two letters in it—GD—joined together to form a sort of symbol.

The sword handle featured a cross at the base of it.

"What is that?" I demanded.

He still didn't speak, instead grunting and gasping for air.

I swung him back over the edge and down onto the rooftop. Once he regained his footing, I shoved him down onto his backside once more and pressed my heavy foot down on his chest.

He kept wriggling, desperately trying to pry my new metal-clad boot from his torso.

"Now that you can breathe, I expect answers."

"You'll get nothing from me, demon," he spat.

"Is that so? Well, I can just kill you now."

"You may kill me. I am ready to die for the cause."

"You gonna end this guy or what?" the voice in my head taunted.

"Not until I get some information."

The sniper's eyes filled with fear. "What?"

"I wasn't talking to you," I snapped. "Who do you work for? I already killed a bunch of your guys back in Mexico. What do you want from me?"

"You know what we want," he sneered. Spittle spewed between his lips as he continued trying to relieve himself of the heavy foot crushing his ribcage.

I inclined my chin as I peered down at him. "And why? Why do you want the medallion?"

"Only the righteous should wield its power."

I nodded. "So I've heard. And yet something tells me you aren't the righteous." The crimson smoke hovered over him like a wild beast ready to consume its prey.

"What is righteousness, Gideon Wolf? Who gets to decide?"

I didn't realize I'd landed in the middle of a theological debate with a guy who was trying to kill me. And I wasn't about to get in an argument with him. I learned a long time ago there were some battles you couldn't win, so don't bother fighting them.

"If you're not going to tell me who you work for, then there's really no point in keeping you alive. And before you say again that you're ready to die for whatever your whole deal is, you can save it. I really don't have any interest in anything you have to say except for answering my question."

He drew a breath and paused, either searching his memory for details I wanted—doubtful—or to consider the next batch of dribble he was going to shovel my way, in which case I would just make him hurt that much more.

"I heard what you did to my brothers in Mexico. There were no bodies to bury. You consumed them."

"I'm going to let you in on a little secret," I said. "I don't consume anyone I kill. See, there's this red vapor that follows me around, shows me who is evil and who isn't. And right now, there's a whole bunch of that mist surrounding you, just waiting to devour you. I know it sounds weird. Believe me, it's a whole lot weirder on this side of things. It's going to consume you when you're dead. The only question is, how much you want to hurt before I let it?"

He only laughed; a disturbing, sickly sound. "Do you enjoy the blood? The taste of it? Do you enjoy the killing?"

"This guy thinks you're a vampire or something," Xolotl said. "Just kill him, and be done. He isn't going to talk."

"I don't enjoy any of this," I confessed. "Quite the opposite."

The sniper glowered in turn at me, unwilling to believe anything I said. "The cardinal does not lie," he blurted. "He is infallible."

I cocked my head to the right. "Cardinal? What cardinal?"

The man's eyes flashed wider for a second, realizing he had made a mistake. He shook his head vigorously. "I'll tell you nothing. Kill me, and be done with it."

"I don't know. Seems to me like you just started opening up. I wonder if I apply a little more pressure to those ribs how much more I could get out of you." I pushed down harder on his torso.

His face reddened, and his eyes bulged in their sockets. I knew the man's lungs struggled to fill with fresh air.

He kept rolling his head back and forth in dramatic denial of my request.

"Are you sure?" I asked. "This is really going to hurt if I keep it up."

He grinned but said nothing else.

I sensed there wasn't much more I could get out of him. He'd slipped up telling me about the cardinal, whoever that was. At least it was a starting point, however vague. And it was way more than I'd gotten out of any of his brothers in Mexico.

There was one piece that bothered me about his leak. Only one organization had cardinals—the Catholic Church.

I refused to believe they had anything to do with these guys. Over the years, I'd read novels and seen movies that picked apart the church, blasting them for all kinds of atrocities and conspiracies throughout history. The attacks seemed unending at times. And while religious organizations in general had done numerous despicable things over the course of history, I couldn't convince myself that the Catholic Church, or any church, had anything to do with what these guys were up to.

Perhaps, the cardinal he mentioned had gone rogue and sought the medallion for his own personal gain. While the faith considered many of these men to be infallible, I knew deep down they were just people, capable of good or evil. And sometimes evil could be masked by religious zeal.

I leaned closer to the sniper. "Who is this cardinal?" I asked one final time. "This is your last chance."

He said nothing while still trying in vain to fill his lungs. His cheeks continued to change colors.

"At least you gave me a place to start," I said and took my foot off his chest. He immediately took in a huge breath.

As he breathed, refilling his chest over and over again, I let him have a moment of relief before I reached down and grabbed him by the neck. I lifted the sniper up off the floor and held him high, taking a quick glance over my shoulder. I suddenly remembered I was on someone's rooftop patio.

"Would be bad form to let someone inside that apartment see you out here, especially what you're doing to this guy. You know, torturing him for information."

"Is someone home?" I asked.

"Doesn't seem like it."

"You're a huge help."

The sniper looked down at me in terror, kicking and squirming to free himself.

"Thank you for your help," I said, and took a step near the edge. "Don't worry. I'm not going to eat you either. But you are going to die for whatever your little cause is."

I extended my arm over the railing. The crimson vapor swirled around him, preparing to consume its next victim. Down below in the alley, several dumpsters lined the walls of the buildings. No one would see him fall. And there would be no body to find.

"You will burn in the eternal fires of hell, demon."

I bobbed my head and shrugged. "I guess it's a good thing I don't believe in hell." I loosened my fingers and let him go.

He screamed as he fell. The shriek was short lived, as was his life after I released him. I looked over the edge in time to see him hit the pavement between two of the dumpsters.

The mist trailed down the shaft between the apartment buildings, twirling through the air until it reached the body, where it began the process of consuming him.

I looked back across the rooftops toward Eliana's apartment but saw no sign of Vero or my Greek friend. I didn't want anyone to see what I'd just done to that guy, though in a crowded city like this the odds were someone might have witnessed it.

I'd taken a pretty big risk changing and leaping across the tops of buildings. Someone probably caught a glimpse of me, but it would be left to hearsay and rumors. I doubted anyone managed to snap a picture.

I needed to get back to Eliana's flat. But it would be better to take the more conventional way.

I vaulted over the railing and dropped down to street level, landing close to where the body was evaporating. Seconds after my feet hit the ground, I transformed back into human form as if nothing had happened.

After a glance down at the vanishing body of the sniper, I took off at a trot toward the intersection.

Whoever these guys were, they knew we were here. They'd followed me to Mexico. And now they'd followed me to Greece.

There was no way we could stay at Eliana's place tonight. It wasn't safe for us, or her. That meant we were going to have to ramp up the timeline and leave Athens sooner than planned.

14

I climbed the stairs to Eliana's apartment, opting for the old-fashioned way over the elevator—just in case.

When I reached the top floor, I stepped out into the corridor and hurried over to the doorway to her apartment. A terrible feeling overwhelmed me with thoughts that someone else had gone through the front door and ambushed Vero and my friend.

I rapped on the door and took a step back to wait, emotions of fear and hope mingling in my head.

After a few seconds, I spoke. "Eliana. It's me, Gideon. You can open the door."

A moment later, I heard footsteps. The doorknob twisted, and the door opened. Fear stretched across my friend's face, and had drained her skin of its usual color.

I stepped inside and closed the door behind me.

"Are you okay?" I asked, gripping her by the shoulders.

She swallowed and shook her head, confusion dripping from her eyes. I saw her searching for answers with her eyes.

"Who was that?" she asked. "And where did you just come from?"

I hadn't thought about that explanation before returning.

"Don't worry about that for now," I said. "Lock the door. I'm going to check on Vero."

I left Eliana behind for the moment, hoping I could buy myself some time to figure out how to answer her question about me getting downstairs. Actually, I really hoped she would simply forget about it.

Hurrying through the room, I stopped at the sliding door and saw Vero still crouching behind the far wall.

She looked over and saw me, and the concern on her face melted. "Gideon," she blurted. "Is it safe?"

"Yes," I answered with a nod. "For now."

I walked toward her, and she stood.

"Are you hurt?" I asked.

Vero shook her head and put on a feeble smile. "No. I'm fine. Are you?"

This woman. In the harrowing experience of being shot at by a sniper, she remained concerned about my well-being—me, a nearly indestructible creature.

I reflected her smile. "I'm fine. It's going to take a lot more than a bullet to hurt me. Plus that new armor Myra gave me... I didn't feel a thing. It's pretty sweet. I'm not going to miss that pain; that's for sure."

She gazed across the rooftop toward where the shooter had been. "Who was that?"

I followed her stare. "I don't know," I confessed. "But we should get inside, just in case. I don't think there are any more of them out here, but if there aren't, it's a good bet reinforcements will be on their way soon."

I ushered her back to the door and inside the apartment, then closed the blinds and the door behind us.

I could tell Eliana was bursting at the seams. Her fingers trembled as she eased herself into a chair at the little table, staring up at me in shock. "Gideon? What is going on? Who was that man? Why was he shooting at us?"

After a glance at Vero, I met her eyes. "Look, El, you're just going to have to trust me on this one. There are some things I can't tell you right now. Those men are after this." I held the medallion up for her to see. "This is an ancient treasure. Its value is beyond price."

My answer painted a dissatisfied frown across her face.

"So, he was trying to kill you for that?" She pointed at the amulet as I tucked it back into my shirt.

"It would seem so. I don't want to put you in any danger. I'm not sure how they found us here, but if they know we're staying tonight, then there's a good chance they'll be back, and in greater numbers. It's not safe to stay here tonight."

The words fell on her ears, but I wondered if she processed them. Her vacant stare told me she felt lost. I also sensed she felt concern for her own safety, which was only logical. This sort of thing wasn't the kind of experience many archaeologists had to endure. Although it was becoming increasingly frequent for me.

"It's not you they're after, El. You're going to be okay. It's me they want."

She looked over at Vero for a second, then back to me. "And what about her?" Eliana asked. "Are they after her too?"

I wasn't sure about that. If somehow these men knew Vero was to be the next guardian, she could well be in grave danger. Without a medallion, she remained highly vulnerable.

One lucky shot could take her out. And that thought shook me to my core. I had to concentrate to force it away, but the idea of losing her rocked me in a way I'd never felt about anyone else.

"She'll be fine," I assured Eliana. I would protect her with all my power, but that confidence was unable to prevent a slight hint of doubt from tainting my answer.

She could have been shot out on the rooftop. If the shooter had been a second faster, that bullet might have killed her.

Had he been shooting at her?

She'd been staring out at the Acropolis in the distance, and was an easy target. The sniper had a clear line of sight to her. If they somehow knew she was the next guardian in line, and had designs on the medallions, that meant they were the enemies of the guardians. And if they were enemies of our kind, then part of their modus operandi would be taking out any future guardians before they received their powers. Much easier to do it that way than after.

"How can you be so sure?" Eliana asked. "You're lucky she's not dead right now."

I nodded and stole a quick look at Vero, who seemed unfazed by the statement. I knew she felt the concern in my heart.

"Maybe you should hang back while I go to Delos," I suggested. "You can stay in a hotel tonight. Much safer there. Like I said, it's me they're after. I'd prefer to keep as much distance between you and trouble as possible."

She scowled at me, and I knew immediately what was coming next. "No way," she countered. "I'm coming with you. You don't have to worry about my safety. I can handle myself."

I sighed at her predictable response. "I know you can, Vero. I'm not questioning that. But that guy nearly killed you."

"But he didn't," she protested. "I want to stay with you."

The words touched me deep in my chest. "I knew you were going to say that."

I turned back to Eliana, who seemed to be calming down from the harrowing episode. "I'll take care of her, El. And you'll be safe. But you should probably leave the apartment for a night or two."

She answered with a weak nod. For the moment, it seemed like she'd forgotten the question of how I got down to the street and back.

To make sure she didn't ask, I redirected the subject to our trip to Delos. "It's probably best we take the next ferry to the island," I said. "Do you think there are any we could catch here in the next hour or so?"

When she answered, her voice sounded distant, her mind still mired in shock. "Yes. Of course. There are several ferries that leave Piraeus each day. I'm sure we can get you on one of them."

"Thanks, El. I appreciate it. This is the last thing I wanted. I had no idea these guys were here in Greece."

She looked up at me again after staring at the table for several seconds. "I have a feeling there's more you need to tell me when the time is right."

"There is," I agreed. "And I will. For now, we should get moving. Just in case."

Eliana took a deep breath and exhaled a long breath, expelling the stress from the incident into the air. "Well then, I guess you'll need a ride. My car is downstairs."

15

U tter, worry-filled silence dominated most of the ride to the port of Piraeus, about fifteen kilometers south of Athens.

I lost count of how many times I looked back through the rear window of Eliana's Audi. Every time I checked, I expected to find some train of pursuers with gunmen hanging out the windows, firing bullets wildly at us. That thought, I knew, was ridiculous, especially when we were in the gridlock traffic of downtown Athens. It became less implausible as we distanced ourselves from the densely packed city, and hit the more open roads heading south toward the coast.

Still, every time I checked I didn't notice a threat.

"For someone with incredible power, you worry a great deal," the voice in my head said after my umpteenth look through the back window.

I'm more concerned about these two, I thought. *They don't have the same protection.*

The notion either appeased the voice or caused it to go into silent reflection. Either way, at that moment I was glad it left.

I'd noticed Eliana watching the rearview mirror while she drove. I wanted to say something to calm her nerves, but I knew that was going to be impossible. I just hoped that she could calm down enough to get some rest later on. Such a traumatic event could have a lasting impact on the human mind, and that was the last thing I wanted for her.

"How did you get downstairs?" Eliana asked abruptly.

The question startled me, and I stalled for a moment, looking out the window at the passing trees and rocky hillsides. A gas station passed, and I took pointless note of a man with a thick mustache filling his subcompact car with gas.

I'd really thought she'd forgotten that little question. But here in the car, there was no avoiding it. I was truly a captive audience.

I had to think about it another second, and Vero looked over at me from behind the driver's seat. I knew she wondered how I was going to answer that one.

"I jumped across the street to the next building, then to the one where the shooter was positioned."

Her eyes darted to me in the mirror, full of cynical irritation. "I don't appreciate the humor right now, Gideon."

"He's not joking," Vero said.

Eliana looked back toward her, though in that spot I doubted she could see Vero. "What do you mean, you jumped? That's impossible."

"Yeah," I said with a nod. "It would be."

"I don't understand. Are you going to be honest with me? There's no way you could have gotten down to the street and back up that quickly. And why would you do that? What were you doing down there?"

I sighed. "I jumped, El. And I killed the sniper."

She looked at me again, even more aghast than before. I expected her to say something, but instead she flipped on her blinker and quickly turned off the road next to a concrete building that looked like construction had been stopped midway through the project. I'd noticed many such structures on other visits to Greece, and never really understood what happened other than to posit that the construction contractors must have run out of money. After all, Greece wasn't the most financially stable democracy.

Eliana stopped the car and shifted it into park, then turned around and looked back at me. Annoyance burned in her eyes. "I want the truth, Gideon. What happened back there?"

Vero kept staring at me, probably glad she wasn't the one on the spot right now.

I glanced at her, then back to my friend. "Get out of the car. I'll show you."

"What?" Eliana's forehead tightened with a frown.

I didn't answer, instead pulling the handle and shoving the door open. I stepped out to the sound of cars passing every few seconds. My shoes crunched on the rocky, dusty ground.

"Come back here," I said into the car to the women who still hadn't moved. "I'll show you."

Eliana looked to Vero for answers, but Vero merely nodded. "Fine."

Eliana stepped out of the car. Vero did a second after.

I walked toward the half-constructed two-story villa, and stepped through the unfinished doorway. It smelled of dust and concrete inside, and the shade cooled my skin. The two women entered the building a few seconds after me—Eliana with a confounded expression stretched across her face.

"What are we doing in here, Gideon?" she asked, her tone forcing the notion that this whole charade was ridiculous.

I retreated deeper into the shadows of the far corner, saying nothing.

She started to ask again, but Vero held up her right hand to suggest silence. The gesture stifled Eliana for a second.

Satisfied no one out on the road could see this far into the building, I summoned the power, and shape-shifted into the creature.

Eliana stumbled back a step, her face twisting with fear. She yelped, but Vero caught her in her arms before Eliana could escape.

"It's okay," Vero soothed. "Just watch."

"What do you mean?" Eliana barked. "He's..." Her voice faltered.

The transformation took less than four seconds, and when it was done, I stepped out of the corner and into plain view.

"It's still me," I said, though I knew the deeper baritone of the creature sounded almost nothing like my human voice. "It's Gideon."

For a few seconds, Eliana simply stared in rapt horror, her head twisting back and forth in an effort to deny what her vision told her to be real.

"That's... That's impossible," she babbled, slowly lowering herself to her knees. "How?"

"Not impossible. There are only a few people who know about this, El. And I would prefer to keep it that way. The medallion I wear isn't just an ordinary piece of jewelry. It's an ancient amulet of power, worn by what many would call gods and monsters. I don't have time to give you all the details right now. But this is why we are here in Greece. There are seven medallions in total. One of them is here in Greece. I must find the other six before evil does."

Her head kept shaking back and forth. "I don't understand," she managed.

"I still don't fully understand it, either. But I thought showing you might help answer your question about how I ended up on your front doorstep after the shooting on the rooftop. When I said I jumped across the street, this is how I did it. I have superhuman strength, and the only way I can be killed is if someone removes my head."

She frowned at the last statement.

"I know," I continued. "Believe me. It's weirder for me than anyone. I didn't ask for this. The man who had Amy killed was after the medallion. I found it by accident when I escaped his tent in the jungle where I was being kept. That's when I learned the truth about who I am, what I am."

She searched my eyes, and I saw the glowing red orbs reflected in hers.

"I have so many questions."

"I did too," Vero injected. "It's a lot to take in."

I still felt a little guilty for not telling Vero the real reason I needed her to come along, but I perished that twist of emotion to the void of my subconscious.

My point proved, I transformed back into my human shape,

looking just as I had before. Eliana watched the shift, mesmerized by the strange visage.

"See?" I asked. "I meant what I said, by the way. I did kill that sniper. My duty is to eliminate wicked people like him, those who would harm the innocent."

She seemed to be slowly accepting things, but more questions still lurked in her mind. "But... the body?"

"Was gone by the time I got back to your door."

"What happened to it?"

I blinked a few times, uncertain how I should answer that one. Then I figured I might as well give her everything. "A red mist surrounds those with wicked hearts," I explained. "Once they are dead, that mist consumes them. And it is as though they never existed."

"I... I don't understand." She lowered her gaze to the dusty slab underneath her, as if it might offer up some sort of easy explanation. Then she raised her head and said, "But I believe you, Gideon. It's hard not to with the evidence you just showed me."

"The man that was shooting at us was after me. And he's part of an organization that's trying to locate the medallions. Once we're gone, they won't bother you. But just in case, I would lie low for a few days until the dust settles. Just to be safe. Can you do that for me?"

She nodded absently. "Yes. I... can clear my schedule."

"Good."

Eliana slowly rose to her feet. "You said that man is with an organization? Who is behind this?"

I sighed and rolled my shoulders. "I don't know. But I'm going to try to find out."

16

The ferry bobbed in a steady rhythm as it cut through the waves of the sea. I've never had problem with seasickness, but that issue hadn't occurred to me in regard to Vero until after we'd taken our seats and the ship departed the harbor. Fortunately, she didn't get seasick either. Since there was no direct ferry from Piraeus Port to Delos, we first had to make the journey to Mykonos, then take a ferry from there. Due to the time of day, that meant we were going to have to spend the night on Mykonos before heading out to Delos in the morning.

Every second we spent searching felt like an anvil hanging over my head. Until she had the Artemis Medallion, Vero wouldn't truly be safe.

The problem with that line of thought was believing that once she did have it, all would be well. Far from it. My issues only just began when I found this thing.

I looked down at the outline of the amulet under my shirt, then over at Vero.

She looked out the window at the whitecaps on the water as the swells rose and fell. Islands passed by, some far off in the distance, others close enough of to make out the details of the hills and trees.

I'd paid for seats with a table so I could do more research on the pressing issues surrounding our voyage.

The first I'd been most curious about—the subject of Drake's journal and maps—had taken a back seat to the newer, shinier problem of just what in the world that sniper's tattoo meant.

I took the phone out of my pocket and performed a search, but nothing even remotely close to an answer popped up.

Vero noticed what I was doing and leaned in closer, curious. "What are you looking for?" she asked.

"I don't know, exactly," I admitted. "The shooter on the rooftop had a tattoo on his forearm. I guess I'm trying to figure out what it means."

"Oh." She shifted to get more comfortable, and her shoulder brushed against mine, sending a tingle across my skin. "What did it look like?"

I'd never been great at drawing, but I figured I could construct a rudimentary example. So, I took out my journal and a pen and drew a rough sketch of the sword cutting between the two letters.

"That's interesting," she said. "I've seen a lot of tattoos. Especially with the cartel around. They always have ink they believe will show off how tough they are, or that might intimidate an enemy. But I've never seen this one before."

"Probably a good thing," I said. "These guys are dangerous. The ones that attacked me on the road near Santa Rojo had some heavy-duty weapons. And they knew how to use them."

I took a breath and continued with a sigh. "None of them would talk, except the shooter in Athens slipped up and gave me one piece of unintended information."

"What's that?"

"He said something about a cardinal."

Her brow furrowed. "You mean, like the bird?"

I chuckled at the question and shook my head. "No. As in a high-level priest."

The answer dawned on her and darkened her face. "As in a Catholic cardinal?"

"So it would seem."

"But why would a cardinal... I mean, how?"

"Those same questions have been gnawing at me since the guy said it. I have no idea. I know that the church has had secretive branches throughout history. But I've never been aware of an elite death squad-style group."

She pondered the information for a second. "And why would they need such a thing? It's not like there is going to be another Inquisition. At least, I hope not."

"Right." Even though I agreed, I wondered if that were true. "The only thing I can think of is that whoever this cardinal is, he has gone rogue. I've heard of high-level members of organizations such as churches or secret societies going off the rails and using their power for nefarious purposes. I can't imagine the church itself is actually behind all this. And since that sniper only referenced the cardinal, I feel pretty confident in that theory."

We both fell silent again, left to consider possibilities.

I entered a few more search terms into my phone but still came up with no plausible answers. It wasn't much to go on—a sword splitting two letters. I found myself quietly wishing the shaman would show up on the boat and tell me who was behind this.

"You know it doesn't work that way," Xolotl said. "That would be reinforcing laziness."

I held back a laugh at the comment.

God helps those who help themselves. I guess that phrase works all the way around, even to an entity like you.

"Indeed."

Still, I felt myself wishing for the tiniest hint, a fraction of a crumb that could point me in the right direction.

I also wished I'd studied more about Catholic history. At least then I may have heard of some militant branch of the organization. Visions of the Swiss Guard popped into my head. While they were certainly elite in many ways, my brief study of them produced only a fragmented knowledge. I seemed to recall they acted more as a private police force for the Vatican. Though not knowing more details nagged at me.

How do I not know more about these guys?

I considered those answers were only a quick web search away, but that would be a distraction. I didn't need to waste time chasing the wrong leads. The men who'd attacked me were hitters, not a defensive or police unit. They were trained assassins. Unfortunately for them, there was no way their training could have included how to take down an ancient mythical monster like me.

"Still thinking about the shooter?" Vero asked, interrupting my train of thought.

"Yeah. As if I didn't have enough to think about already."

"I'm going to go to the bar and get a drink," she said, standing abruptly. "You want something?"

"Actually, I would love another coffee." Travel fatigue was already setting in. Despite the supernatural powers given me by the amulet, I still fell prey to the ordinary rigors and problems every human body faced.

I started to fish my wallet out of my jeans, but she waved it off and shook her head. "At least let me pay for your coffee. You've taken care of everything else."

"I also got you shot at," I added dryly.

"I'm still here," she said and walked away, disappearing around the corner.

I watched her leave, catching myself admiring her figure as she walked, then immediately snapped my attention away to the window and the infinite waves of the sea.

Why was this puzzle so hard to figure out? I felt like the answer was right in front of me, staring me in the face. But how could it be?

I shook off the frustration and reached into my bag, pulled out the Wells diary, and flipped it open.

I carefully turned through the pages until I reached a point where the late reverend had stopped writing. I scanned through the words with a quick pass, but my eyes caught something on the next-to-last page, and I reread the passage more intentionally.

Despite the allegiances I've forged, the pressure is growing more intense. At first, I thought the threat from Rome wasn't something I should worry about. After all, we're supposedly working for the same team. But now I'm not so sure. I must be vigilant against these men from the so-called Gladius Dei, just in case they decide to turn on me.

I didn't take a breath for several seconds. There it was. I blinked a dozen times as I reread the passage.

Wells had been concerned about a group from Rome called Gladius Dei. I didn't need a Latin-to-English translator on my phone to know what that meant. It translated to "sword of God."

The sword tattoo with the two letters made perfect sense now. But that fact brought about several more questions.

Who were these guys, and perhaps most importantly, who was the cardinal apparently giving them their orders? The only clear fact I could glean was that they were obviously willing to die for whatever cause they'd attached to their organization's goals. But to what end?

It definitely wasn't world peace.

The red mist surrounding every one of them I'd encountered virtually guaranteed me of that.

"Remember what the shaman said," the voice said to me as clearly as if speaking from the chair to my left.

"Remember what?" I wondered. "He said a lot. And he was pretty vague." Despite the question, my intuition poked my attention and brought a reminder to the front of my mind.

He'd said the forces of evil were bent on consuming the souls of mankind, or something to that effect. I now knew they were being driven by a single dark force, the one the shaman had called Ahriman. And that being's minions were spread all over the world—even in the Catholic Church.

It reminded me of what I'd been taught growing up, how when we were born, we were constantly watched by two angels—one good, and one bad. The good was there for our protection, while the bad perpetually attempted to lead us astray toward things and actions that would eventually lead us to ruin.

As a child, I'd easily accepted this notion, though in adulthood I had questioned it off and on. Kids accepted things so easily, and I'd been no different. Santa Claus was real to me until I accidentally saw some toys in the trunk of my parents' car at one point around the age of eight.

Believing in supernatural beings had never faded, though, even though I'd asked some hard questions about that once I was in college and beyond. And every now and then I would hear a story about someone's experience with an angel that reinforced the concept to my often-skeptical mind.

I'd heard the usual stuff, of course—tales of how someone survived a car crash or something along those lines when they shouldn't have. That sort of thing was always up for debate. Was it just luck? Or was there really some kind of otherworldly intervention?

But there was one story that stemmed the doubt for me forever.

I'd met an older lady at a church one day—not my usual sanctuary. I don't know what it was about me, but she latched on to me at the church potluck lunch after the service and kept asking me questions about what I did for a living.

Eventually, the pastor came up to her and asked if she'd like a ride home. She matter-of-factly replied, "No, he's going to take me home."

The statement caught me off guard, but as the pastor looked to me for confirmation, I simply nodded and said I'd be happy to.

After the meal, I helped the woman into my car and drove her back to her single-wide trailer. The humble home was parked on the edge of a farm in a beautiful, green valley in the hills of southern Tennessee.

When I entered the trailer, it instantly reminded me of my grandmother's place from when I was a kid. Her home had been a double-wide, though as a youth I didn't know the difference between that and a regular house. I'd grown up in something similar, though I had asked my parents at one point why our house had wheels on the bottom of it.

Looking around the tiny living room, I noticed the same kinds of afghans, homemade pillows, and quilts adorning decades-old fake leather sofas and chairs. The television along the far wall sat in a relic of an entertainment unit probably left over from the late 1970s. Part of me wondered if that television and the furniture it sat on was an upgrade. I remembered the system my grandmother had—a huge wooden cabinet with doors on either side of the tube television that came built into the thing. It was a far cry from the lightweight, high-definition jobs of modern times that you could lift with one hand. I recalled trying to help my dad move that monstrosity after my grand-mother passed away and thinking a forklift could have come in handy.

I spent the next two hours talking to that woman, though I'd lost most of the conversation to memory. One thing, however, stuck out, and I figured it always would.

She told me a story about the day her husband died at the age of 81. She said she woke up that morning and had gone into the kitchen to get a drink of water. When she returned to the bedroom, she claimed it was bathed in a radiant golden light, and standing next to her husband's body was a being of incredible beauty. She told me this figure looked over at her and smiled, and that the golden light seemed to pulse from his face.

"It was an angel," she'd said.

Then, she told me that the angel looked down at her husband's motionless body, put his glowing hand on the dead man's chest, and closed his eyes as if in a silent prayer. The next instant, the angel was gone, and the room was left in the relative darkness of early morning dawn.

To this day, I don't recall anything else that lady said to me. But that story burned in my mind's eye as if I'd been there to witness the whole thing in person.

Thinking about it on the ferry only reinforced the concepts of angels and demons in a constant battle for the souls of mankind, the great controversy that waged beyond the veil of human senses, just out of sight but always with and around us.

"How's the book?" a male American voice asked from just over my right shoulder.

I turned and looked back, startled by the sound. Then I saw a familiar face. Two faces, actually.

"What are you—" I started to ask but was stopped with an interrupting hand.

"We are just keeping an eye on things," Agent Gabriel Keane replied with a cool look around the room.

I glanced around the area, following his gaze, and realized that we were oddly alone. There'd been other passengers in there, all minding their own business in their seats, conversing, looking at their phones, reading books or magazines. But now, the cabin was empty.

"They can't see us," Agent Az Miller explained. "We are between the veils right now."

I stood up and turned around, again sweeping the room with my gaze as I tried to understand what was going on.

A splinter of panic stuck my chest. "Vero will be—"

"She's still at the bar getting your coffees. She won't know we were here," Keane explained.

"What are you doing here?"

"You needn't worry about us," Keane said. "Remember, we are on your side."

"Yeah. So you say."

"Have we given you reason to think otherwise?" Miller asked.

"No," I said with a twist of the head. "But you haven't exactly defended me either."

"You seem to be doing just fine."

Out of instinct, I looked toward the corner where Vero had gone, still thinking she might reappear any second.

"Why are you here?" I asked. "Are you going to help me out, or are you going to just stalk me while I run all around the world trying to locate these medallions?"

"Who said we aren't helping you?" Keane asked. Then his eyes shifted slightly, looking just beyond my right shoulder.

I narrowed my eyelids, then followed his gaze, turning to look behind me. A chill swept over my skin, raising the hairs across my body.

At the other end of the room, two more agents, dressed in similar black suits, stood in the entryway to this part of the cabin. They lurked on either side of the archway, arms crossed as they spoke to each other.

"What are they doing here?" I demanded in a whisper.

"Same thing we are," Keane answered. "Well, except they're not on your side."

"No, I definitely got that vibe. But what do you mean, same thing you are?"

"They're watching," Miller replied.

"Okay..." None of this was making sense. I recognized the Sector agents standing at the doorway, although it didn't seem like they knew I was talking to a couple of their Division Three rivals.

"They cannot see us at the moment," Keane said, making me wonder if he could read minds.

"You sure?"

The agent snorted, which seemed strange coming from him. "Yes. I'm sure."

"So, the four of you follow me around. You're supposedly on my side, and they aren't, yet neither of your groups has done anything except watch. No offense, but that is really creepy."

"Is it?"

"Uh, yeah. It's very creepy. And how in the world do you split, what was it you said, veils of reality?"

"That's a secret of the universe for another time and place," Miller said after a quick look to his partner. "But you are incorrect in thinking that we've done nothing to help you."

I searched his gray eyes, then Keane's. They shimmered like crystals and seemed to change colors randomly, shifting from gray to blue, to green, and back again.

Then it hit me.

The second the epiphany dawned on me, the two agents smiled. I looked back at the two on the other side of the room, and immediately I recognized huge differences. The Sector agents wore black shirts with black ties, and that contrast with the white shirts the Division Three agents wore was easy enough to spot. But there was something else about the Sector guys.

They appeared angry. Their faces wore dark expressions as if they'd never experienced or sought joy before.

"We are always with you, Gideon," Keane said. "Always have been. While we don't often intervene directly, unless the timeline dictates, our primary objective is to make sure they observe the rules, and likewise don't intervene."

I exhaled sheer disbelief. "Are you saying...?"

The two agents beamed at me. And not just smiling. A sort of golden light radiated from them, like an aura from a distant sun.

"Yes, Gideon. We are."

I finished the answer. "Angels."

17

"I have so many questions."

"Yes, we know," Keane said. "And someday, you will get the answers. But not right now. For the time being, just know that we always have your back when it comes to the fallen ones. We will make sure those two, and the rest of their colleagues, do not meddle directly with your mission."

I noticed a recurring theme and had to address it. "You keep saying the word directly. What exactly do you mean by that?"

Miller cracked his neck from side to side as an ordinary human might. "We are not permitted to touch a human being; neither are they. However, we are allowed to influence people. Usually, this kind of direction is done through premonitions, intuition, or now and then verbal communication through a conduit."

"Conduit?"

Miller's grin widened. "You've heard of the text about being kind to people because there are angels that you're unaware of?"

I felt my eyes widen. "Yes. So, you mean in disguise."

"Correct."

I shook my head, still trying to process all this, and again looked off to the side in the direction Vero had gone.

"But what about the stories I've heard? The ones where people have encountered you guys? If you aren't allowed to touch us or intervene, how is it that—"

"We saved your father in that car crash?" Keane finished.

I blinked and nodded, my mind tracing back to the story my dad had told me when I was a kid.

He'd been driving on a country road, one lane on either side. Back in those days, seat belts were nothing more than a suggestion rather than a rule. He wasn't speeding or anything crazy. But as he went around a bend in the road, another car in the other lane veered over across the yellow lines and onto my dad's side.

Dad said he jerked the wheel out of instinct to avoid hitting the other car, which sent his own vehicle careening off the road and into a ditch.

What happened just before the car hit the embankment was something that had a profound effect on my father for the rest of his life. By all accounts of physics, with no seat belt on, the impact should have sent him flying through the windshield, and likely killed him.

Instead, he said he felt something hit him hard on the back on both shoulder blades, effectively shoving him down so that when the car struck the ditch, most of his inertia got caught wedged between the seat and the wheel.

After the dust settled, and my grandparents picked my father up from the scene, he went home—bruised and aching, but alive. He took off his shirt in the bathroom, and turned on the shower, but when he spun around to inspect the two sore spots on his shoulder blades, he nearly fell over in shock.

There, on my dad's skin, were two, unmistakable handprints.

I felt a tear pushing against the corner of my right eye, and I had to choke it back. "Yes. How did you save my father if you're not permitted to intervene?"

"That, Gideon, is a question many humans have asked for millennia. We are only allowed to step in when one of them breaks a rule. Every now and then, they push the boundaries, usually when they see something in a human that concerns them and the success of their mission."

I considered the statement. "Their mission, as in mankind consuming material things until they've abandoned all thought of spirituality."

"Very good," Keane nodded. "In the case of your father, they perceived him as a threat to that goal, so the dark ones tried to take matters into their own hands—thinking we wouldn't be able to react fast enough."

"I didn't think time was something relevant to your kind."

"It isn't. Not in the way you mortals understand it. Time for us flows in all directions, which can make it tricky sometimes if one of the others tries to slip by us. But that hasn't happened yet. And that isn't to say bad things don't happen. That is the nature of the life you live on this planet. But when the balance is tipped, guardians have always come to reset it and bring justice and good back to the world."

We were getting pretty deep into the weeds now, and I wondered how far this conversation was going to go.

"Unfortunately," Miller said, "we have never in Earth's history seen the balance shift to the side of light. Always to the darkness it slides. The adversary's temptations are many. He and his agents know the minds of every human better than you know your own."

I'd heard that before, but never really pondered it much. "Like the Screwtape Letters by C.S. Lewis," I muttered.

"Very much so. They have a plan of attack for every human who has ever lived, or ever will be born on this planet."

A single question dominated all the others rattling around in my mind. I had to ask it.

"Will it ever end? This conflict between good and evil?"

Both agents smiled at me. Their expressions softened, and I could see the pity filling their strange eyes.

"We are not allowed to tell you the future, Gideon. And the decisions of every person in their individual lifelines alters everything, much like a pebble tossed into still water—the ripples carry on until they reach the shore."

Keane turned to Miller and nodded. "We must go. Just know that we are always with you, Gideon. Even if we cannot see you."

"Thank you," I said with an appreciative nod. "I have so many other questions."

"We know. Those answers will have to wait for another day."

"Take care of Vero," Miller added. "We know you will."

A swish of air blasted over me. I blinked and looked around. I was back in my seat, as if I'd never moved. Wells' journal still sat in my lap. The other passengers were in their seats just as before.

I looked to the doorway at the other end of the room, but there was no sign of the Sector agents I'd seen a moment before. I turned in every direction and likewise found Agents Keane and Miller had disappeared.

I sighed as I sat back in my seat, feeling suddenly fatigued. It was difficult to process it all. I'd spoken to... angels. I couldn't help but appreciate the timing, moments after I'd just been thinking about that very topic. As if my thoughts had called them.

I dispelled that notion. They weren't lackeys sitting around waiting to attend to my every whim. The two had alluded to orders. That brought to mind more visions of the angelic hierarchy on both sides, something I'd only come across on rare occasions when researching ancient theological concepts.

I could have sat there pondering all these things for an hour and never found the answers I wanted. But I only had a few seconds.

Vero rounded the corner and walked toward me, holding a cup of coffee in each hand. She beamed at me as she approached.

"Sorry that took me so long," she said. "The line was like six people deep."

I shook off the apology. "Were you gone that long? Didn't seem like it."

She tilted her head at the comment and handed me the cup from her left hand. "Oh. Well, in that case, I'm not sorry." She giggled and sat down next to me.

Vero turned her head toward the window again and peered out through the glass, studying the waves and another island that passed by in the distance. After a minute, she looked over at me and frowned. "You okay? You look like you've seen a ghost or something."

I huffed at the comment. "Yeah. Or something," I muttered.

"What?"

"Nothing," I said, raising the cup to my lips. I watched the steam drifting out of the little hole in the lid, then cautiously took a sip. The hot liquid nearly burned my tongue, and I pulled back from it to let it cool for a minute or two. "Whew, that's hot."

"They just made a fresh pot," she explained. "I guess that's why the line was so long. You didn't say you wanted creamer or anything. I forgot to ask you."

"No, it's fine. I like it black."

"Me too."

I felt a warm, welcoming feeling at the pointless banter. It was a soothing embrace after the incredible experience I had while she was gone.

"But everything's okay, yeah?" Vero asked. "Did you find out anything from that book?" She motioned to the journal still sitting on my lap.

"Actually, I did," I said. "Wells mentioned a group called Gladius Dei."

The blank look on her face told me she needed the translation.

"It means sword of God," I clarified. "I can't be sure, but I think it might be a secret offshoot of the Catholic Church."

She nearly spit out her coffee. "So, wait. You think the church is trying to kill you?"

"No," I quickly shook my head. "I doubt the church knows anything about it. If I had my guess, I believe they're a rogue element, acting without the Vatican's knowledge." I felt weird talking about it, especially as a non-Catholic. But that was my best guess.

I recalled the situation that went down in Waco, Texas, back when I was in high school in the early 1990s.

David Koresh had convinced a bunch of people that he was the messiah. Most people in the United States heard about the situation and the standoff with federal authorities. The undertone of the story, however, was that the core denomination he was affiliated with was somehow responsible. His sect was a far offshoot of the Seventh-day Adventist Church, which had nothing to do with what happened in Waco, or with Koresh. But that didn't stop wild rumors and accusations from flying.

Koresh had acted alone—a loose cannon with a wild idea that somehow resonated with a group of followers.

Was it possible this cardinal the sniper in Athens mentioned was doing the same thing?

"Of course it's possible," Xolotl said. "All things are possible."

I didn't respond to the voice, but I accepted what it told me.

"I'll have to do some more snooping around," I said, realizing I'd been silent for nearly a full minute. The second the words were out of my mouth, I remembered someone who might be able to help me out with this issue.

I had a friend in Rome, an expert in not only Roman history but the history of the Catholic Church.

He'd committed to becoming a priest at one point but backed out one week before he took his vows because he changed his mind about having a wife and family. He had remained a devout Catholic after giving up the priesthood.

If anyone in my network had information about Gladius Dei, it would be him.

Vero stared at me over her coffee lid, expecting me to say something as if she'd been waiting for five minutes.

For a second, I wondered how long I'd been lost to my own thoughts. Had it been five minutes?

"Sorry," I said out of instinct. "I just remembered I have a friend who might be able to help with this question."

"Who's the friend?" Vero wondered.

"His name is Lorenzo Tonali." I rubbed both cheeks with thumb and forefinger as I thought. "Historian. Specializes in Roman and Catholic history. If he doesn't know what this Gladius Dei group is, I'm not sure I know anyone else who would."

"Well, I suppose you could ask around if this Lorenzo can't help."

She was right, of course. I knew who to call, and who to ask for at a dozen or so universities and research facilities around the world. Maybe more. But I didn't like asking for help from people I didn't know. It was one thing to call on a friend, quite another to knock on the door of some archaeologist I'd never met.

Fortunately, I hadn't pissed off many people in my field. I had a nice guy reputation, which made the fact that I could turn into a sort of berserk monster more than a little laughable.

"I tried to always practice something my mom taught me when I was young," I said. "She told me to be nice. It doesn't cost any extra. Maybe I've built up enough goodwill that if Lorenzo can't help us, someone else probably can. But I'm going to reach out and see what he says. Maybe we'll get lucky."

I found his contact in my phone and typed out a message. I tried to be as brief as possible, though I wanted to give Lorenzo as many details as I could. Before I sent the text, I hesitated.

Vero noticed my reluctance. "What?" she prodded. "You going to send it or what?"

I blinked a few times as I stared at the screen. "Yeah, I just... this Gladius Dei group, they may have their grubby fingers into more than I realize. This text thread isn't encrypted."

"You think they could be tracking your phone?"

"Possibly. I don't even know how any of that stuff works, to be honest. If something happened to Lorenzo because of this message, I couldn't forgive myself."

She studied my face for half a minute. I glanced over at her and caught her sympathetic expression. "If you're that worried about it, don't send the message. Just call him."

I grumbled something unintelligible as my thumb hovered over the send button. "I'm being paranoid."

Then I selected the entire message and hit delete.

Before Vero could say anything else, I typed out a much shorter message and hit Send.

"That's smart," she said when I was done.

"Thanks." I slid my phone back into my pocket. There was no

telling how long Lorenzo might take to get back to me. For now, it was enough to be on the way to Mykonos, and tomorrow morning Delos.

I'd done the right thing to keep my friend safe. As safe as possible, anyway. Now, I had to figure out how to let Vero know she was a guardian. Then again, maybe that would take care of itself as it had for me.

I guessed we'd find out soon enough.

18

The sun dipped low in the western sky over the Mediterranean as the ferry pulled into the harbor at the island of Mykonos.

We filed out with all the other passengers, along with the cars and delivery trucks that had made the voyage. As we descended the stairs toward the exit, I kept looking back over my shoulder in case one of the Sector agents had snuck behind me. I hadn't noticed them ahead of us, but now that I knew what they really were, I realized it was entirely possible they could shift into human form, disguising themselves from being noticed.

I wondered how many times that had happened in my life, moments I'd bumped into an angelic being from either side without knowing it.

That kind of thing could drive a person crazy, so I did my best to let it go as Vero and I stepped out onto the shore and walked toward the shops across from the landing.

"What do you want to do?" I asked, partly to shut down the thoughts overtaking my brain.

Vero looked over at me with a tired smirk. "What do you mean?"

"Well," I said, tightening the straps on my backpack, "I know we're tired from traveling, but we've been going this long, and we can't go to bed yet or we'll be useless tomorrow. I was thinking maybe we could go walk on one of the famous beaches here, maybe watch the sun set, then grab a bite to eat before we check into the hotel."

She seemed impressed by the offer. "That's ambitious."

"Which part?"

We kept walking toward the street where several cabs waited, along with a dozen ride share cars, to take travelers to their destinations.

"All of it?" she said in a mocking question. "I thought you'd be too tired to do anything else tonight. Maybe that medallion gives you a little juice."

"Nah. I wish. More like a shot of adrenaline when I need it. Okay, a shot of adrenaline on steroids. But hey, if you're too tired to go exploring a little, I understand. We can just go get dinner then head to the hotel."

She laughed at me. "Are you kidding? Of course I would love to go check out one of the world-famous beaches on this island. After all, who knows when I'll get a chance to come back here? And since we're pressed for time, I doubt we'll be able to take a proper tour on this trip."

I hummed a regretful sound. I wished that I could give her a proper tour of this place. I'd never been here either, and there was so much to see and do, it would take us a week to get it all in.

"Let's do it, then," I said decisively. "Only live once, right?"

She grinned with excitement as we approached the line of ride share cars and cabs. I made my way toward the cab in the front of the line where a man in his mid-forties leaned against the driver's side door with his arms crossed. He wore a white short-sleeve button-up short and gray slacks. His hairline started high on his forehead, but the hair that remained was thick and curly, dangling down just behind his ears.

He nodded to us as we approached, and stood up as if at attention. The man didn't even ask if we wanted a ride. He simply opened the back door to the cab and motioned us in.

"Can you take us to the nearest beach?" I asked.

"Certainly," he said in a thick local accent. "Only fifteen euro."

I squinted at him as Vero waited next to the door, trying to decide if she should get in or wait for me to negotiate. Normally, I would have haggled him down to ten or twelve as was the custom now and then with drivers in this country, but I decided to let him have this one.

"Cool," I said, finalizing the deal. I gave a nod to Vero, and she climbed into the back, then slid over to the far side.

I got in after and set my bag in the middle next to hers. The cab driver closed the door with a loud thump and got behind the wheel. He flipped on the meter and stepped on the gas.

"Here on vacation?" the man asked, making polite conversation. As cordial as the question was, he said it in a gruff tone that gave the impression he was just trying to squelch awkward silence until he could drop us off and collect his fare.

"Yes," I said quickly, deciding brevity was best.

"First time here on Mykonos?"

"It is."

"Oh. Well, welcome to the island. I am sure you will enjoy the sunset from the beach. Of course, some of our beaches are more crowded than others. But this time of year is not so bad. More people come here in the summer."

"So, you're still a few months from that, huh," Vero said.

"Yes. But it is still a popular place, particularly for Europeans from the colder nations. I must say, we don't get many Americans here this time of year."

He drove through the intersection when the light turned green and made a sharp left turn. A gray hatchback in front of him stopped, seemingly for no reason, and our driver decided to shoot past him on the left, weaving into the other lane for a second before swerving back as another cab approached in the other direction.

The maneuver reinforced what our driver in Athens had said, and the thought caused a nervous smirk to spread across my face.

"Only ten minutes to the beach from here," he said.

I felt a tickle of relief at the statement. The less time we spent in this car, the better.

"Are there any ancient ruins we should see here?" Vero asked, egging on the conversation.

"A few," he answered. "Though most of the more famous ones in this area are on the island of Delos."

The name of the island sent a spark through my gut, reiterating why we were here.

"It isn't far from here," the driver added. "Short ferry trip. Maybe thirty to forty minutes."

I didn't feel the need to let him know we'd already figured that part out. Instead, I steered the conversation elsewhere as I looked out at the colorful buildings along the street and hillsides. Most of the homes going up the slopes glistened with the famous white exteriors seen in so many postcards and touristy videos.

"So, you like history?" the cabbie asked.

Vero nearly giggled. She knew she'd set me up. "He's an archaeologist," she answered. "So, you could say that."

"Oh! Wonderful. We get many historians and archaeologists here to the island. I suppose I don't have to tell you about the mythologies of Mykonos and Delos."

"Actually," Vero said, leaning forward with piqued interest, "I would love to hear about those."

Maybe she thought I'd be annoyed at the conversation, but I wanted to know more about the area just as she did. While my expertise was more centered around Central and South America, I always enjoyed learning about stuff from other places in the world.

"Ah," our driver went on, sounding happy to be able to enlighten us on the subject, "as the legend goes, Mykonos was where Zeus fought and conquered a mighty Titan. Then there's another myth that followed it, a story of how Hercules battled twelve giants. The legend says that after the giants were defeated, they were turned to stone, and those rocks became the island of Mykonos."

"That's cool," Vero said, satisfied with the tale.

"Yes, well, it's a good story. The mythology of Delos is not as exciting, but still quite interesting. According to the legend, the twin gods Artemis and Apollo were born there. I sometimes wonder where these stories came from so long ago. There was a temple there, although now it is only ruins. Still, the place attracts many tourists throughout the year, though far more in the summer."

I heard everything the driver said, but my attention locked on to the part about Artemis being born on Delos. The second he'd mentioned her name, I felt a chill shoot over my skin.

Vero looked over at me. I loved that mischievous grin she wore. She appeared unfazed by the time change and the long travel day. I knew she was at least a few years younger than me, maybe as many as five or six. But it wasn't her youth that fueled her. It was her curiosity. I saw it in her eyes.

"Where are you staying for your trip?" The driver interrupted our shared silence.

I snapped my head away from her and met his eyes in the mirror. I gave him the name of the hotel, and he informed me that the place was only a short walk from the beach where he was taking us.

"Very convenient, that hotel," he explained. "Many good restaurants and tavernas within walking distance. You picked a nice one."

Vero raised her eyebrows at me. "Oh, fancy."

"Yes, well, if you're going to visit Mykonos, you may as well do it right."

The driver laughed a booming, hearty sound. Then he flipped on his blinker almost at the same time he veered to the right into a narrow parking spot along the sidewalk.

To our left, the sun dipped low in the west. Its bright yellow glow faded into deeper and deeper orange, reflected in the shimmering surface of the sea.

The cabbie opened his door and stepped out, quickly pulling my door open, then moving around to let Vero out. I walked around and met them on the sidewalk, fishing a ten and a five note out of my wallet. I handed him the bill and thanked him for the ride.

"Enjoy your time here," he said cheerily as he stuffed the money into his pocket.

"Thanks," Vero said.

He gave a curt nod, then hurried back around to the driver's door that hung precariously out into part of the road. So far, the cars passing by swerved slightly to miss it, but I was once again reminded of how some drivers in this part of the world either didn't consider the rest of the people on the road or did and simply didn't care.

The driver closed the door the second he was behind the wheel and sped out in front of a line of cars with only a meter or two to spare.

"Interesting guy," Vero commented, watching the car meld into the rest of the traffic.

"Yes. Friendly as they need to be, that sort. But they have to hustle to pay the bills. At least he didn't try to scam us." *Too much,* I thought. I indicated a crosswalk at the intersection. "Shall we?"

We walked over to the stop light, then crossed the street when it changed. Several resorts lined the coastline, and we passed between two white hotels before reaching the beach where hundreds of umbrellas and beach chairs were set up in neat rows on the sand.

Most of the beachgoers were gone. A few dozen or so walked lazily along the water's edge, dipping their toes into the sea, some holding hands, while others simply stood there with their feet in the sand, staring out at the sunset as it smeared the sky with colors of pink, purple, and faint orange.

The sound of waves gentling rolling onto shore filled our ears. I inhaled the salty breeze and felt momentarily renewed. I'd always imagined having a beach house, and part of that longing was simply to enjoy the salt air as it cleansed my nostrils.

I had a friend who'd owned a place on the coast of the Florida panhandle, and he'd always said that the salty air could cure just about anything.

I doubted the absolute medical truth behind that statement, but I knew that whenever I was by the ocean, my allergies seemed to disappear, and I never had any sort of sinus issues.

So, maybe there was some truth to it after all.

I exhaled with a long, satisfied sigh and looked over at Vero.

"This is beautiful," she said, taking in the view. "Come on. Let's go to the water."

We still hadn't set our bags down, but that was fine. Now that we were here, I started wishing I hadn't suggested the idea. Fatigue and gravity worked together, begging me to sit down on one of the beach chairs, but I wasn't going to ruin the adventure with a little laziness.

I followed her through the maze of chairs and umbrellas until she stopped where the water touched the sand in slow, rhythmic waves.

Vero sucked in a huge breath of air and smiled as she blew it out. "I could get used to living in a place like this."

I nodded. "Yeah. It doesn't suck. That's for sure."

I caught a subtle movement to my left and looked that direction. A woman with thick gray hair shuffled along the sand in a light blue dress. She was coming our way, but her head was down as if scanning the sand for something.

I heard her mumbling something as she approached, and for a second I didn't know if she would see us or bump right into me.

At the last second, she looked up and into my eyes. "Oh, I'm so sorry," she said. Her accent sounded like she might be from around here, but also different, as if she'd moved here from somewhere else in her youth.

"No problem," I said, and stepped back out of the path she seemed so intent on following.

"I seem to have lost something, and I have looked up and down this beach for it for nearly an hour."

"Oh no," Vero joined in. "What was it you lost?"

The pleading look on the woman's face drew both of us in. "It's a locket given to me a long time ago. A family heirloom, you see. It's in the shape of a vase. It has been in my family for generations, and now I fear I've lost it. I hope someone else didn't pick it up and claim it for themselves."

I felt a complaining part of me want to wish the woman well and send her on her way while I enjoyed a peaceful sunset with Vero, but I could tell by the way the lady looked at me that she wanted me to help.

I groaned on the inside, and I wondered if the voice in my brain was going to tell me to let the stranger figure out her own problems. He remained silent, so I shoved aside the selfishness tugging at me. That wasn't who I was anyway. I'd always been the type of person to help someone in need, even if their need was a result of carelessness.

"What did this locket look like?" I asked, already scanning the sand for any sign of something I assumed would be gold or silver, and probably in the shape of a vase.

"Oh, thank you, young man," she said with grateful relief dripping from her eyes. "I truly appreciate it. You are so kind to offer your help."

"It's okay," I said. "But it's getting dark, so if we're going to find it we should hurry. Hunting for something like that after nightfall will be nearly impossible."

She nodded urgently. "Yes. Yes. Of course. It's a golden locket in the shape of a vase."

"A vase?" Vero asked just to be sure.

I also thought that an unusual design for a piece of jewelry like that.

"Yes. You will know it when you see it. But it is small. If someone hasn't already picked it up, it could have been accidentally covered with sand." The woman kept looking around at the ground, hoping she might get lucky. Her face darkened with worry, and she teetered on the verge of crying.

"We'll find it. I'm sure it's around here somewhere," I encouraged, though I didn't really believe the statement myself. That thing was probably long gone, most likely scooped up by some random person who thought they just found a little treasure in the sand. I doubted there was a lost and found around here.

I motioned to my left along the water's edge. "You two look that way. I'll go this direction. You think it was close to the water?"

The lady nodded. "Yes. Oh, thank you so much, dear. I hope we can find it."

I waited a second for Vero and the lady to go the other way before I turned my back on them and slowly walked along the hard, wet sand. There was no point in looking in the wet area. If so, the sea would have taken it and there'd be no finding it. Ever. So, I shifted my track slightly onto the soft, powdery sand a little farther from the lapping waves.

I swept my gaze left to right and back again, covering a ten- to fifteen-foot swath as I moved. But I didn't see anything. A minute passed. Then two. Then five.

I glanced over my shoulder and saw Vero and the other woman were at least a hundred yards away, maybe more.

Didn't seem like any of us were moving that fast, but I'd been so focused on the sand at my feet I guessed I didn't realize how far I'd gone.

I looked back down at the ground again and kept going, though I wondered how much farther I needed to go before turning around and returning to the other two. The lady hadn't been clear about how much beach she'd covered, or an approximate area where she may have dropped the locket.

I briefly considered turning around and heading back to catch up to them. The term needle in a haystack started pricking at me, and I felt like somehow this was worse.

Figuring I should at least give an honest try, I pressed on. It was a perfect day. Weather was warm but not hot, a gentle breeze coming off the ocean, and one of the most spectacular sunsets I'd ever seen.

I guess the reason I was annoyed by this silly side quest was that I'd been pulled apart from Vero, and I'd really wanted to spend the sunset on the beach with her.

Not that I thought it was going anywhere. At least not on this trip. I just thought it would be nice to watch the sun go down in a special place.

Who was I kidding? I liked her. And I knew it was too soon to move on after what happened to Amy. Then again, Amy had moved on a long time ago. And I wasn't dead.

The nagging sense of contempt snaked through my gut and chest. I dispelled the emotion with a long sigh and then caught a glint of something in the dying rays of sunlight a few yards away.

"No way," I said, and picked up my pace, covering the last couple of paces quicker than before.

As I drew closer to the anomaly in the sand, another wave crashed onto the shore. This one was stronger than the others before, and I realized the tide must have been rising. The sea licked at the golden locket, now embedded in the sand. White foam surrounded it, and I wasted no time reaching down to snatch the thing lest the water take it away for good.

I stared down at the item, studying it front and back.

The golden locket was indeed shaped like a thin vase and even had a golden cork in the top of it. The tiny piece of jewelry fit easily into my palm with room to spare.

I held the thing aloft and watched it sparkle in the sunlight, almost as if the gold were mixed with glitter. It seemed to have a glow of its own, and I leaned in closer to get a better look.

Then, out of nowhere, I felt something wrap around my left ankle and jerk me off my feet and into the sea.

19

I n the field of archaeology, I'd heard plenty of stories—legends of monsters from ancient times and the heroes who slew them. Sea monsters were always on the menu in that regard, particularly when it came to the study of maritime history.

Down through the ages, sailors from every corner of the world had a myth or legend they feared, a leviathan that could destroy well-armed ships with a single devastating attack.

The kraken came to mind. And as I felt an incredibly tight, slimy grip wrapped snugly around my ankle, I found myself wondering if that one was real.

Fortunately, I had the presence of mind—and I don't know how—to take a huge breath the second before the creature dragged me under.

I somehow managed to hold on to the locket, though I wasn't sure why that felt important at the moment. A massive sea monster was pulling me down into the depths of the Mediterranean.

It took a Herculean effort to keep water from shooting up my nose as whatever this thing was pulled me away from shore. I'd never been great at holding my breath, and even though I figured inhaling the water that would normally kill an ordinary person probably wouldn't do that to me, the process sounded extremely painful.

"You just gonna let that thing pull you to the bottom of the sea or what?" Xolotl asked.

He didn't have to speak twice.

With nothing more than a blink, I summoned the power of the medallion. The monster's grip on my ankle loosened for a second as my leg doubled in size. The turbulence of the enveloping water still made any controlled movements difficult, and I felt the pressure in my ears increasing. Again, being crushed in the depths wasn't a form of death I had any desire to test out.

I contorted my body, hoping I could lean over and pry away whatever gripped my leg, but the speed of the water rushing by made that too difficult.

My lungs tightened, and I knew I'd need air soon. The surface above rippled with the last light of day, fading as I descended deeper into the swirling darkness.

Desperation hit me, and I did the only thing I could think of. I used my right foot and dug the claw of my big toe into the creature's tissue, jabbing it deep into the slippery surface.

The grip weakened, though not entirely. Encouraged by the effect, I stabbed harder, pushing the sharp claw deep into the creature.

That did the trick.

The thing wrapped around my ankle immediately released me, and a strange howl echoed through the depths, like a mangled cry between a whale and a cat in a rainstorm.

The sound pierced my ears, but I squinted it away and kicked hard toward the surface. I pulled myself up through the water, pushing my arms and legs to their max. Surprisingly, I found I was a powerful swimmer in beast form, and I climbed faster than I ever could have as a human.

Just before I reached the precious air above, I glanced down as I heard something stirring in the sea below. The face that stared back at me was unlike anything I'd ever seen. Nothing could have prepared me for it, even considering the bizarre experiences I'd been through over the last few weeks.

The creature swam toward me at incredible speed. Yellow eyes fixed on me, set in a brownish-green face that looked like the images of velociraptors I'd seen in movies or on toy shelves. But this monster's body was longer, something akin to an alligator, but with longer legs and arms. Its massive tail whipped back and forth, propelling it toward me much faster than I could swim.

I kicked as hard as I could, fearing the thing might grab me before I could reach the surface. Its eyes remained locked on me as if ready to devour a meal.

Unexpectedly, my head breached the layer between water and air, and I felt my head burst into the light. I sucked in air like it was the last in the galaxy and managed to get four huge gulps before I felt the slimy claw wrap around my ankle again.

The creature pulled me under again, but this time I was ready. As ready as I could be for whatever this was.

I leaned my head down as it pulled me close. The monster grabbed at my right arm and brought me to eye level with it. The thing opened its jaws and bared sharp, pointy teeth—ready to bite.

It twisted its head at an angle and snapped forward, but I shoved its reaching arm away and ducked to the side. As its mouth shut, clamping down on ocean water, I quickly wrapped my thick arms around it in a tight bear hug and squeezed.

The monster instantly went into a fury, jerking its head around wildly, suddenly desperate to free itself from my powerful grip.

It felt like riding one of those mechanical bulls that certain bars offer for patrons drunk enough to think they can stay on. Except this bull was underwater, and I knew I had only seconds before I'd need to swim up and get another breath of air.

The monster clawed at my arms, digging into my flesh. Pain screamed from the fresh wounds, but I wouldn't let go. With the beast preoccupied with my arms, I twisted my body and wrapped my legs around its neck. That really made it mad, and apparently more desperate. With its neck between my thighs, I squeezed hard, crushing the creature's throat. I didn't know if the thing was breathing water or just holding its breath for a long time like a frog, but choking it seemed to be working, so I tightened my grip even more.

The giant lizard twitched wildly, and its body started to go rigid. Meanwhile, I fought my own need to climb to the surface again for another breath of air, and I knew I could only hold out for a precious few seconds more.

Then, the monster's struggle weakened. I wasn't about to risk it faking death. I flicked out a sharp claw on my right hand-paw and raked it across the creature's neck where I'd felt a strong pulse against my leg.

I dug the claw deep into the leathery, slick skin and felt it drag through an artery.

The lizard's body only gyrated one more time from the mortal wound, then it lost all strength, and I felt it get heavy in my grip. I released the monster and looked down as it slowly fell away, a trail of inky blood pluming from its neck and mingling with the water.

I kicked up to the surface with only a few swings of my legs and breached the air again. I dog-paddled for a second, catching my breath while still looking down into the water beneath my feet—just in case.

The monster never reappeared, instead fading into a nondescript dark mass slowly succumbing to the blackness of the deep.

I'd felt a wave of relief and renewal course through me, as if I'd just taken an ice bath. That relief faded when I realized I'd released the lady's vase during the fight. Regret rapidly replaced the other emotions. That locket had clearly meant a lot to the woman, and now I'd let it go. To be fair, I had probably the greatest excuse of all time. But I also knew there was no way I could tell the lady about this. She'd think I was certifiably insane.

Still, I wished I could have salvaged the locket for her.

I began to swim back to shore, only now realizing how far the creature had taken me out to sea. The beach had to be three to four hundred yards away. I hadn't realized how fast we were moving as it dragged me from the shore.

I'd only swung my arms a couple of times before I spotted something shiny bobbing in the water. I froze. "No way," I blurted.

There, only five feet away, floated the woman's locket.

I paddled over to it, eyeing the thing suspiciously as if it might attack me as the monster had done. Then I snatched it and held it up so the last orange beams of light danced on the wet golden surface.

"That's lucky," the voice said.

I looked up toward my forehead as if I could see him. "Yeah. And thanks for the word of warning about whatever that thing was."

"You seem to have gotten out of it unscathed."

"Unscathed?"

My arms hurt where the lizard had dug its claws into my skin, but the wounds were already healing.

I didn't say anything else and started swimming back toward shore.

When I was a hundred yards from the beach, I spotted Vero and the lady, still with their backs to where I'd been before being attacked. From the looks of it, they were still searching for the lady's locket and hadn't seen what happened.

With fifty yards to go, I willed myself back into human form and made the shift as I continued swimming.

The last stretch of water was more difficult without the super-human strength of the chupacabra, but I managed, and finally felt the sand under my feet as I made it to shore.

Utter exhaustion gripped me, and gravity suddenly felt like it was working double time.

I fell to my knees, bracing myself with palms in wet, foamy sand as I dragged myself out of the water and onto the beach.

I collapsed there for a minute or three, catching my breath and letting my muscles rest. After the respite, I turned my head in the direction Vero and the woman had gone, and saw them making their way toward me.

I rolled over onto my rear and sat there for another minute, watching the top rim of the dull orange sun disappear behind the horizon on the sea.

Then, I stood up and slowly trudged toward the two.

As I drew near them, I noticed the forlorn look on the woman's face, the sadness tugging on her eyes.

I held the locket in my fist and slowed down as we met.

Vero looked at me like I was wearing a pink tutu. "Did you... go for a swim?"

"I... found this in the water," I said, extending my fist toward the lady. I peeled open my fingers to reveal the golden locket in my palm.

Her face lit up in an instant, as if reflecting the golden hue of the vase. "Oh my," she exclaimed. "You found it. You found my locket."

She plucked it from my hand and pressed it to her chest. "Thank you. Thank you so much, young man. How can I ever repay you?" She started to weep as she stared down at the heirloom in her open hand. This locket obviously meant even more to her than she'd let on.

I shook my head as I ran my fingers through my wet hair. "Don't mention it. I'm happy to help."

"How did you ever find it in the water?" she pried.

"It was in the sand. The tide is rising, so the waves were encroaching a little higher on the breach. I spotted it just before the water pulled it in. Or buried it in the sand."

"I can't thank you enough," the lady said, holding the locket out to examine it again.

"Well, I'm just glad I was able to find it."

Satisfied with having the item back in her possession, she finally seemed to notice how wet I was. "Did you say it was on the edge of the water? What happened?"

"Good luck with this one," Xolotl whispered in my ear, returning to his usual annoying self.

"I... lost my balance and fell in just as a big wave crashed onto the beach. I felt kind of like an idiot. Glad the two of you didn't see it."

She studied my face for several heartbeats, as though she didn't believe the lie. It seems reasonable enough, but this woman seemed to see right through it.

"Well, I'm glad you didn't get hurt," she said.

If only she knew.

"Yeah, I'm fine. Just a little clumsy. That's all." I piled on the details to hammer the deception home. No way I was telling her the truth.

Vero's suspicion was evident in the incredulous expression on her face.

"Have a good evening," I said, deciding to end the conversation and get somewhere I could dry off.

"You too," the lady replied with a warm smile. "Perhaps if I see you again, I can repay your kindness."

"No repayment necessary, but you're very welcome."

She bobbed her head and turned in the other direction, cradling the golden vase in her hands as she made her way down the beach.

I wondered where she was going, but I figured she knew, and there was no sense in prying.

I watched her for ten seconds before I realized Vero was still staring at me by my side. "What?" I asked without meeting her accusing gaze.

She put her hands on her hips, and I finally rounded to face her. "Fell in the water?"

I pressed my lips together and inhaled through my nose. "Yeah..."

"You going to tell me what really happened?"

I swallowed the lie and looked around for a towel rack. I spotted one in front of the resort directly behind where we stood. From the looks of it, the white outdoor cabinet was still open.

"Yeah. But let's get moving. I need to dry off. It's getting chilly."

As we trudged through the sand, our feet sinking awkwardly with every step, I relayed the story of the attack, how the lizard-like monster had grabbed me just as I found the woman's locket, and how it tried to take me down to the bottom of the sea.

Vero listened without judgment, wearing only a look of concern as the tale fell on her ears.

"Wow," she said when I finished. "You know, Gideon, all of this would be hard to believe... normally. But based on everything I've seen with you lately, I actually believe you. It shocks me to say, but I believe you."

I removed a white-and-blue-striped towel from one of the shelves put out by one of the beachside hotels and rubbed my hair with it, then did my best to dab my wet clothes, which proved an effort in futility.

"What do you think it was?"

I rubbed my ears to get them dry as I answered. "I have no idea. That's the first time I've encountered anything like that. I mean, a monster of any kind. I thought those things were just... you know, myths."

The irony wasn't lost on me even as the words spilled from my lips.

Me, a monster of folklore, calling out another such beast. I did find it oddly humorous, despite the sobering situation.

"If that creature is out there," Vero theorized, "then there are probably others. Perhaps many more."

"Yes," I agreed with a nod. "I'm afraid you're right." Another thought occurred to me, and Vero noticed.

"What?"

I looked down at the sand for a second, then out toward the beach where the lady had gone previously. There was no sign of her now.

"It sounds weird, but I'm glad that thing attacked me and not some innocent person walking on the beach. An ordinary human wouldn't have survived that, unless they happened to have a harpoon gun on them. Or maybe a really big knife. Even then, unlikely."

"You think it was targeting you specifically?"

"I don't know. Seems strange that if it was looking for a meal it picked me instead of all the other tourists walking the sand."

"Much easier targets than you," she said with a flirty grin.

I blushed, which felt nice since I was getting colder by the second. "Can we talk about this more in the hotel? I need to warm up."

"Oh yes. I am so sorry. Let's get going."

"Don't be sorry. It's okay. It's a short walk from here."

I pointed down a path that went to the left of the resort where we stood. "Should be just that way."

As we started down the sidewalk that ran perpendicular to the water, I felt a sense of concern simmering inside me like a long-dormant volcano preparing to erupt. I glanced back over my left shoulder in the general vicinity of where the attack happened. My own words echoed in my head over and over again. *What if there are more of them out there? And if so, how long until they start attacking ordinary people?*

20

Checking into the hotel was a comedic episode—me standing there in soaking wet clothes, handing over a damp credit card for incidentals, and unable to come up with a story for the curious eyes of the concierge.

Curious judgment smeared across her face, though she didn't venture to ask the question as to why I was soaked and my companion was not.

She finished checking us in to our rooms, then handed me a pair of small envelopes containing our key cards. I passed one of the two to Vero, who glanced at the room number written on the outside, then at mine.

"Separate rooms?" she asked.

I felt my face warm again. "Um, yeah. I... thought... Well, it's just that...."

"Smooth," Xolotl said. "Real smooth."

Shut up.

"No," Vero said. "It's fine. I understand."

The brunette concierge behind the desk watched the interaction with subtle amusement.

"I'm sorry. I thought—"

"No. Really. It's okay. We discussed it before."

I saw the concern in her eyes, and that was enough to kick my insecurities to the curb.

I turned to the concierge and placed my keys on the counter. "I'm sorry. I guess we will only need one room."

The woman appeared both annoyed and pleased, the latter part being the hopeless romantic hiding under the professional exterior.

She invalidated the keys, and explained my refund would show up on the credit card in the next forty-eight hours.

Vero smiled at me, relief spreading across her features. It hadn't been desire that changed my mind, though there may have been a little of that. I'd seen fear in her eyes. I couldn't blame her.

What if another creature appeared, and ventured into the hotel? That seemed unlikely, but anything was on the table now. More likely, agents of evil like I'd encountered before were lurking in the shadows, just out of sight.

I looked around the lobby but found nothing and no one suspicious. "Come on," I said. "If you don't mind, I'd like to take a hot shower before dinner."

She smirked; a wry expression that drove me wild on the inside. "Is that an invitation?"

If my cheeks were pink before, they'd turned beet red now. "Um. I—"

"I'm kidding, Gideon. Relax. Come on. You need to get into some dry clothes."

She reached out and grabbed my right hand, pulling me away from the prying eyes of the concierge, who stood there as if watching a romantic comedy play out live in front of her.

Alone on the elevator, I felt a million emotions racing through my head. "I just didn't want to be inappropriate," I said. "I want to make sure you're comfortable. That's all."

Vero looked over at me. Her eyes brimmed with understanding, but also something else—a look I hadn't seen in a long time, at least not from my wife.

Then, as soon as the ride up had begun, the elevator dinged, signaling that we'd reached our floor.

I cleared my throat awkwardly as the doors opened.

"If you were waiting for the opportune moment to kiss her, big guy, that was it," the voice taunted me.

I rolled my eyes. "This is us, I guess." I extended my hand to allow Vero to exit the lift first.

"For a smart guy, you sure can be an idiot."

Not helping. The more I thought about it, the more I felt like the voice didn't do a whole lot to help.

"That hurts, Gideon. I help when it's needed most. But that's mostly limited to combat. You know this."

I followed Vero out onto the fourth floor and turned into the hallway, where it split in two directions, then went to the right, watching the doors pass by until we found our room number indicated on a black-and-gold placard to the right.

Vero slipped the key out of her envelope and scanned it on the reader. The mechanism beeped then clicked. She pushed down on the handle and shoved the door open. I held it for her once she was across the threshold and then followed her in.

The door closed on its own behind me as I inspected the room. A bathroom to the left with a white barn door featured white counter tops with black cabinetry and a shower with gray tile that looked like faded slate. I admired the rain shower head and the pair of horizontal nozzles.

Farther in the room, two queen-size beds occupied space to the left, separated by a single black nightstand. Silver sconces acting as night-lights hung over the headboards. A flat-screen television hung on the wall to the right over a black desk that extended from a matching closet to the right, over to a gray chair in the corner.

Long curtains from the ceiling to the floor hung bunched at the left side of a sliding door that provided an unimpeded view of the sea. A crescent moon loomed in the clear night sky, its pale reflection rippling and muddled on the choppy water.

"You can take whichever one you want," I offered.

"How chivalrous," Vero said, stopping at the balcony door to look out through the glass. "It doesn't matter to me."

"You really are gun shy, aren't you?" Xolotl noted.

I ignored him.

"I'll take the one by the door," I said, my rationale being if someone broke in, I'd be closest to the trouble.

She accepted my decision by setting her bag down on the gray blanket atop the mattress.

"You mind if I—" I jerked my thumb toward the bathroom.

"No. Please, get warmed up," she insisted with a smile, looking back at me over her shoulder.

"Thanks."

I took my bag into the bathroom and slid the barn door shut, then turned on the shower to let it warm as I undressed.

Thoughts of what happened in the hotel in Guadalajara pummeled my brain.

"They aren't here, Gideon," the voice said.

"You sure?" I whispered.

"I cannot give some of the answers you seek, simply because I do not have them. But when it comes to immediate threats, I will always have your back."

I stepped into the shower and tested the temperature. It always amazed me how quickly hotel showers heated up.

"Look," I breathed, "I appreciate it. I apologize for acting like a baby with all this. It's a lot to take in."

Xolotl chuckled. It was a strange sound, especially coming from that entity. "You should have seen some of your ancestors. One of them thought he was going mad. Took him a few weeks before he came around to the idea."

I leaned my head forward into the shower stream and let the hot, soothing water pour over my head and the rest of my body. It felt so good after being chilly for the last half hour or so, made worse after entering the cool air inside the hotel.

"What were they like?" I wondered as the water dripped off my nose and chin. Steam swirled around me.

"Your ancestors? How much time you got?"

I chuckled at the answer.

"They were all very different, had various interests and goals in life. Some were humble farmers. Others were wealthy merchants. But they all had one thing in common."

"You?"

"No." Another laugh. "Besides me. They were all good people. Each one of them was honorable."

I reached over to the shampoo dispenser hanging on the wall and pumped out some of the goo onto my hand, then rubbed it into my hair, lathering it before sticking my head back under the water to rinse it out. It smelled like rosemary, a popular scent here, and I hoped it'd wash out the stink from the sea—and the sea monster.

"I don't know how honorable I am," I said. "I've done things in my life I'm not proud of."

"All have sinned and fallen short now and then, Gideon. No one is perfect. The fact you can admit the things you've done wrong, and face them, proves you are just as honorable as any who came before. I know your kind dwells on mistakes of the past, as if you will be punished for them in your future. That is in direct conflict with what so many great messengers have taught in the past, that your present moment is all that is real."

I turned and pumped some conditioner into my palm, rubbed it together with both hands, then worked it into my hair, massaging my scalp as I did so. "You sound like a guru or something."

"Search your feelings, Gideon. You know this to be true. The past has nothing to do with the choices you make right now, in this present moment. You can choose to be honorable, or evil. You cannot choose to be that in the past. And you cannot choose it in the future because that moment has yet to come."

Forgiveness, I thought. *Forgiveness transcends time.*

"Yes. It is the great equalizer, and one of the purest forms of love. There is nothing you have done in the past that is not already forgiven, so long as you continue to strive in the present moment to do what is right."

I nodded. "This was an unexpected sermon," I joked, shoving my head back into the stream to rinse out the conditioner.

The voice said nothing else, leaving me to consider the words, and my thoughts.

I finished washing off, thinking of the young woman in the room mere feet away from me. I wondered how she would handle the voice once she attained the Artemis Medallion tomorrow. The thought hit me as surreal.

Tomorrow, her life is going to change forever.

I wondered if I should tell her, but no one told me. Then again, I might have appreciated it if someone had.

I switched off the water and grabbed a white towel hanging on the rack just outside the open shower and dried myself off. Then I slipped into a T-shirt, a pair of sweatpants I'd brought, and brushed my teeth.

When I was done, I took a deep breath, picked up my bag, and stepped out into the room. For a second, I still worried I'd find members of Gladius Dei, or some other agents in the room, but all I found was a beautiful young woman standing outside the open balcony door, leaning over the railing, watching the waves roll into shore in the moonlight.

I smiled and walked over to the corner, set my bag down on the floor next to the chair, and then joined her out on the balcony.

"Beautiful, isn't it?" I asked, feeling like I'd already said that when we first arrived in the room.

Vero whipped her head around, slightly startled. "Yes. It really is. Thank you for bringing me."

I felt the need to tell her the truth about why she was here. It tugged at my throat, but I couldn't get out the words. I guess I felt like she might run, though I wasn't sure where she would go.

"What is it?" she asked, sensing my apprehension.

I shook my head. "Nothing. You can use the shower if you like. I'm done."

She smiled back at me. "Thanks. I need to get cleaned up."

Vero went back into the room, grabbed her things, and disappeared into the bathroom. A minute later, I heard the distant sound of the shower running, leaving me alone with my thoughts once more.

I spent a few more minutes on the balcony, contemplating what Xolotl had said about the past, the present, and the future. They were wise words, and I knew that deep down in my heart I hadn't truly forgiven Amy. I also didn't know if I was ready to do that yet.

The betrayal was still fresh and bleeding inside of me.

I left the balcony and returned to my belongings in the corner. I remembered I'd left my phone in my pants pocket and reached into the bag to get it out. I checked the screen but still hadn't received a message from Lorenzo.

That was odd, but I also realized I had several friends that were less than quick responders to text messages. My friend Jason in Las Vegas was one such type. He actually preferred to communicate with email, which seemed archaic to me, but I didn't judge. Much.

I set my phone down on the desk and plugged it in to let it charge overnight, then took the tablet out of my bag and walked over to the bed. I slumped down heavily onto the mattress and realized just how tired I was.

It had been a long day, and all I wanted to do was read a little then fall asleep. Other thoughts, tempting ones, drifted through my head as I heard the shower running just around the corner. I dispelled them at once and opened the last article I'd been reading about Artemis.

I'd only made it through a few paragraphs when I heard the shower cut off.

I wasn't sure what to expect, but when Vero reappeared holding her bag, wearing a white tank top and a pair of pink athletic shorts, something stirred in me like I was in high school again.

"Thanks for leaving me some hot water," she said as she floated by. She set her bag down next to mine and then padded over to her bed and sat down on the edge. She stared at me expectantly.

"Sorry. I didn't mean to use it all." I thought she was being sarcastic.

"Oh no. You didn't. There was plenty."

I set the tablet down on my lap.

"What are you reading?" she asked.

"Just catching up on my Greek mythology."

"Heard anything out of your friend?"

"No. Not yet. But I will. He's probably just busy with his research."

She nodded her acceptance of the answer, then plugged her phone into the nightstand USB outlet underneath the switches for the reading lights.

I felt myself teetering on a precipice of emotions.

"You know I like you, right? We don't have to sleep in separate beds if you don't want to."

The words sent my heart racing. I panicked, but I couldn't think of the right words to say.

"Unless you do want to," she added quickly.

I choked back fear and doubt, took a deep breath, and sighed. "I just think it's best to take things slow. Okay? I like you. A lot. And I've only known you a short time. I want to make sure I honor you in every way possible."

It sounded like the words coming out of my mouth weren't my own. But I kept going.

"But I would like to hold you," I said. "If that's okay."

She stood up and took a step to my bed, a warm smile on her face as she nodded. "I'd like that. You're not like the other guys out there, Gideon. You know that?"

I shook my head, lowering my gaze to her feet. My heart continued pounding.

"Thank you," she said, lifting my head up with a finger under my chin. I met her eyes and fell into them like two dark vortices pulling me in.

All I could do was smile back.

I scooted over to the other side of the bed, and she climbed in after me, slipping under the covers. I put my arm out across the pillows, and she tucked in close, resting her head on my chest.

"Thank you too," I said.

We were both so tired we forgot to order dinner.

21

I woke abruptly to the sound of my phone vibrating on the desk across the room. The bright light of morning shone through the balcony door and the curtains covering the glass.

For a second, I didn't know what was happening.

Then I realized someone was in the bed next to me. My memory quickly caught up to what happened in a second. I still had my T-shirt and sweatpants on.

I exhaled in relief. I hadn't screwed it up. Or maybe I had. Hard to say. A quick check to my left, and I saw Vero still had her nightwear on as well. She was facing the other way, head on her pillow, still breathing in the steady rhythm of slumber.

I quietly slid out of the bed and tiptoed over to the desk where my phone danced on the desk surface and picked it up.

I hit the green button at the same time I saw Lorenzo's name on the screen and pressed the device to my ear.

Waiting until I was at the balcony door, I pushed it open and stepped outside as my friend said, "Hello? Gideon? You there?"

I closed the door behind me before I answered. "Yeah, Lorenzo. It's me. Sorry."

"Hello, my friend! So wonderful to hear your voice again. Where are you?"

I looked out across the water and down at the beach below with the rows of umbrellas and chairs just as they were the day before.

"I'm on Mykonos right now. Doing some research."

"Mykonos? I am so jealous! I love that island. So much fun there. You had a chance to partake in the party scene?"

I chuckled. Lorenzo had the reputation of someone who enjoyed a good party—particularly if there was wine involved.

"No. We just arrived last night."

"We?"

My cheeks burned as I realized I'd just opened that can. "Yeah. I brought a friend with me."

"Who? Do I know them?"

"No. You don't know her."

"Her?" Lorenzo exclaimed. "Good for you, Gideon. I heard what happened to Amy. But between you and me, I never—"

"Lorenzo, I appreciate your candor, but I'm still trying to process things." There was no way he'd known about my late wife's indiscretion. *Or was there?* Either way, I didn't feel like talking about it, even though my friend was clearly glad to hear or, at least perceive, that I'd already moved on. "It's not like that. She's a friend. That's it."

"Okay. I understand." His Italian accent reminded me of a restaurateur I'd met in Chattanooga on one of my weekend visits there. The owner and head chef hailed from Milano. The times I'd been there, the man seemed genuinely happy to have patrons grace his restaurant, and even happier to cook for them personally.

"I got your message," Lorenzo continued. "I apologize for not responding sooner."

"It's okay. Really. I figured you were busy."

"Indeed I was. We were conducting research on some new tablets that were brought in. Very old. Early Bronze Age."

"That's cool." I meant it. Hearing him talk about something so simple made me miss the old days. And by old days, I was thinking like a couple of months ago. "I look forward to hearing about it."

"Yes, well, there is much to do before we know anything worth relaying, but I will happily keep in touch. Speaking of getting in touch, your text message had a pretty loaded question in it. I have to ask; how did you find out about Gladius Dei?"

Suspicion laced his voice. I drew in a long breath of salty air. It cleansed my nostrils in a single inhale, and I felt the fog of slumber wash away with the tide.

"Before I say anything..." I looked back through the window, but the curtain still blocked my view inside. For a second, I wondered if I should open it just in case. But Xolotl had said he would let me know if trouble was nearby. And so far, he'd said nothing.

"Correct," the voice said.

I wanted to tell him how unnerving it was that he could read my thoughts and just interject whenever he wanted, but I didn't want to keep my friend on the phone waiting. Or have him thinking I was crazy.

I'd nearly forgotten what I was saying. "You're alone, right?" I asked.

"Yes. I am in my office right now. Why?"

"I am being followed, Lorenzo. By men from this Gladius Dei group. I don't know anything about them, so I was hoping you could fill me in since you know so much about that stuff."

"Following you?" Concern tainted the Italian's voice.

"I can't give you all the details, but one of them tried to kill me. I think they're after an artifact I found. And they will do anything to get it."

"Artifact? Gideon, are you all right?"

"I'm fine. But I need to know everything you can tell me about Gladius Dei."

For a dozen seconds, my friend remained silent. I wasn't sure if he was trying to think of what to say next or if something had happened to him.

"You there?" I pressed.

"Yes. Sorry. It's just an odd topic." He cleared his throat as if about to begin a lecture. "Gladius Dei is an old sect of zealots that branched off from the Catholic Church long ago."

"How long?"

"No one is certain, but more than four centuries. There's some speculation that they go back to around the fifth century."

Wow. That is old.

"There isn't much information available out there, and for good reason. There is a strange relationship between Gladius Dei and the church. On the one hand, the zealots believe in all the doctrines and the position of the church in the world. They diverge in their beliefs on how things should be carried out. I've stumbled upon a few pieces of documentation referring to them, but I'd largely discounted them as myth, or at the very least a benign, silent wing of the church that never bothered anyone."

"That doesn't sound like zealots."

"No. From what I gathered, and according to much speculation from others, they believe they are protectors of the church, and will only rise when called upon, when great evil threatens the world."

There's a dose of irony.

"It sounds like the church doesn't condone this group."

"Indeed. Rumor has it that Gladius Dei was responsible for a number of atrocities around the time of the Renaissance, though no one has been able to prove that. As far as I know, there is no documentation for such a claim." He paused in the middle of his thought for a breath before continuing. "You say you believe they attacked you in an attempt to steal an artifact?"

"Yes."

He hummed a short, contemplative sound. "How can you be certain it was Gladius Dei and not some other black-market organization?"

A breeze rustled through my hair. I rubbed the back of my neck as I recalled everything that had happened.

"One of the men had a tattoo. I connected the tattoo to Gladius Dei. I didn't know what it was at first, but I thought maybe you might. It seems that hunch has proved correct."

"But why would a religious organization such as this target someone like you? What artifact could they possibly want unless..."

"Unless what?" I wondered where my friend was going with this. No way he knew about the medallion, or any of the ancient guardian amulets. *Was there?* I blew off the notion. I'd never heard of them until that fateful night Vicente Carrillo approached me. I wasn't so full of myself that I thought I'd heard of every little thing in the world of archaeology, but something such as this would have certainly crossed through my feed at some point online, or even in some of my professional circles.

"The artifact, what is it? Is it something of religious significance?"

I trusted my friend, but I didn't trust cell phones at this point. "It could be," I hedged. "But I don't think so. It's not related to anything in Christianity, which makes their actions seem even more out of character."

"Hmm. Yes, it certainly does. Well, if it isn't a religious relic of some kind, I'm afraid I don't have a theory as to why they would want it, unless they are so ostracized by the church that they need funding to carry on. It's possible that they've taken to the black market to bring in money. Still, very odd that a group of religious zealots would attack an ordinary civilian in such a way. Where did this happen?"

"Multiple places," I blurted. "Mexico. Then yesterday in Athens."

Silence took over for ten seconds. "Mexico," Lorenzo breathed. "And now in Greece? What were you doing back in Mexico? I would have thought you wouldn't go back there for a long time after what happened."

"It's complicated," I offered and left it at that. "But if these guys have that kind of global reach, they must be everywhere."

"Yes. So it would seem." Another thoughtful hum. "Well, I'm afraid I don't have any more information on this subject at the moment. But I will snoop around and see if I can find anything, though I suspect I've reached the end of the road as you Americans say. There simply isn't much out there about this organization."

"I understand. And you've actually been very helpful, Lorenzo. I really appreciate it. Given me a lot to think about."

"I don't know how helpful I've been, but thank you. When will you be coming to Rome? It's been too long, my friend."

I smiled at the question. "You never know. I'm definitely due for a trip to Italy soon."

"It seems you've been traveling everywhere else. Might do you some good to come see an old friend, have some proper food and wine, enjoy the sites, the history."

He knew how to speak my language.

"All that sounds amazing. And when I can, I'll take you up on it. Promise."

"Well, don't wait too long. Life is best lived in the present."

I liked that, and found myself repeating it in my head. I looked down at my watch and realized what time it was. "Thanks again, my friend. I need to get going. I have a ferry to catch. Speak to you again soon."

"Sounds good, Gideon. Ciao."

The balcony door slid open behind me, and I spun around to find Vero standing there, hair tousled and looking as beautiful as ever, even with the fog of waking in her narrowed eyes.

"Good morning, sleepyhead," I said, trying to sound cute despite using the cliché.

She grinned at me and took a step out onto the balcony, squinting against the bright morning sunlight.

"Were you talking to your Italian friend?" she asked as she drew close. She stopped next to me and rested her arms on the railing, leaning forward.

"Yeah. That was Lorenzo. He'd heard of Gladius Dei."

I filled her in on the few details I'd been able to glean during the conversation but went over it quickly since we needed to get going to catch the ferry to Delos.

"That's very interesting," she said when I was finished. "And kind of scary. It sounds like the Vatican doesn't know anything about this."

"Yes," I agreed. "That's what I think."

Neither of us said a word for a minute. I leaned against the railing, staring at the glass door, then realized I was missing precious minutes of this incredible view. I turned around and joined her in gazing out at the water, the people walking lazily along the sand.

"I could get used to a view like this," I said. "Sure is pretty here. And relaxing."

"You'd get bored of it," Vero countered.

I was surprised at the statement.

"I would too," she added.

"I'd like to try."

She looked over at me and grinned. "I would too."

We shared a laugh, then went back to the sounds of waves crashing and a sea breeze blowing through our ears.

The moment lasted a few minutes, but it had to end eventually. The calm always preceded the storm. And I had a bad feeling a big one was lurking just beyond the horizon.

22

The ferry to Delos took a little under forty minutes. It had proved uneventful, though I'd been unable to relax for a second during the voyage. Fortunately, I slept pretty well the night before, probably due to sheer exhaustion.

We stepped off the boat onto shore and then onto the walking street that led toward the village. White buildings with blue windows and doors lined the street and crowded the slope up a hillside. Several of the iconic white windmills I'd seen in pictures dotted the top of the hillside nearby.

To the right, tourists ambled along the ancient thoroughfare toward terraced ruins on another hillside across the bay.

"I guess that's where we need to go," I realized, pointing to the ancient village.

It struck me as strange that the people of this island built a town over there so long ago, and a new one just across the water. I was glad the modern Greeks had done it that way, but so many humans throughout history simply destroyed the old to replace it with the new.

It happened all over the world, and frequently in the United States.

Sailboats sat anchored out in the water not far from the shore, some with people milling about on them, others appearing to be empty at the moment.

I wondered what that life would be like, to sail around the world, or even just the Mediterranean on a vessel like that, anchoring in ports on various islands, sampling the food, the nightlife, the culture, the history.

I found myself wanting that more than I'd ever considered before, and wondered if a life like that could ever really be mine.

It felt doubtful. Maybe before all this had happened, that may have been possible, but now the weight of enormous responsibility drowned out any chance at having a relaxing life full of casual travel.

My once-simple life I led as an archaeologist had been replaced by something otherworldly, in some senses, literally. I looked back over my shoulder just in case one of the Sector agents was behind me.

"They are," Xolotl said.

I shuddered at the statement and searched more frantically for the men in suits.

"So are the other ones," he added. "You sure are jumpy."

"Maybe lead with the good guys first," I muttered under my breath.

"What's that?" Vero asked.

I shook my head. "I said maybe we should head over there first," I said, quickly pointing toward the ruins on the hill. "I believe that's where we'll find the temple. Or what's left of it."

"Nice recovery," the voice said.

I rolled my eyes at him and led the way around a rope on the edge of the pier.

"This place really doesn't have much to offer in the way of accommodations," Vero noticed as we strolled along the wide pedestrian road. "I can see why we stayed on Mykonos."

"Yes. Pretty isolated place, Delos." I tried to be subtle as I looked around, scanning the area for trouble.

Some tourists took pictures of the ruins from a distance. Others talked as they moved slowly, unhurried, to and from the ancient site.

A sixty-foot white yacht drifted into the bay away from the other vessels. I didn't know much about boats, but I felt certain this one must have cost seven or eight figures.

"Something wicked this way comes," Xolotl warned.

Frowning, I narrowed my eyelids and peered out at the boat as it slowed to a stop. I saw traces of swirling red mist within, but I'd seen that everywhere. Not with every person, but enough to be disconcerting for the fate of humanity.

Who are they?

The voice didn't say. But I got the feeling I already knew.

Gladius Dei.

I found myself picking up the pace as we neared the ruins at the base of the hill. The stacked stone walls lined a pathway around a bend that had to be more than four to five thousand years old. Perhaps older.

A few white clouds drifted through the sky overhead. A strong breeze blew across the island, seeming to carry them away.

"I bet this place is pretty crowded during peak season," Vero theorized.

"Yes. Good thing we're here now. Hopefully, we can conduct our search without being bothered."

We reached the base of the first ruins and found a path that wound its way up the hillside toward columns that marked the scattered remains of the temple to Artemis.

"It should be up there," I said, indicating the spot with a wave of my right hand.

I let Vero take the lead, primarily so I could keep an eye out behind us. I glanced back over my shoulder at the yacht in the harbor, but it seemed no one was stirring on the boat. If they were here for me, parking in that spot didn't make any sense. There was no good place to come ashore, so they'd have to jump into the water and swim over. Unless there was a small lifeboat on the back, which I didn't see from this angle.

"You coming?" Vero asked, looking back at me from twenty feet up a set of old stone steps.

"Yeah. Sorry." I hurried and caught up, following her through what must have at one time, so long ago, been a bustling little island village.

Delos had been attacked and ravaged by Mithridates in the year 88 BC. He looted and pillaged the place, leaving it a wreck. Then nearly two decades later, in the year 69 BC, one of his pirate allies returned and finished the job. After that, the island's population deteriorated, and the town was abandoned until much later, when resettlement began across the harbor.

Even with the destruction of the original village, it was remarkable to bear witness to the remnants of buildings and statues that remained intact. To think that human hands laid these stones many thousands of years ago was a haunting thing to consider. I could almost feel those people still here, going about their day, toiling at their jobs, laughing, drinking and eating, watching the sunset to the west.

I wondered what their lives must have been like. Their daily reality was likely beyond my imaginings, and I knew that no history book could ever truly relay that sentiment, that emotion, that real-world experience—the smells, sights, and sounds—of what it felt like to live in this place, in that time.

Standing in places like this, as I felt so often when in historical locations, was like being on holy ground for a historian—if there were such a thing.

Vero and I reached the top of the hill and paused to catch our breath. We turned around and looked out over the harbor and the sweeping vistas of the island and sea beyond.

"You know," she said between breaths, "I didn't think this hill was that high, but it offers quite the view."

"It does indeed," I said with a nod.

Behind us, several stone columns stood erect, surrounded by low walls—broken in some places.

"This is the temple," I said, jerking my thumb in that direction.

"Now you going to tell her?" Xolotl asked.

For a few minutes, I'd almost forgotten he was there. Almost.

I didn't answer, and surprisingly, he didn't press me further.

Courage bubbled up somewhere deep inside me, and I felt like this was as good a time as any to tell her the truth, to let her know who she really was.

But just as the words reached the tip of my tongue, she interrupted them.

"So, what are we supposed to do here? Say some kind of incantation or something?"

I smiled at the suggestion. "No. Nothing like that." Then the realization hit me. "Crap."

"What?" The breeze coming off the sea whipped her hair around, and she tried to fight it by pulling strands back behind her ears.

For a second, I couldn't think of anything else but how beautiful she was.

"Um... so, we have a slight problem."

She took a step closer, and once more her perfume weaved its way into my nostrils, sending my brain to another reality, one where none of this stuff was happening except she and I standing there, looking into each other's eyes just before I pulled her close and kissed her.

"What's the problem?" she asked, planting her hands on her hips and tilting her head to the side.

Just when I thought she couldn't get any cuter.

"Well, see, I might have forgotten that the hidden temple only appears at sunrise. At least, that's the way the last one was. I assume that's how this one works."

"You assume?" Vero teased me playfully. "You know what happens when you assume, right?"

"I thought that was an American expression."

She shook her head, and her hair danced around her shoulders with the motion. "Nope. It's international. In English anyway. Doesn't really work in Spanish or other languages."

My grin stretched to both corners of my jaw as I looked around the site.

"That's not how this one works," Xolotl whispered.

The voice sounded like the entity was standing right next to me, and for a second I almost thought I felt breath from it on my left ear. I quickly dispelled that notion as merely the product of the wind. But I snapped my head around anyway out of pure instinct.

"What?" she asked.

"Nothing," I answered, shaking off the paranoia. "I just wonder if this temple is different. It would suck to have to stay here overnight."

Vero made a show of looking around the island, taking in the view of the sea and the rocky, rolling hills, the town down near the port. "Sorry, what would suck about this? It's amazing. And quiet. Not too many tourists here. I wouldn't mind staying the night if we could find a place."

"Yeah. I mean, that part wouldn't suck. Just slows things down."

She took a step closer to me, and I felt a magnetic force drawing me toward her. The energy was real, tangible, undeniable.

To distract myself, I slipped my backpack off my shoulders and set it on the ground, determined to figure out exactly what the voice in my head meant when he said this temple site doesn't work the same way as the other.

"I'm just going to see if there's something maybe I missed in Wells' diary," I said. Her feet stopped inches away from my bag, and she hovered over me like a hawk circling its prey.

As I rifled through the pack, she set hers down next to mine, and unzipped the top. I felt the magnetic energy dissipate, and sensed disappointment radiating from her. I was disappointed in myself. What was I doing?

The voice in my head remained silent on the matter. I figured he'd said his piece and wasn't going to keep at it.

No. I wasn't going to blow this. Vero was into me. Nothing could make me doubt that. She'd come halfway around the world with me to find a mystical artifact that may or may not exist, or be here. And her reason for coming along wasn't purely due to the search.

My fingers touched the leather journal stuffed down into the side of my backpack. I hesitated as she rummaged through her own bag, I guessed to find a bottle of water or something.

Right then, I made up my mind. I wasn't going to miss an opportunity like this. I wanted her, and she felt the same. Maybe it was a rebound thing. Maybe not. But I wouldn't know unless I tried.

I summoned the courage to move closer to her, even as we both squatted there next to our backpacks.

The angle was less than ideal, but I'd manage.

What better place than this—an island in the middle of the Mediterranean with the sounds of the sea rolling into shore, the breeze blowing through our hair, and even the ancient ruins made the scene better.

I looked over at her, with her hair hanging around her face like dark brown drapes. My heart raced, and my breathing quickened. It had been so long since I'd had a first kiss, and there hadn't been many in my life. But each one had sent raging butterflies through my gut.

I'd always thought it was a weird description of anxiety to call it butterflies in the stomach. Butterflies were beautiful, majestic creatures—delicate and gentle.

To me it felt like someone had dumped a bucket of acid into my belly.

I choked down the nerves and moved a little closer, leaning toward her.

She didn't seem to notice, focused solely on the contents of her bag.

"What the—"

Her unfinished question doused the burning in my stomach, and curiosity instantly overwhelmed my anxiety.

She pulled a small, golden cylinder out of her bag and held it up to inspect it. The shiny yellow metal gleamed brightly in the unimpeded rays of the sun.

"What is that?" I asked, shuffling closer.

Vero stood upright and turned the solid tube over in her hand. I took a step closer and stopped when our shoulders touched. The incidental contact sent a spark through me, but I pushed it down for the moment.

"I have no idea," she confessed. "It's not mine."

"What do you mean it's not yours? How did it get in there?" The notion this thing was in her bag without her knowing seemed irrational. Then again, most of my life now defied logic and reason.

"I mean it isn't mine. I don't know what this is?"

"May I?"

"Sure."

She passed me the cylinder. The object looked like it was made of solid gold, which should have been heavy in my hand, but as I held it, I realized the thing was only about the weight of a baseball. Maybe a little less.

"If this is gold," I said, "it should be two or three times this heavy. At least."

I held up the tube and looked at the top, then flipped it over and checked the bottom. Both were solid, with no openings.

"You don't know how it got in your bag?" I pressed, trying not to sound accusatory.

"I swear. I don't even know what it is."

I shrugged. "Well, maybe someone put it in your bag by mistake. You didn't notice anyone strange at the airport getting close to it, did you?"

"No. And besides, I would have seen this last night or this morning as I went through my stuff. I emptied the entire bag last night."

"Hmm." I thumbed my chin and surveyed the area. Surprisingly, no tourists were up here at this spot. The ferry horn blew down at the port, and within a few seconds the boat churned the water behind it into a white foam as it departed.

"You think someone on the ferry might have put it in here?" she asked, following my gaze to the vessel.

"That's the only explanation that makes sense. But why? Seems strange. It doesn't appear to be dangerous. Even though it looks like pure gold, it can't be, unless it's hollow on the inside."

I handed the cylinder back to her. "It's yours now, I guess. Whatever it is."

As the metal touched her palm, a bright flash of light blinked from the center of the tube.

"What the—" I blurted, echoing her sentiment from before.

Greek letters started appearing on the shaft, as if being written out by an unseen hand in glowing, white ink. As each letter completed itself, they darkened and appeared as if they'd been carved into the metal.

"Gideon? What's happening?" Her voice trembled with a touch of fear.

I shook my head. "I have no idea."

"What does it say?"

I tilted my head to get a better angle, and translated the Greek letters. "Artemis, guardian of Greece."

The second I finished reading the words, a loud ringing filled our ears. It wasn't piercing, or painful, but it wasn't pleasant either. It sounded like a constant tone in alpha waves, similar to some I'd listened to while meditating. Except much louder.

"What's happening?" Vero asked, a sliver of worry tainting her voice.

I didn't have an answer, and even if I did, it would have been interrupted by what happened next.

23

"**G**ideon," she said, panic taking over. "This thing is vibrating."

I reached my hand out to touch it, but before I could, something clicked from inside the cylinder.

I froze. Then I watched in rapt astonishment as the ends of the tube expanded, lengthening itself like some kind of liquid metal, stretching out from both ends until it was roughly six feet long.

The bottom of the shaft rounded itself out to the shape of a half sphere, while the other end sharpened to a fine point. Where Vero held it, the cylinder shaped itself into a sort of handle.

"It's... a spear," I realized, barely able to speak over my disbelief.

"Yeah. What am I doing with a magical spear?"

"If you were thinking about telling her the truth, big guy," Xolotl said, "you aren't going to get a better time than now."

Thanks, Captain Obvious.

Vero looked over the strange weapon, inspecting it from tip to base.

"Vero," I began. "There's something I need to tell you. And now that I've seen this, and the inscription on the spear, it confirms my suspicions."

"Suspicions?"

I nodded, and ran my fingers through my dark hair. "Yeah. You're much more than you realize. You're—"

"Over there!" A man's voice interrupted.

I whipped my head around and looked down the staircase we'd ascended a few minutes before.

Three men in black tactical gear rushed up the last few steps and spilled out onto the plateau, each extending pistols toward us.

I put out my arms and placed myself in the line of fire, stepping in front of Vero so they couldn't hit her.

One of the men stayed near the top of the stairs, while the other two fanned out, effectively rendering my plan of being a human shield as useless. I tried to back up a step, but felt Vero's hand bump into my lower back.

I had to think fast.

"Put it down," the gunman directly in front of me ordered. "Now."

Red mist swirled around him and the other two. I also noticed the ink on his inner wrist—the mark of Gladius Dei.

"You guys are everywhere," I said casually.

Right on cue, two more emerged on the plateau behind us.

Not good.

"You think?" Xolotl taunted.

I thought you were supposed to warn me about this kind of thing.

"We are on a sacred site. There's an energy here that is messing with my ability to detect trouble."

Well, it's here now.

"Put it down or she dies now," the leader barked. His accent sounded Italian, Florence if I wasn't mistaken. *How did I know that?*

I turned my head back and forth, watching the men as they tightened the perimeter around us. There was nowhere to run. And unfortunately, if I shifted into the beast, within the second or two that transformation took, they could gun Vero down.

I swallowed hard and thought. *How do we get out of this?*

My mind raced. But one thought broke ahead of all the rest. I remembered how I got away from Carrillo's men down in

Mexico. I'd escaped the tent and run when a jaguar attacked their camp. I doubted we'd find any such wildlife here. But after that, some of the cartel goons had chased me through the jungle. And that's when I stumbled, quite literally, into the hidden temple.

"The temple," I whispered.

"What?" Vero asked, fear evident in her voice.

"Okay," I said to the leader. "We're unarmed. Just... lower your weapons."

"That isn't going to happen. Drop the spear. You have three seconds to comply."

The guy sounded like an Italian robot.

"Gideon? What should I do?" Vero asked.

Then it hit me.

I remembered studying Artemis, both early on in my career and, more poignantly, in the last few days. I'd read about the Greek goddess, trying to learn as much as I could before we arrived here. I figured it was just a prudent thing to do. But now, the answer screamed at me from my memory.

"All right!" I shouted. "She's going to drop the spear. Just, don't shoot."

"One," the leader answered, beginning his count.

"Relax. She's going to drop it."

"Prepare to fire," he said to the other men.

"Vero," I said, looking over my shoulder at her standing behind me. "Trust me. Flick the spear. Do it like you're throwing it, but subtle."

"What?"

"Two," the leader announced.

"Just trust me. Flick it away from you."

She met my intense gaze with hers full of fear. Then she nodded. "Okay, Gideon. I trust you."

Before the leader said three, Vero twitched the hand holding the spear and released it. To her surprise, the weapon zipped away from her as if guiding itself.

The gunmen followed the shimmering golden spear as it flew, skirting the circle they'd formed around us.

I feared one may open fire, which would cause the others to do the same, but instead they merely stared in fascination at the bizarre flying shaft.

Then, abruptly, after making three passes around the perimeter, the spear shot up into the air, soaring a hundred feet over our heads. The gunmen stared at it, and for a brief second I thought that was my chance to transform and go berserk on the enemies.

But I too found myself oddly mesmerized by the flying spear.

Just as suddenly as the gilded weapon took flight, it dove down from the sky toward me and Vero. I reached out to push her clear, but the sharp point of the spear struck the rocky earth and plunged the tip deep between us.

The ground shook as though a meteor had smashed into it. The tremor rippled across the plateau. A shock wave blew out from the spear's shaft. The blast of energy didn't touch me or Vero, but the surrounding men fell back like they'd been hit by a hurricane-force wind.

A bright light pulsed from the spear, like a star shining from its center. Then the light grew and encompassed the entire plateau, wrapping around us in pure radiance.

And then, as abruptly as it all happened, the light blinked out, and we were in utter darkness.

I spun around in a circle, peering into the black.

"Gideon?" Vero's voice cut through the eerie space, and I immediately felt relieved that she was here with me.

I didn't see any sign of the gunmen, or the red mist that surrounded them.

"They cannot be here in this place," Xolotl said.

That's good to know.

"I'm here," I answered her.

As soon as the words spilled from my lips, a torch burst to life, hanging in a sconce on a stone wall.

The light from the flames illuminated Vero's terrified face, and the moment she saw me she quickly stepped over and wrapped her arms around me.

"What's happening, Gideon? Where are we?"

"It's okay," I answered.

More torches bloomed to life along the walls surrounding us.

"This is the temple."

"The temple?"

I retreated back to arm's length, still holding her, and looked her in the eyes. "Yes. They can't come in here. We're safe for now."

She shook her head, confused. "I thought you said we could only find the temple at sunrise."

"I thought so too." I looked around, assessing the surroundings. The chamber was similar to the one in Mexico only in that there were torches hanging from the walls that seemed to ignite themselves. I didn't know what kind of magic that was, or if it was magic at all.

It could have simply been an optical illusion, a ripple in the reality around us. The torches had been a secondary thought to me after all the wild events in Mexico and thereafter. But now, my natural curiosity begged the question I'd never really thought could be pertinent.

Is magic real?

"What's going on? How did those guys find us?"

"They must have followed us." I wondered if they'd been on the yacht that pulled into the bay, but it would have taken them too long to get to shore that way unless they had, as I'd considered, a lifeboat. Or jet skis were a possibility. I'd seen those on the back of boats before. For the time being, it was enough to know they'd found us and leave it at that.

"Now what do we do?" she asked, her voice calming despite her head twisting around in every direction the way people do when they're certain something frightening is lurking in the shadows.

I indicated a path leading away from the circular room where we stood. The corridor narrowed to around six feet wide and eight feet tall, rectangular in shape.

On the floor at our feet, Greek blessings were carved into the stone in a spiral that swirled into the center where the spear stuck up from the ground.

I reached out and took the weapon, inspecting it as I held it up in the torchlight.

"Did you know it would do that up there?" Vero asked, running her fingers along the shaft as if somehow familiar with the ancient spear.

"Actually, I thought it would do something else."

"Something else?"

I nodded. "I remembered reading about the spear of Artemis. She carried a few weapons. The more famous of her arms were the bow and arrow, but the legends about the spear stuck out in my memory. As the lore has it, when she threw the spear, it never missed its target. When I realized this was that same spear, I figured if you threw it—"

"It might take out all those gunmen?"

Just then, the spear melted back into its original form, retracting down to nothing more than a cylinder the size of my hand.

"That's wild," Vero gasped.

More torches ignited in the passage leading away from the chamber.

"It gets wilder," I said.

"What's that supposed to mean?"

I reached out my hand to hers and gripped it gently. "Follow me. I'll show you."

She squeezed my fingers. "Okay. I trust you."

A pulse of energy shot through me. It was exciting and nerve-racking at the same time.

Together, we walked ahead into the corridor. It reminded me of that fateful night in Mexico when I'd made this journey alone, finding my way through that tunnel to the altar, and the medallion that changed my entire existence.

I felt glad to be here with her. I didn't want her to have to do this alone. As the first guardian to return, maybe it was my job to walk her through it.

She kept squeezing my fingers as we passed pairs of torches on both sides of the corridor. I knew there had to be a million questions in her head, wondering how far this thing went, what we would find at the end of it, and if there was a way out.

It was a lot to take in.

After walking fifty yards, the flickering light of the torches cast their orange yellow glow on a wall straight ahead. I watched the floor, ceiling, and walls on either side as we approached the end of the passage just in case there might be some kind of ancient booby trap we could trigger.

That's ridiculous, I thought. The last place didn't have any such mechanisms. The secret nature of the temple and how it was discovered seemed to be all that was needed for its protection.

"What is that?" Vero asked as we approached the end of the tunnel. She looked over at me, concern filling her eyes. "Is there no way out of here?"

We stopped where the passage ended abruptly with a huge stone slab blocking the path. It had been fit into place so perfectly; there were no visible seams, making it appear as though whoever had carved this corridor simply stopped right there.

I inspected the slab from top to bottom. "Strange," I said. "There wasn't anything like this in the temple in Mexico."

"Gideon? Please tell me we're not stuck in some ancient mystical cave."

The worry in her voice swelled.

"It's going to be fine," I said, though I wasn't sure what was going on. And the voice in my head apparently didn't feel like helping with this one.

I reached out my right hand and pressed my fingers against the smooth stone, brushing them across the surface. The moment I touched the slab, something black, like ink, appeared on it, as if being drawn by an invisible hand.

I stepped back and watched with Vero as the image of Artemis drew itself on the wall before us. Her likeness was split, one half showing the goddess in all her radiant splendor—the other the shape of a raging bear. As the image completed itself, a hole opened in the center of the slab, right at the midpoint of the strange drawing.

"What is this?" Vero asked.

"It's the door into the chamber of the Artemis Medallion," I answered, a little hopeful.

"A door? How does it open? Doesn't look like a door to me."

I wasn't sure, but my eyes kept looking back to the hole in the center. "I have an idea."

The gold cylinder felt warm in my hand. Odd for a hunk of metal. I lifted it up toward the door, paused for a second, and then touched it to the opening.

I expected it to fit in easily. To my surprise, the hole closed as if it were some malleable, semi-fluid substance. I pulled back the cylinder, fearful the magical slab might swallow up the golden relic and it reopened.

"What was that?" Vero asked.

"I don't know." I shook my head. Then I had another idea. "Here," I said, holding out the collapsed spear to her. "You try."

Vero frowned, giving me a doubtful look. "Me? Why would it be different for me?"

"Just... try it." I took her hand, opened her fingers, and placed the cylinder in her palm.

Instantly, the spear extended out again into its full form. Vero took a step back and held her hand out, fearful the thing might accidentally stab her.

"Try inserting it into the slab," I suggested.

Vero breathed, still staring at the ancient weapon with intense uncertainty.

"Are you sure?" she pressed.

"Not really," I admitted. "But it's this, or we're stuck in here for who knows how long."

She sucked in a long breath through her nose, then turned toward what I hoped really was a door.

Turning the spear, Vero leveled it horizontally. To both of our surprise, the long shaft shortened, as if accommodating the length for her to make inserting it into the opening easier.

She froze for a second, unsettled by the transformation.

"It's okay," I said. "You can do this."

"I hope you're right. I don't feel like starving to death in a mystical cave."

"That makes two of us."

She held the point near the hole, hesitated for a second, and then slipped it through.

The ground rumbled under our feet, and the walls shook.

"Gideon? What did I do?"

I touched her shoulder, doing what little I could to comfort her.

"It's okay," I said.

"Are you sure?"

The earth itself seemed to tremble, filling the corridor with a deep groan.

Then, the slab began to swirl slowly around the spear. Vero briefly let go of the shaft.

"Don't let it go," I said.

She looked up at me, her face an ocean of mixed expressions.

The stone appeared as though it had turned to a thick liquid, gradually twisting in a slow vortex around the spear, folding into the golden weapon.

Gaps opened around the edges, growing wider and wider as the ethereal matter disappeared into the vortex.

A white light pulsed, dimly at first, and then stronger until the entire door was engulfed by it. Then, as quickly as it had appeared, the light blinked out, revealing an opening where the stone door had been only moments before.

Vero and I looked beyond the threshold into another chamber, where torches hung from the walls, all seeming to cast their dancing glow on a stone altar in the center.

She glanced back at me again, as if asking if we should enter. I answered with a single nod and, holding her hand, stepped through into the new room.

A gust of wind washed over us, and I looked back to see the door close behind us, the liquid stone material reforming out of the center. Vero saw it too, and checked with me again with a quick look.

"Let's just keep going," I said.

I allowed my eyes to sweep the vast room. Its rectangular shape, with high walls, cedar ceiling, and Greek columns lining the interior gave a glimpse into what the temple of Artemis had looked like so long ago.

Four deer made of pure gold—two bucks and two does—stood at each of the four corners of the altar. The metallic animals bowed to the altar with their foreheads only an inch away from the stone.

A wooden chest with a golden clasp rested atop the plinth.

Now was the moment I would finally tell Vero who she really was, that she was meant to be a guardian.

We approached the altar cautiously, more for her sake than mine, and stopped next to it.

"What's inside this chest?" Vero asked, not taking her eyes off it.

"The Medallion of Artemis," I answered. "Open it."

She looked over at me. "You sure that's a good idea? You're the one with"—she waved her hands around in a swirling motion—"the superpowers and all that. You've done this before. What if some ancient magical power devours me for doing something I'm not supposed—"

"Vero," I said in a soothing tone, smiling confidently at her, "you are meant to open it."

"What?" The question mirrored in her eyes, and across the lines in her brow. "What do you mean?"

I tilted my head toward the box. "Just open it. And you'll see."

"You're sure?"

"I'm sure."

Semi-convinced, she returned her gaze to the chest and warily reached out her right hand to the golden clasp as if afraid to even touch it. She paused, then unhinged the metal. With one last look for approval from me, she put both hands on either side of the lid and lifted it up.

A swirling blue mist drifted out of the interior and evaporated into the air.

For what was probably a minute, we both stared silently into the ancient, mystical container.

Finally, Vero cut the silence without taking her eyes off the chest. I couldn't look away either. "It's empty."

24

"Why is it empty?" Vero asked. "Does that mean someone else has the medallion?"

I blinked rapidly, looking around the room in a near panic. The torches continued to flicker on the walls, the steady roll and crackle of the flames filling the chamber.

"I don't know," I admitted. My eyes drew back to the chest, then the pillar, the gilded sculptures, the floor around it—all in hopes of finding a clue as to what could have happened to the medallion.

Vero spun around, searching the room. She inclined her head and checked the ceiling. I knew what was coming next, and I'd be lying if I said I wasn't thinking it too.

"Gideon? Are we going to be able to get out of this place?"

The split second of hesitation before I answered probably told her the truth of what I feared, but I forged ahead with an uncertain, hopeful answer anyway. "Yes. We just have to figure it out."

"Figure what out?" she asked. "There's nothing here." She put her hands out by her sides, a gesture that sent more guilt rippling through my body than I'd ever felt in my life.

If there wasn't a way out of here, I'd just sentenced Vero to an unimaginable fate. We'd be stuck here forever, or at least until we starved to death.

I didn't even know how that was possible. Walking between the veils of reality, in my mind, should have some kind of a limitation, a time boundary that kicked us back out to where we belonged.

Just thinking about that stuff felt insane.

"There must be something we missed," I said. "Before we panic, let's take a closer look around and see what we can find. Search every corner. The floor. The walls. All of it. I'm sure there's a clue."

The despondence on her face told me she didn't believe a word of it, or have the slightest glimmer of hope. But she nodded anyway. "Okay."

"I shouldn't have brought you here," I said. "I should have known better. It's just that..." I stopped midsentence.

"Just that what?" she pressed, taking a step closer.

"There's something I haven't told you."

Pain streaked through her eyes. "What?"

"I... you..." I faltered, and she reached out and took my hand, which only made the guilt in my chest that much worse.

"You can tell me anything, Gideon. It's okay."

I took a deep breath, teetering on the cliff's edge. I didn't know how she would take it—if she'd be furious at me. The last thing I wanted was her angry at me over all this. Well, maybe that was a close second to not wanting to be stuck here until we died.

I swallowed, then just blurted it out. "You are a guardian, Vero. You are the one who is supposed to wear the Artemis Medallion. That's why I brought you here, so that you could get it from this place."

She puzzled over my statement, still holding my right hand in hers. "That's it?" she asked.

I felt my brow furrow almost on its own. "What do you mean, that's it?"

She inched closer to me. "The only reason you brought me here was so I could retrieve the medallion?"

I still didn't catch her drift, or why she was taking this so well.

"Um... yeah? I mean... I—"

"Oh," she said, dejected. Her eyes dropped and I felt her grip loosen. In that instant, I knew what she was getting at.

I tightened my fingers against her palm, and pulled her close. "And this," I said, feeling the magnetic pull to her I felt before.

I looped my free hand around the back of her head, threading my fingers through her hair, and pulled her close.

Our lips pressed together, and for an instant, she stiffened, then relaxed and kissed me back.

I felt an exhilaration pulse through me unlike anything I'd felt in as long as I could remember. My senses tingled, and my heart pounded like a racehorse in the final furlong. I tasted the lip gloss on lips that felt like soft, plump fruit against mine. For a few seconds, I stood there kissing her with my eyes closed.

Then, I retreated to catch my breath and look her in the eyes.

She stared up at me, her face beaming with a pleased smile. "I was hoping that was the other reason you invited me on this trip."

"Yeah, well, I was trying to be a gentleman."

She wrapped her right hand around my head and pulled me in for another, this time more vigorous than before.

A minute later, she let go, licking her bottom lip with satisfied desire.

I looked around the room, desperately trying not to feel awkward. "I would have preferred a better place than this to do that."

She shook her head. "It was perfect." Then she glanced around too. "That said, I would like to find a way out of here."

I nodded. "Yes. That would be good." I stared into her eyes, pleading for forgiveness before I even apologized. "I'm sorry I didn't tell you. I should have."

"Oh yeah, well, it's okay." She angled her head bashfully. "I already knew."

"Wait. What?" I wasn't sure I'd heard right. "What do you mean you knew?"

She beamed at me. "Well, Myra told me. She *is* an oracle, after all."

Then it hit me. "Of course. I guess I didn't consider she would do that. Well, now I feel like an idiot."

Vero tugged me close again and kissed me. "It's okay. I think it's cute you were trying to surprise me."

That wasn't entirely it, but I let the notion slide. Pulling my gaze away from her, I searched the dark temple chamber for any sign of an exit.

"There has to be a way out," I said. "Come on. Let's have a look around."

I pulled her with me and walked over to the wall. "This is as good a place as any to start," I suggested. "Check the floor, the wall, the torches, anything for a sign or a clue."

"You want to split up?"

It would have been faster, but I didn't care about that at this point. I just wanted to keep her close to me.

"No," I said. "Two pairs of eyes are better than one."

The comment stretched her smile a little farther, and we began our search, scanning every inch of the rectangular stone temple layout as we moved slowly around the perimeter to the first corner, then the second, the third, and eventually the fourth.

By the time we reached our starting point, discouragement had taken hold again, and I started wondering if there really was a way out of here.

Vero, however, didn't seem as worried about it as she had at first. "Maybe there's something we missed over by the altar. Let's go check there again."

"Okay," I said, though doubt fluttered in my gut.

I followed her over to the center again and stopped at the altar next to one of the golden bucks.

I admired the intricate detail of the sculpted beast, marveling at the workmanship of some long-gone artist from ancient times. The antlers branched out from its head, twisting and narrowing to a fine point at the tip of each one. The ears, eyes, nose, mouth, even lines defining the musculature of the creature displayed impeccable attention to every feature.

You really could help me out here, I thought, hoping the voice in my head would lend a hand for something other than the usual trouble-related alert.

I knew he wouldn't answer, and that expectation wasn't disappointed. All I got was silence.

Vero shifted sideways and then turned her back to me to inspect a doe opposite of the buck I stood by.

She tilted her head to the side and gently reached out and touched the top of the animal's head to feel the smooth metal. "These really are remarkable," she noticed. "I wonder who made them."

The second her fingers brushed the beast's head, a gust of air blew through the chamber. There were no windows or doors—none that I could see.

The baffling burst of wind was only the appetizer of strange occurrences. The doe sculpture Vero touched suddenly came to life, as if awakened from a long slumber. The animal moved slowly at first, stretching its neck and torso.

Vero snatched back her hand, terrified at the abrupt and unexpected movement of something that we both believed to be inanimate.

"What's happening?" she asked.

The deer shook its tail, then the rest of its body in a shiver. It looked up at her with vacant golden orbs, blinked a few times, and then bowed low to her.

I had an idea.

"Vero," I said, excitement returning to my voice. "I think you just figured it out."

She turned her head, still unclear. "Figured what out? I just touched that thing."

"Yes. Come here." I stepped out of her way and motioned to the buck next to me. "Touch this one, and see if the same thing happens."

Vero took a reluctant step forward, then another. She paused, hovering over the buck as if the thing might attack her if she touched it.

"It's okay," I encouraged. "Artemis was a protector of animals, but she had a special connection to deer. Hence these sculptures."

She blinked several times, then looked back at the doe. The figure held its kneeling pose toward her.

"Okay," Vero said. "But all I did was touch it."

I nodded.

She stretched out her right hand, this time with more apprehension than the first, and grazed her fingers across the back of the buck's skull.

The thing shivered, then turned its head and looked at her, blinking slowly. As with the first, it stretched its neck and legs, then bowed low, tipping its antlers toward her.

Vero smiled at the metallic creature, as if the beast were truly alive. Then, she lowered her head toward the animal in a respectful bow.

"Now the others," I suggested.

"You think this will open a way out of here?"

"Only one way to find out."

She bobbed her head and stepped around the buck to the next corner. She held her hand over the statue of the second doe, then lowered her palm to its head and ran her fingers along the smooth surface.

Just as before, the creature roused to life, and repeated the same waking process before it bowed at Vero's feet.

She sighed and moved over to the last buck. I watched her hold out her hand and then carefully caress the animal's scalp. The deer shook its head gently as it roused. As the others had done, it looked up at her, then took a step back with its hind legs, and bowed low.

Vero smiled at the gentle animal, and for a moment it seemed as if that were the end of it.

After a breath, a golden light appeared from within the empty chest.

We both faced the container and inched closer to it.

"What is this?" I found myself asking out loud.

A papyrus scroll with a dark blue ribbon tied around it lay in the bottom of the chest. The light radiating from it dimmed slightly as we neared.

I started to reach out to take it, but then I thought better of it. This was her mission. "Take it," I said. "See what it says."

Her eyes remained fixed on the scroll for a few seconds, then she looked up at me. "You sure? This isn't some kind of booby trap, is it?"

"No. I don't think so."

"You don't think so?" She emphasized the word *think*. "Gideon, I would prefer you know the answer."

"It isn't. This must be a clue as to where the medallion is."

"Did you have something like this when you found yours?"

"No," I admitted. "The amulet was waiting for me in the hidden temple. There must be a reason for this, though. I would pick it up, but it is yours."

She inhaled deeply then slowly let it out. "Okay. But if this thing unleashes some kind of a deadly trap—"

"It won't."

The statement seemed to solidify my resolve with her. "All right, Gideon. I trust your judgment."

She held out her hand over the box, about to reach in and take the scroll, but to our surprise, the papyrus suddenly jumped out of the chest and into her palm, as if called by some unseen magnetic force.

The unexpected act startled us both, and Vero took a step back in reaction.

"Wow," I breathed. "That was cool." I smirked. "See? It *is* meant for you."

She didn't respond for half a minute. Instead, she just breathed as she held the scroll in her fist, gripping it gently. Then she swallowed and lowered it to waist level and started untying the ribbon.

She let the strand fall to the altar next to the chest, and gradually, cautiously unrolled the papyrus.

When the scroll was rolled out, she held the top edge with her right hand and the bottom with her left. I maneuvered around the statues and joined her on the other side of the altar to see what it said.

Vero stared at it, shaking her head.

"What does it say?" I asked as I stopped next to her, centimeters away.

Her head turned back and forth. "Nothing. It's blank."

I leaned closer. "Blank?" It only took a quick check to confirm what she'd said. Before I could ask how or why the scroll was blank, and why it had magically appeared within the chest only to give us false hope, the golden glow we'd seen from it before returned, only this time in a radiant ink that etched across the papyrus as if written by some unseen hand.

"Look at this," Vero exclaimed. "How?"

"I don't know. I'm new at all this too."

The letters continued to scribble across the page in fluid, artistic cursive. Based on the style, I reckoned it was from sometime several hundred years before, though that was sheer conjecture.

The glowing ink stopped writing, finishing its message in a single sentence, followed by the signature of a name I recognized immediately.

"The compass shall show you the way." — Sir Francis Drake.

My eyes were as wide as an owl's.

"Francis Drake?" Vero said. "The famous privateer you told me about?"

I looked to her, momentarily tearing my eyes away from the page. "It would seem so."

"The way to what, though?"

"That, my dear, is the million-dollar question." My voice echoed throughout the temple as I finished. Then I looked down into the chest and saw something else that hadn't been there before.

It materialized from nothing, as if previously hidden by some mysterious power. "Look," I said, pointing into the box.

A bronze compass lay on the bottom, with the needle pointing west.

Without being told, Vero reached into the chest and picked up the strange object. She frowned as she studied it. "Isn't the needle supposed to point north?"

"Yes," I said, nudging her shoulder with mine as I leaned closer to inspect the compass. "But this one seems to be pointing west. Or...." I stopped in midsentence.

"It's pointing to the medallion?" Vero finished.

"Exactly."

As if triggered by our words, the scroll glowed again. This time, instead of words, the invisible pen began drawing.

"What is that?" Vero asked as curving lines, and erratic shapes formed.

"It appears to be a map," I realized.

"A map? A map of what?"

Within seconds of her question, the map finished drawing itself, and I immediately recognized the area.

"That's the Caribbean," I said, pointing to a patch of islands. I traced my finger down from Jamaica to a black X close to the point where Central America met South America. "This is Panama."

"Panama? Is that where the medallion is?"

"Sure seems that way. Looks like we flew all the way across the world and the thing was much closer to Mexico the whole time."

Vero shook her head, still puzzled by... well, probably everything.

"But why would the medallion be in Panama?"

I already had the answer, though I never suspected as much before now. "Because that's where Drake was buried at sea."

25

The torches on the wall flickered, then faltered. The warming light they cast throughout the room faded, and we found ourselves descending into darkness once more.

"Gideon?" Vero grabbed my arm.

"It's okay. We'll be back on Delos when all this disappears."

"You sure about that?"

I scanned the room, turning my head in every direction to assess the situation. "Pretty sure."

"You're not exactly instilling me with a lot of confidence."

"It's okay. The last time I was in a place like this, I woke up in the jungle near your village."

The flames continued dying, spitting out the last of their flames.

"Just stay close to me." I put my arm around her and pulled her close.

"Here," she said, placing the compass in my palm. "Hold on to this."

"What?"

"In case we get separated. Those guys are still out there," she explained. "If something happens, we'll each have a piece of the clue."

I had to admit that was a smart idea and wished that I'd thought of it. "Okay," I said. "But let's hope that doesn't happen."

The last tongues of flame lapping the air from the torches sparked, then died, plunging us into total darkness.

"Gideon?" Vero said. Her voice sounded distant, and it came to me as though through a tube.

"I'm here."

Then, as suddenly as the blackness had overtaken us, a dim gray light surrounded me. I felt something hard and crumbly underneath me. I opened my eyes, squinting hard against the blurry fog, like waking from a bizarre dream.

"Vero?" I rolled over onto my back and looked left. She lay there on the ground next to me. At the sound of my voice, her head lolled to the right.

Her eyes cracked open, and she offered a faint smile. "Wow. That was weird," she said, rolling up onto her side.

I sat up and surveyed the area, suddenly aware that the gunmen were probably close by—depending on where the temple spat us out.

A quick survey told me we were still on Delos, but not within the temple grounds anymore. We were somewhere else.

Then I heard the men's voices, shouting at each other in... was that Latin?

I looked back over my shoulder and realized where we'd been dropped off by... whatever power or magic fate seemed to be using.

"Crap," I breathed. "We're on the other side of the temple."

"Other side?" Vero followed my gaze and came to the same conclusion. "Do you think they know we're here?"

"Not from the sounds of it, although my Latin isn't what it used to be. Not sure why they're using that language."

"Latin?"

I didn't answer the question. The far more pressing issue at the moment was putting as much distance between us and the Gladius Dei agents as possible.

"Let's move. We'll work our way down the hillside and then back over to the walkway to the ferry. Another one should arrive soon."

I checked my watch. Just as I'd suspected, almost no time—if any —had passed while we were in the temple.

We could have been in the mystical chamber for what felt like hours, perhaps days, situated between constructs of reality, and yet here only seconds or minutes would have passed.

"What if they see us?" Vero hissed. She crawled to her feet but crouched low in case one of the gunmen ventured close to the outer wall of the temple ruins.

"If we stay here, they will see us," I answered. I extended my hand to her. "We have to make a run for it."

"Bad idea," Xolotl warned.

"What?"

"I didn't say anything," Vero said, looking at me like I was bonkers.

"Sorry. Not you. Ugh. Trust me. When you get your medallion, it's going to be an adjustment.

"You should fight them here," the voice continued. "You have the element of surprise. It is the only way to protect her."

That doesn't make sense. She is vulnerable right now. Without a medallion—

"Yes, they could kill her. But not if you kill first. Take them out, Gideon. It is the only way."

I sighed, exasperated that I had to make such a huge decision with virtually no time to weigh the consequences.

Xolotl was there to help me in situations just like this. But was he always right?

"Yes."

Shut up. Let me think.

"You're running out of time, Gideon. Kill them now."

Part of me wondered if the ancient power within me simply wanted the mist to feed on the wicked, like some kind of deranged, starving beast kept in a cage that needed to be sated every so often to keep it quiet.

No answer to that one.

"Come on," I urged Vero. "Let's get out of here."

She nodded and took my hand.

"You're making a grave mistake, Gideon," the voice said. Then it went eerily silent.

We scurried down the hillside, picking our way through loose rock and clumps of ancient ruins from the old village.

Halfway down the hill, we passed a collection of statues shaped like lions. Their forms had remained relatively intact for thousands of years, with only fragments missing from random places such as a nose, a foot, a tail.

From our vantage point, I saw a ferry approaching in the distance, slowing down as it approached the port. "Right on time," I mumbled. As if the captain heard me, the ship's horn blared across the harbor.

I stopped at a six-foot-high wall of what was probably someone's home four thousand years ago and ushered Vero behind me. I peeked around the corner of the hut, looking up the slope to the side of the temple. No sign of the gunmen yet.

"Okay. We should be in the clear. Make straight for the port. Once we're at the bottom, we should be able to blend in with the—" I turned to look at Vero, and was met with a nightmare.

A man in the same black outfit the rest of Gladius Dei wore stood behind Vero, holding a pistol muzzle against her head.

"Now," the man said. "You have something I need."

I breathed hard as anger and ancient power mingled in my blood, beckoning me to summon the monster.

"The chamber was empty," I snarled. "The Artemis Medallion isn't here."

The gunman frowned, obviously not believing a word I said.

"Then I suppose we don't need her." His finger tightened on the trigger. "Of course, not all is lost. There is, after all, still the medallion you wear. Take it off."

My heart thumped in my chest. I should have listened to Xolotl. He tried to warn me to fight them at the top of the hill.

"Yes, I did," he said.

Would it have made a difference?

"She wouldn't be held at gunpoint right now; I can tell you that much."

I watched the crimson mist swirl around the man. I'd seen it kill one of Vicente Carrillo's men in a dream or a vision, I wasn't sure which. And I'd even managed to control it once or twice.

I calmed my nerves and the fear racking my body and spoke to the fog through the desire of my heart.

The mist danced and churned faster. It climbed up the man's legs and wrapped around his torso, then his neck.

I smiled devilishly at him. "You should have let her go," I said.

"If you try to use that mist on me, the gun could go off," the gunman said. The statement rocked me like an earthquake. *How did he know about that? I was the only one who could see it. Had he learned of it some other way?*

"You must be wondering how I know," he realized.

All I could do was breathe, my nostrils flaring with every exhale.

"You'll soon learn we know a great many things about the medallions, and your pathetic order of houses that have dealt so much wickedness to the world. At least, you would learn if you weren't going to be dead soon. Step back."

I choked back a response and took one step away from the two. "Let her go," I demanded. "It's me you want. She's nothing to you. Not without the Artemis Medallion."

"Oh, I think she may still be some use to us." He tilted his head to the right, and looked at her hip.

"If you so much as—"

"What is in your pocket?" he asked, cutting me off.

I traced his gaze down to Vero's jeans and saw the scroll sticking out of the front right pocket. She must have stuffed it in there when we reappeared from the temple.

Before she could answer, the gunman reached around her waist and nicked the scroll. "What is this?" he asked.

"It's nothing," Vero answered quickly. Too quickly.

The man kept the gun against the side of her head as he used his other hand to unroll the papyrus on her upper back.

It was all I could do to keep the beast within bridled. But I knew one wrong move could send a bullet through Vero's skull. I'd already seen that happen once—with my late wife.

"Ah," the gunman said with sinister delight. "A map. I wonder where this leads. The medallion, perhaps?"

"You'll never find it," I snapped.

He cocked his head to the side at an angle, a look of mocking pity drawn across his face. "Oh, you're wrong about that. With this, we will have no trouble locating the medallion that heathen donned so long ago. Your pagan gods can't help you now."

"They weren't gods. Just people who did extraordinary things. But there's no accounting for research versus propaganda, is there?"

He only clenched his jaw at me. "It matters not. Soon, you'll be dead. As will she. Now, take a step back, and remove your medallion."

I shook my head, but deep down I knew there was only one way this could end. If I took off the amulet, I'd be vulnerable again, and the second I removed it, this guy would kill me. But it would buy Vero some time. Maybe she could escape somehow. It all sounded hopeful and vain, but that was all I had left at this point.

"Do it. Or she dies now in front of you."

I held out a hand to settle him down. "Okay. Take it easy. I'll remove it. Just... don't hurt her."

"Gideon. Don't," Vero pleaded. "You can't."

I took another step back. Then I reached into my shirt and pulled out the medallion. The shimmering metal glistened even in the muted light of the overcast sky. A gust of wind rolled in from the sea, blowing hard across the hillside.

"You can't," Xolotl cautioned. "If you do, all is lost. There is no other way now, Gideon. If she dies, she dies. There will be another."

"Not for me," I said, shaking my head.

I carefully reached my hands around to the back of the necklace holding the amulet, and felt for the clasp.

I hesitated for a second with my finger on the hinge.

"Do it," the gunman ordered, his body shrouded in red mist from the waist down.

Vero shook her head vehemently, but the man tightened his grip on her, forcing her to stop moving. Tears brimmed in her eyes. One snuck by her defenses and rolled down her cheek, falling from her jaw down to the dry earth.

"I'm sorry," I said. "I'm so sorry."

My apology had barely left my throat when I heard the sound of a muted gunshot. I felt the impact of the bullet hit the back quarter of my skull and exit out the other side. It sounds horrific, but honestly doesn't hurt that much for the first few seconds. It feels more like getting hit with a hammer—blunt, and somewhat painful, but more jarring than anything.

I fell over on my side, my vision blurring as I hit the ground.

Vero screamed. "No! Gideon!"

Then I heard another woman's shrill voice mingle with Vero's. It came from somewhere down the hill.

I blinked away the fog enough to see a gathering of tourists less than a hundred feet away at the base of the slope.

The gunman holding Vero hostage spat something unintelligible, but I felt like it was some kind of swear word.

I blinked again, and he was gone, darting behind the corner of the ruins, dragging Vero with him.

The entry and exit wound in my skull began healing, the bones and tissue rebuilding themselves in mere seconds. After ten seconds, I regained my senses enough to stand up.

"Now will you kill them?" Xolotl pressed.

I nodded. "Suits me."

A pop echoed from the hilltop, but my armor flashed across my skin as I transformed into the monster. The bullet pinged off my shoulder, which was where my head was a second before in my shorter, human self.

I turned to face the gunman who stood forty feet away with a pistol extended at me. Two more rushed to his side and immediately opened fire.

I stalked toward them, rounds ricocheting off my armor. More tourists screamed from the base of the hill below. I imagined they were all running toward the port now, desperate to get on the ferry to escape the firefight—and now the terrifying creature.

The gunmen emptied their magazines, ejected them, and retreated a few steps as they reloaded.

I shook my head at them, then ducked to the side out of sight behind another building. Skirting behind a wall of stacked stone, I sprinted along a path behind another structure. Moving faster than any human could, I knew the men didn't see me, or if they did, all they could make out was a shiny, furry blur.

At the next corner, I looked down the path, but there was no sign of Vero and her captor. I needed to find them. But they couldn't get away that easily. By the time they got to the harbor and either the ferry or their getaway boat, I'd have dealt with these guys, and would catch up to the one in charge.

I hurried up the path, between the ancient rubble and crumbled structures, picking my way to the top of the hill. There, I stopped behind a column at the corner of another hut and took a peek around it.

The three gunmen were still facing down the hill, though now they'd fanned out, putting space between each of them.

While the tactic made sense, it wasn't going to save them.

Once I emerged from my hiding place, the closest guy would spot me. Not that it mattered. These men may as well have been armed with peashooters.

I looked down at my feet and noticed a piece of wall that had broken away. I grinned and picked up the five-pound stone as if it were only a tennis ball. Then, I reared back, stepped around the corner, and threw the rock at the nearest gunman thirty feet away.

The heavy stone struck him directly in the left temple, crushing skull, bone, and brain—killing him instantly.

Before the man hit the ground the red mist around him began flowing into his mouth and nostrils, beginning to consume him as he fell.

I ducked back around the corner before the man in the center of their column could turn and see me.

No doubt, he was looking at his fallen comrade, wondering what happened. I grinned knowing that panic would settle in, even with the most hardened, well-trained warrior.

I backtracked down and around the building and over to the path that snaked through the ancient village. The second gunman's next move would be to check on his dead team member.

At the bottom corner of the next hut, I paused and looked up the slope. Just as I suspected, the second guy hurried over to assist the one I'd hit with the rock. It must have been harrowing to see the dead man's head caved in on the left side, along with the body disappearing before his eyes as it was devoured by some—to him—unseen force.

The instant he disappeared from view around the upper wall, I pumped my legs and surged upward.

I covered the distance between the two of us within three seconds, barely enough time for the man bending over his dead comrade to twist his head to the side before I grabbed him by the throat and lifted him off the ground.

His gun fired impotently as he twitched the trigger. Even with the muzzle pressed against the armor on my side, I felt nothing. Not even a tickle.

"Drop him!" the third gunman shouted as I held his partner up with only my right arm.

I looked around my victim at the last one, bared my teeth in a devilish grin, and nodded. "With pleasure."

I lowered the man down to the ground for a second, just enough so his feet could brush the dirt. Then I pushed hard with my leg muscles, and forklifted the guy up into the air.

He sailed sixty feet up before gravity fought back and turned the tide of his momentum. I stared at the last guy, marching toward him as his comrade fell to the ground behind me. I didn't look back, but from the sound of it, I guessed he'd hit headfirst. That popping, cracking sound was pretty unmistakable.

I flicked my wrist, signaling to the mist to finish the job.

The last gunman shook his head, as if that could deny the terror that approached him. He took a step back, then another, then faster as he kept firing his impotent weapon.

Finally, thirty feet away from him, his gun clicked empty. I snarled at him, and he turned and took off running.

"Really?" I growled.

I lunged forward, covering half the gap between us in four huge, bounding steps. The man looked back over his shoulder, fear glaring back at me from the whites of his eyes. I pounded the ground underfoot, then leaped into the air, covering the rest of the distance in a split second.

I raised my right fur-covered hand over my shoulder as I descended from the sky, and just before I landed, I swung hard with my palm.

The hand cracked the back of the gunman's skull, and the force of the blow along with my inertia drove him face-first into the rocky ground. The crunch of bone against stone would have turned anyone's stomach—even mine in my past life. Now, though, there was something grimly satisfying about it.

These men had tried to kill me, and they'd abducted Vero. Making them pay for such acts felt noble in my mind.

I twisted my head at the sound of the ferry horn in the harbor and knew I needed to hurry, though I doubted these guys were waiting on that boat. My money was on the yacht in the bay.

Just to make sure this one was dead, I flipped over the limp body. I first noticed his bloody, mashed face as the crimson fog seeped into him. But the second thing I saw sent a shiver through my spine, and a chill across my furry skin.

"Oh, come on," I complained with a sigh.

26

After the blast, everything went black.

There was no way I could have known the guy had a grenade in his right hand—and the pin for it in his left. In hindsight, maybe I should have been prepared for that.

But I wasn't a trained soldier. I'd never gone through any sort of military exercises, so when I flipped the dead guy over, the last thing I expected to see was an explosive device.

I guess he knew he had nothing to lose after seeing what I'd done to his two comrades. Out of ammunition and facing a nightmarish monster could—I supposed—make a person pretty desperate.

The last thing that went through his mind must have been "If I'm going to die, I might as well take him with me."

Except the explosion didn't kill me.

It was, however, extremely painful.

My armor took the brunt of the blast, but there were gaps between the metal that allowed the ordnance to cut through.

I was lucky, I supposed, in some ways. The explosion could have blown my head off my body, which would have been the end for me. Fortunately, I ducked my head down just before the blast, and my helmet took a considerable amount of the concussion and shrapnel.

My hands, arms, and legs were badly damaged—all from the few gaps in the armor. Even so, before my vision returned, I felt my body healing itself, repairing the muscle, tissue, and bone.

I rolled over onto my side and tried to sit up, but the pain was too much, and I had to lie back once more, resting my head on the ground. I focused on breathing, just breathing in and out to calm my mind as I waited for the healing to complete.

Vero. I needed to get to her. But I couldn't do anything except lie still and wait, biding my time.

My ears rang to cap off the list of problems I was dealing with. The high-pitch hum distorted my thinking, and the fact I couldn't see anything made it nearly impossible to focus on anything else.

"Ugh," I groaned. "Any time you want to make this ringing in my ears go away, I'd appreciate it."

I expected to hear a wisecrack from the voice in my head, but instead I heard the sound of a woman's voice say, "Oh, settle down. You'll be fine in a few moments."

I sat up, pushing through the pain in my extremities. I looked around, twisting my head one way then the other, even though I still couldn't see anything.

A dim light peeked through my vision. It was orange like candle-light but not distinct, not at first.

"Who's there?" I demanded.

I realized my armor was gone, and I was no longer in the form of the chupacabra.

"Relax," the woman said. "Quite the mess you were when I found you."

"Found me?" I blinked rapidly, desperate to clear the darkness from my eyes. "Who are you?" The voice sounded vaguely familiar, though I couldn't place it. There was a kind, grandmotherly tone to it.

My sense of smell hadn't been warped in the explosion. I detected the scent of roasting meat in the air, along with cardamom, black pepper, onion, coriander, and garlic. The next thing to hit me was the realization that I was not on the ground. Instead, a smooth, hard surface supported me from below.

"Where am I?" I asked, panic creeping around the corners of my mind. "What's going on?"

"You really don't understand the word *relax*, do you, Gideon?"

"She's got you pegged," Xolotl gauged.

What is going on here?

"You went off script," the voice in my head told me. "You should have listened to me. I have one job. I did that job. And you ignored my counsel."

Yes. Yes, I get that. I should have killed those men when you told me to.

"Well, at least you can admit when you're wrong."

My vision continued to clear, and I made out faint shapes in the room. A room. I was in a room. That was a start.

"Who are you? What is going on?" I asked.

I saw the form of a woman in a flowing beige dress pass in front of me, but the details still hadn't cleared up yet.

"Here," she said from my side, as if she'd appeared there like a ghost. "Drink this."

I twisted my head toward the source of the voice. "Drink what?"

A shadow passed in front of me. I sensed heat wafting up from it. Then ceramic touched my lips. I jerked back, hesitant.

"Oh come now, you big baby. It's just matcha."

"Matcha?"

"Yes. Incredible drink, matcha. Anti-inflammatory. Loaded with antioxidants."

"Antioxidants?" I found myself saying the word as if in a trance. Her voice sounded haunting, hypnotic in a weird way.

"Yes. And full of healing properties."

"Healing properties," I repeated as the cup touched my lips again. I felt the hot liquid slip into my mouth and onto my tongue. The heat, at first, caused me to twitch back, but I adjusted quickly and took in a long sip.

"I put a little fresh mint in there to help with the flavor," the woman said.

I swallowed, then let out a relieved sigh. It *was* good.

My vision cleared faster, and within seconds the layout of the room came into view. I was in a kitchen. It looked like the interior of a traditional Greek home, with exposed timbers supporting the roof and white stone walls behind the appliances.

I turned my head left and nearly jumped off the floor.

"You," I blurted. "It's you."

The gray-haired woman smiled at me. I recognized her through the tempest of confusion in my brain. Her kind blue eyes shimmered in the candlelight. I looked down on the floor and spotted five candles set in a circle around me, each atop a symbol or rune. The woman standing before me was the same woman from before, the one who'd lost her locket on the beach on Mykonos.

The emblems surrounding me looked like things I'd seen before from Ancient Greek culture.

"What are you doing here?" I asked. "What am I doing here?"

"It's okay, Gideon. You were badly hurt. Lucky I came along when I did."

"Came along?"

"Shh." She raised the cup to my mouth again. "Drink."

I shook my head, but she forced the rim against my lips and tilted the cup up. The hot liquid spilled onto my tongue again, and I felt compelled to swallow once more.

I wiped my lips with the back of my hand and tried to stand, but my legs felt weak. I checked my neck, suddenly afraid I might have lost the medallion. Fortunately, my fingers found it right where it belonged against my chest.

"Yes, your medallion is still where it belongs," the woman confirmed. "You're lucky to still have your head."

I winced, squeezing my eyes shut tight for a moment, then opened them to full clarity. Finally.

"Vero. Where is she?" I stood up and searched the room.

My host put out her right hand to calm me down, while setting the cup down on an end table made from a tree trunk to her right.

"They took her," she said. "The men who were trying to kill you."

"Where? Where did they take her?" I felt anger boiling inside me, and the beast begged to come out once more.

"Calm down, Gideon. She isn't here."

"Where is here?" I asked, still twisting around to reign in my surroundings. "Where am I? And... how did you—"

I faltered in the middle of the sentence.

"You're safe," she said, her voice still calm as ever.

"You're the lady with the locket. But I don't—"

"Take a few breaths," she said.

"You should listen to her," Xolotl added.

I clenched my jaw, furious at the voice in my head.

"What is going on?" I asked, doing all in my power to settle down. "Who are you?"

Her smile never wavered as she answered. "You never know who you might meet on the beach here in these ancient lands. You could run into all manner of creatures." She paused on that last one. "Or, in my case, an oracle."

My heart skipped a beat. "Wait. Did you just say oracle?"

"I did," she said with a single, slow nod.

"Okay, I did not see that coming." More emotions rushed through me. "I need to find her." Then I stopped myself. "I'm sorry. I didn't even catch your name. You seem to know mine."

"I do, Gideon. All the oracles know the names of the guardians. Especially yours." She paused and let me absorb the statement. "My name is Andora. I am the current oracle of Delphi."

I couldn't say a word for nearly a minute. All I could do was stand there and stare at the woman in disbelief.

Finally, when the words came to me, I shook off the cobwebs. "I'm sorry. I didn't mean to be awkward."

"It's fine. It isn't every day you meet an oracle. Although I understand you have met Myra. She gave you a nice armor upgrade, yes?"

"Yes, ma'am," I said with a sheepish nod. "Am... I supposed to bow or something? I gotta say, this is a weird moment for me. I've read all about you, at least in the history books."

"You probably read about my predecessors. I have only been an oracle for a thousand years."

Again, the words evaporated in my throat.

"It's much to take in," she said. "I understand. Of all the oracles on Earth, my position is the most well-known. It was a much more difficult position for those who occupied it a few thousand years ago. Dealing with some of those tyrant kings, despicable priests, and of course the ones mortals called gods. You, however, understand what those gods truly were."

I nodded. "Heroes of epic proportions."

"Yes. Well, some were heroes. Others, not so much." A hint of sadness darkened her face. "But that is a story, perhaps, for another time. I know you are worried about your friend. She is still alive."

"She is? How do you—"

"Oracle."

"Right." I nodded, pressing my lips together.

"I sense you are eager to reach her. Understandable. Wicked men, the ones that took her. They act under the pretense that they are warriors of God. They are, as you well know, anything but."

"Who are they?" I asked bluntly. "I learned a little about them from a friend, but he was sketchy on the details."

"Gladius Dei? A rogue band of elite agents, guided by an evil man whose sole purpose is to cleanse the earth of anyone he deems unrighteous."

A single thought emerged in my head. "The cardinal."

"Yes," she confirmed.

"But who is he? Where can I find him?"

"To your first question, his name is Virdago Bocello. As to the second, that I do not know. Locations are tricky for my kind. We see things in the background of those we observe, but specific places are often blurry."

"Often?"

"Now and then, we can see through the veils more clearly. But those moments are rare."

I sighed. Virdago Bocello wasn't a name I knew. Not that it mattered right now. I had more pressing issues to contend with.

"Are you able to see where they took Vero?"

Andora offered a pitying smile, then turned and walked over to the kitchen. She picked up a wooden spatula and stirred whatever was cooking in a steel wok. The contents sizzled and sent a plume of steam into the air. She wafted the aromas toward her face with her left hand and inhaled deeply.

"Never gets old," she said, "not even after a thousand years."

She set the spatula down and faced me again. "You already know where they took her, Gideon."

I frowned at her insinuation. "How would—" Then it hit me. "Panama? They took her to Panama?"

"Yes. Along with the map she found in the temple of Artemis. I suspect they will be there soon."

"Soon? How could they be there soon? They just left the island." My eyes darted from one side of the room to the other. "Wait. Are we on Mykonos? Surely, they would have come here first before going back to Athens. They were in a boat. A yacht, actually. Pretty sure, anyway. They don't strike me as the type to use public transport like the ferries. We need to search the ports for—"

"Yes, you are on Mykonos, Gideon," she interrupted. "But they are not here. They flew out of Athens yesterday."

I blinked a hundred times as if it were ten. "What did you just say?"

She merely arched her right eyebrow in response.

"But... that's impossible," I struggled. "How could they have left yesterday? I just fought them a...." The words faltered. "Wait a minute." I searched the room as if it would give the answers. "How long have I been here? How long was I out?"

"Explosions take longer to heal, Gideon. Even for a power as great as the one you wield. I brought you here to speed up the process. I would urge caution in the future when dealing with things of that nature. There won't necessarily always be an oracle hanging around to help you. Fortunately, the rest of the men who attacked you left Delos. Had they found you before I did, well..."

"I'd be dead." Resignation filled my voice.

"Yes. But do not dismay. Vero is still alive, as I said."

I looked down at the floor, dejection and sadness tugging at my heart. "What does it matter? I can't get to the other side of the world in time. If they're already in Panama, and they have the map, I'm already too late."

"Not true," Andora disagreed. She tugged at the thin gold chain around her neck, and the locket I'd found for her on the beach appeared at her fingertips. "Do you know what this is?"

"Um, a locket?"

She smiled at me, again an expression of pity she might give a simpleton. "It is, yes, but it's what's inside it that makes it special."

"I thought it being an heirloom is what made it special."

Her eyes glazed over, and for a few breaths she seemed lost in a long-distant memory. "The container, yes. But what it can do makes it powerful. And it is that ability that will help you now."

"I'm listening."

"The other night on the beach, when you helped me... that was a test. I needed to measure you."

"Measure me? I thought you knew I was a guardian."

She waved a dismissive hand my way. "Oh, of course, but I needed to see for myself, if your heart was a selfish one, bent on only satis-fying your deepest desires, or if you would help a poor old woman who'd dropped her necklace in the sand."

I felt a slight twitch of irritation but expelled it quickly. "You sent the sea monster?"

Andora looked surprised at the question. "The Mornok? Oh, goodness no. I don't control such creatures."

"But you knew it was there. You knew it would attack me."

A single nod. "I did. I also knew you could handle it."

"I could have—"

"Died? I don't think so. Not unless that thing cut off your head. Come to think of it," she turned and looked over at the far wall as if an idea hung on it next to a bookshelf, "it may have done that at some point."

"That doesn't make me feel better. You know that, right?"

"Of course I know. I'm an oracle."

She turned her attention back to the food in the wok and stirred it again before turning off the gas stove.

"Mornok," I muttered.

"Yes. Nasty monsters, those. I can't tell you how many ships that thing has destroyed over the centuries, how many lives were lost to it. You did the world a favor killing that creature."

"Thanks. I guess." Still didn't feel good that she knew about it and basically led me straight to it. "You said the locket... What's in it can help me?"

"Yes. But first you should eat something."

"Eat something? Listen, I don't mean to be—"

"Sit down, Gideon." Her voice boomed, and the candles on the floor and around the room shimmered as if a gust of wind had blown through. The house darkened for a second, and I felt fear stab at my chest.

"Okay. No problem." I eased into a chair at a table just behind me and waited.

The second I sat down, the candles resumed burning as before, and the shadows that had encroached into the room retreated to the corners. The pleasant look on my hostess's face returned as she spun around and scooped a pile of meat and vegetables onto a wooden plate.

"Time," she said, tapping the plate with the spatula to get off a slice of onion clinging to the edge, "is a construct of our invention."

Didn't realize I'd sat down in a physics lecture, but I listened anyway.

She brought the plate over and set it down on the table before me, then stood back and waited. "Go on," she insisted. "Try the lamb."

That's what it was. Lamb. I thought I recognized the scent.

I leaned over the food and let the rising steam work its way into my nostrils. It smelled amazing, and I suddenly realized how hungry I was.

I picked up the fork and stuffed a piece of meat into my mouth. It tasted even better than it smelled. The salty, peppery flavor combined with the onions and garlic exploded on my tongue.

"This is amazing," I said.

"I thought you were hungry. It's been a day since you ate, after all."

The reminder of how much time had passed didn't alleviate my concerns about Vero. "I thought you said time was a construct of our invention."

"It is. And as such, most of us play by the construct's rules."

"Most of us?"

"That, Gideon, is for another time... perhaps. Finish your meal. Then I will send you on your way."

"Send me—"

"Finish," she said with a raised finger and a mischievous grin.

I nodded and returned to devouring the food. It didn't take long. I was famished, and could have gone for seconds, but I didn't want to waste... right, time.

I stood up when I was done and started to take the plate to the sink.

"Just leave it," she said. "I'll take care of it when you're gone."

"Okay," I said, reluctantly setting the plate back on the table. "I'm not used to letting people wait on me."

"I know. Now, grab your bag over there." She pointed to the nearest corner.

To my surprise, my gear bag was sitting against the wall. I obeyed her and swung it up onto my shoulder, then slipped my other arm through the loop.

"So, are you taking me to an airport or something?"

Andora shook her head and scowled. "Goodness no. Planes are far too slow. You'd never get there in time." She took the necklace off and turned toward the circle of candles where I'd woken up a few minutes before. Then she pried the lid off the vase-shaped locket and tipped it over.

A glowing blue liquid dripped out of the container onto the floor. "Just a few drops should do it."

I couldn't say a word. I simply watched as the blue droplets congealed on the hardwood floor and then began to grow outward, doubling in diameter, over and over again until it had swelled into a four-foot-wide puddle of shimmering, ethereal liquid.

"What in the world—"

"It's a portal," she answered before I could finish. "This will take you to Panama. From there, you will be on your own."

"My own? But how will I find Vero if—"

"You do have one item that can help," she cut me off again. Her eyes wandered down to my right pocket, and I became aware of the item tucked inside.

I stuffed my hand in and pulled out the familiar object. "The compass," I realized. I remembered Vero handing it to me just before we were ambushed.

Andora beamed at me. "That will show you the way to Sir Francis Drake's final resting place. But you must hurry. Gladius Dei cannot be allowed to obtain the Artemis Medallion."

"Yeah, I figured as much."

I stepped toward the glowing puddle. "So, how does this thing work? I just step in, and it will spit me out in Panama?"

"Basically."

"There's not a downside to this, is—"

Andora stepped forward and put her hand on my back. "It was lovely to meet you, Gideon. I believe I will see you again at some point. Until then..."

She shoved me forward with more strength than I could have believed possible from a woman her size and age. I stumbled into the puddle one foot after the other and dropped through the floor into a swirling blue light.

27

I could have sworn I heard David Lee Roth's voice an instant before the spinning blue tunnel around me vanished.

I hadn't known what to expect from the magical portal, if it would feel like falling into a hole or simply walking through a door. Turns out, it was a little of both.

In the blink of an eye, I found myself in a completely different place than where I'd been just a second before. The Greek home was gone, and now I stood in an empty... warehouse, from what I gathered.

The metal building, supported by steel beams and girders, was riddled with holes in the roof, more broken windows than not, and an array of mechanical tools, crates, pallets, and drums left here by whatever enterprise had once occupied this space. The smell of dust melded with the acrid scent of a workshop, much like I recalled in my grandfather's garage.

Funny how odors produce such strong connections to memories.

My eyes flashed one way then the other, but I detected no danger, and Xolotl didn't say anything.

He did, hum, though. I thought I recognized... a melody?

"Was that you?" I asked, searching the dim, derelict building for a way out. I spotted an exit in a nearby corner where two metal doors were cracked open but held shut with an old, rusty chain.

"Was it me what?" the voice asked in a coy tone.

"You were singing Van Halen, weren't you?"

"David Lee Roth or Sammy Hagar?"

"Sammy didn't sing Panama," I replied as I made my way toward the door. Broken glass, fragments of metal bars, and other debris littered the floor.

"I guess DLR, then," he said.

"I didn't know... beings like you were privy to such things as rock and roll."

"You act like I've been stuck in an ancient, hidden temple for a thousand years or something."

"Wonder what gave me that idea." I shook my head and moved toward the exit. "I was always more of a Sammy Hagar fan, personally."

"Of course you were."

I rolled my eyes as I stepped over a pile of worn-down wiring. I hoped the electricity wasn't on in this place. From the looks of it, there'd been no power here for a while.

"I have to ask," I said upon nearing the doorway, "were you really stuck in that temple for all that time, you know... alone?"

"No," the voice answered. "We are everywhere and nowhere."

"That's an... interesting and confusing concept."

"We are watchers, Gideon. Wouldn't be much help if we didn't have a handle on the current, and past, state of affairs. Not to mention, could you imagine how boring it would be if we were stuck in a single location for all that time?"

"Like a genie in a lamp," I thought out loud.

"Yes. Exactly like that."

It sounded like he shivered, which was a strange thing to hear.

"Wouldn't want to be one of those."

I wondered silently if genies were real but let the thought go when I reached the door. I pulled on the handle and jiggled the chains. "Locked," I grumbled.

"Seriously? It's a simple chain."

"Right." I closed my eyes for a second, inhaled deeply, and called on the ancient power. I didn't want to shift completely into the monster. Not yet anyway. From the rays of sunlight breaking through the many openings and cracks in the façade, I knew it was daytime out there. I couldn't hear much in the way of noise, other than the sounds of distant traffic—car engines, tires on asphalt, and the occasional car horn.

Then I heard a much louder horn, similar to the ones on the ferries in Greece. I ripped the chain from the door with a single pull. It surprised me how little effort it took. Breaking the links felt more like snapping a toothpick.

The chain fell to the concrete with a clank, and I quickly pushed the door handle. It squeaked loudly as I nudged the door open and stole a peek outside.

My suspicions proved true. Beyond a raggedy fence surrounding an asphalt loading and parking area in front of the warehouse, thousands of shipping containers in tall stacks filled the space beyond, creating an unusual skyline of red, black, blue, green, and orange steel.

I stepped out into the open, quickly scanning the area to the left then right. No sign of trouble here. I let the door close behind me, surprised the pneumatic hinge still worked.

I could hardly believe it. I was in Panama, on the other side of the world from where I'd been just minutes before. The portal created by Andora had transported me all the way here in an instant.

Incredible.

I wondered where Vero was, if she were okay. A few troubling thoughts fired through my brain. *Had they tortured her? Was she still alive?* I didn't expect Xolotl to say anything, even though I had a feeling he knew the answers.

I needed to find her, and sooner rather than later. Every second that ticked by put Gladius Dei closer to locating Drake's coffin, and the Artemis Medallion.

The final resting place of Sir Francis Drake had been a mystery for centuries, befuddling professional historians and archaeologists, as well as amateur treasure hunters.

I knew the story of the man as well as any. He'd been a childhood favorite when I was just a boy. The way he'd swashbuckled his way through life, along with the many adventures and close calls he'd survived, was the stuff of legend—especially for a young kid with an interest in history.

Despite dodging death and seemingly insurmountable odds, the great captain died in an ordinary and miserable way. On January 28, 1596, Drake succumbed to dysentery during a sea voyage.

Now I wondered what really happened. If he'd possessed the medallion, that sort of thing should have been easily overcome.

"That's not how it works," Xolotl reminded. "You cannot be killed, save for having your head taken. Natural causes or disease, on the other hand, are not bound by that rule."

Right.

Seems like I knew that.

According to the story, Drake had been buried at sea off the coast of Portobello, Panama. I figured Andora's portal had dropped me off at the nearest possible location, and in a place where no one would notice my sudden appearance.

The oracle, it seemed, had thought of everything.

If I was going to locate Vero and the men who took her, I'd have to be smart. Just getting to the spot wasn't going to be enough. I took the compass out of my pocket and held it in my palm. It pointed to west, as it had before.

I looked that direction but couldn't see through the stacks of containers, and the cranes hovering over them.

"Okay. So, I need to go that way," I mumbled to myself. "If the stories are true, and he's buried at sea in a lead coffin, then I'll need a boat."

"Unless you feel like swimming out into the open ocean," the voice said.

I ignored him.

I knew there must be a place to rent boats near here, but no ordinary vessel would do. If I took a cabin cruiser out to find the coffin, I'd be easy to spot. Any kind of pleasure boat would arouse suspicion. What I needed was a fishing boat. Something old, unremarkable.

I snugged the backpack on my shoulders and set off across the asphalt to the fence. Then, after a quick check in every direction, slipped through a gap in the gate and out onto a thoroughfare between shipping containers.

I doubted I would find a fishing boat out here. Certainly nothing but huge ships waited in the harbor.

What I needed to find was a marina, or even better, a quiet little fishing village. That thought brought another idea.

I took the phone out of my pocket and checked the map of my current location. "Colón Province," I said. I exited the map and entered a search for Portobello. I tapped the link on the first results and was met with information about the area's history and images of the bay, an old church, and the ruins of an old Spanish fort.

In the background, several fishing boats sat in the water in what passed for a marina in a quaint, tiny village.

"That what you were hoping for?" Xolotl asked.

"Yeah," I answered absently, already returning to the map to find directions. I entered the location and waited for several seconds before the app provided me with the fastest route and the amount of time it would take to get there via car—fifteen minutes.

That sounded great, except I didn't have a car. But I heard the sounds of a semibusy street coming from behind the warehouse. Perhaps there I could find a cab or a ride share.

I hurried around the perimeter fence, turning left at the first corner. There, I found an alley between another warehouse and the one where I'd landed. Through the passage, I spotted the street only two blocks away, where vehicles intermittently passed.

I picked up the pace, running at about 80 percent of my max speed until I arrived at the corner. I spotted a red compact four-door with a black-and-white taxi sign propped up on the roof and waved to the driver just before it reached where I was standing on the sidewalk.

The guy immediately jerked the vehicle over to the curb and slammed on the brakes to the tune of another driver mashing the horn in frustration as they passed by, narrowly missing the bumper of the sidelined taxi.

I stepped up to the passenger side and opened the back door, slid my backpack off, and plopped into the seat.

"Gracias," I said.

"Where to?" the driver asked in English.

He had thick black hair, a light blue linen shirt, and gray linen pants. A look between the front seats gave a glimpse of his feet clad in brown leather sandals. I figured the guy was probably in his mid to late fifties due to some patches of gray mixed into his black beard and a few strands salting his head.

"I'm trying to get to Portobello," I said. "I believe there is a fishing village there near the fort?"

"Of course. No problem. Ten dollars. I take you there. I know a shortcut."

"Shortcut?" I wasn't sure I liked the sound of that. But I wasn't in any position to argue. I knew relatively little about Panama, other than a sparse knowledge of some of its history. In other countries, if a driver claimed to know a shortcut, very often they took a longer path to get to where the patron needed to go and then ended up charging more for the "scenic way."

"Yes. Very fast. Don't worry. I'm not going to cheat you. I know Americans are worried about such things. I pride myself on being honest."

"Okay," I relented. "Thank you..." I looked at the license on the dashboard, along with the guy's permit to operate a cab. But I couldn't make out the name.

"Enrique," he said. "I'll have you to the village in no time."

He flipped on the meter, flicked his turn signal—which seemed to be optional—and pulled out onto the road, shooting between a delivery van and a couple of guys on mopeds who honked angrily. Their frustration was lost in the pathetic, puny sounds their rides offered.

"So, what brings you to town?" Enrique asked.

For a second, I felt the urge to complain in my mind about the guy being one of the talkative types. All I wanted to do was get to the village, procure a boat—I still wasn't sure how that was going to happen—and find Vero.

Despite that, I decided to be polite. Something Andora said stuck out in my mind, and it wasn't the first time I'd heard it.

"I'm here on business," I said, internally convincing myself that I wasn't lying. Then again, that was easy enough to do. I was here on a mission to locate an archaeological artifact that hadn't been seen in over four hundred years. Just so happened I also needed to save someone's life—potentially—and take out a bunch of bad guys.

"Sounds like business to me," Xolotl chimed.

Do I ever get thoughts or time to myself?

"Yes. All you have to do is ask. And, also yes, I will not be around if you and she ever... you know."

"Okay, that's enough," I blurted.

"Señor?" Enrique asked, puzzled by the sudden outburst.

"Nothing. Sorry. I was... just checking the markets on my phone. Looking like a good time to sell."

"Oh." The driver seemed to accept the answer with a dramatic series of nods.

"Wow. So smooth," the voice derided.

Worked, didn't it?

"Is that what you do for business? Stock markets and that sort of thing?" Enrique asked as he whipped the vehicle to the right through an intersection, narrowly missing being hit by an oncoming light blue hatchback. Again, he received a honk for his efforts.

Out of habit, I gripped the handle above the door. Enrique didn't realize he was the only one on this ride that could die in a crash. Unless he was an oracle too. Seemed like there were more of those folks out in the world than I ever could have imagined.

"No, I'm an archaeologist," I confessed. "But it never hurts to pay attention to the markets. Gotta have a retirement account, after all. Live for today. Plan for the future."

"You know, I was just telling my wife that the other day. That's one of the reasons I am driving a cab on my days off. I'm trying to save up for retirement."

"Smart," I said, realizing I'd been catfished into the conversation now.

He jerked the wheel to the right and whizzed by a guy on a motocross cycle with plastic satchels on the sides. The rider in the white helmet only glanced over at Enrique as we blew by him and accelerated through traffic.

I suddenly felt like I was in a Panamanian version of the taxicab from the movie *Scrooged*—the one driven by the reckless Ghost of Christmas Past. The only thing missing was the cigar and the annoying laughter and heckling.

At least this guy was friendly. Unsafe, but friendly.

I guess his version of a shortcut was just driving as fast as he could without regard for anyone else on the road.

"Yes, you never know what will happen. Good to have money set aside." The driver continued to press forward down the financial conversation trail.

"Isn't that the truth," I said. Melancholy hit me then, and I found myself going down a different road in my mind. Amy's face popped into my imagination. Then her father. That one lasted longer. I'd been surprised, though only a little, by the revelation of my late wife's indiscretion. Deep down, I felt like I'd always suspected even if I never truly confronted that notion.

The visage of Amy's dad standing there with a gun, pulling the trigger, then hovering there thinking he'd just killed me was a difficult thing to grapple with. I never got the impression that the man liked me. Not more than a surface, publicly polite sort of vibe. But I never thought he would have gone to such an extreme.

Initially, I'd thought how I would react if I had a daughter and believed her husband killed her. My response would have likely been similar, if not pulled back a measure or two. But when I found out the truth regarding him, and what he was up to, that changed everything.

Dealing with Gladius Dei and investigating their role in all this,

I'd temporarily forgotten Amy's father, but something told me he had just as much stake as before. Was there a connection between him and the offshoot zealots? And did he have a dealing with this mysterious Cardinal Virdago Bocello?

Too many questions and not enough answers.

"So, what are you doing over in the village?" the driver asked. "If you're here on business? Something to do with the fort?"

"He's got you now," Xolotl teased.

"Actually, I'm checking out a lead regarding the burial place of the great privateer, Sir Francis Drake."

"Drake?" The man's dark brown eyes flashed in the mirror, checking to see if he'd heard right.

"That's right. I'm a big fan. I thought I might charter a boat, troll around out in the bay a little. Who knows? Maybe I'll get lucky."

Enrique laughed. It was a nervous, unsteady sound. "Many have come to this place for the same reason as you, my friend. Treasure hunters, mostly. Some of them visited the bay with huge boats and teams of researchers. None were ever able to find it. Not yet anyway. I'm sure the coffin will be located by someone at some point. But I'm not sure I'll still be around to see it.

"You sound like you've driven some of them around."

"Oh, of course. A friend of mine runs a charter fishing operation in the village. Nothing fancy. I told him he would make more money from tourists if he upgraded his boats. But he insists they run fine, and if that's the case he doesn't need to waste money on getting new ones."

The cliché *if it ain't broke, don't fix it* danced on the tip of my tongue, but I held back, due in no small part to the new information my driver had just so generously offered.

"Did you say your friend runs fishing charters in the village?"

"Sí. You interested in going out for a ride?"

I nodded. "Actually, that would be great. Could you take me to his place?"

Enrique grinned, showing off crooked, stained teeth. "Of course. We will be there in five minutes, amigo."

28

Enrique dropped me off outside what was little more than a shack. It reminded me of the Champy's Chicken locations in Chattanooga, Tennessee, and around the Southeast—tin walls, roof, screen doors, and an open patio looking out on the water. Well, Champy's didn't have the water view.

The aesthetic intent of those places had been to replicate old juke joints.

Here, it was just the way things were. And I liked this spot immediately. Far too often, people got hung up on the newest, latest, state-of-the-art things. I usually discovered that the old ways were best; tried and true.

My driver assured me this was the place and that his friend—a guy named Tómas—would be happy to help me.

The place looked empty, much less open for business. But as Enrique had suggested, a couple of aged boats sat moored alongside the rickety dock beyond the tin walls. The twenty-foot wooden-hull vessels were equipped with center console controls inside a tiny wheelhouse that looked like it could fit two adults.

If fishermen coming to Panama for a little excursion were looking for a no-frills kind of fishing experience—this charter outfit was the poster child. It just so happened that no-frills was exactly what I needed. These boats screamed local fisherman and wouldn't arouse suspicion from Gladius Dei—were I to bump into them.

Then again, their agents would be on the lookout for me, and even a boat such as one of these would likely draw a watchful eye. I'd need a better plan that simply trolling through the open waters with fishing lines out if I had any chance of rescuing Vero.

"You looking for a boat?" a man asked from my left.

I looked that direction, through an open window to find the source of the gravelly voice.

"Actually, yes," I answered upon seeing the guy I assumed to be Tómas. He wore a red bandana on his head, and the voice matched the face. A scraggly, long, patchwork brown-and-gray beard hung from his face. He grinned back at me, missing at least two prominent teeth. His darkly tanned skin told of decades out on the water in the warm Panamanian sun.

The old man raised a cigarette to his lips and took a drag. The tip glowed bright orange as he inhaled, a stark contrast to the shadowy interior surrounding the man.

"I can take you out," Tómas said. "But this time of day I'm not sure we'll catch anything."

"That works out fine for me," I said, fishing a hundred-dollar bill out of my wallet. "I just want to go out on the water." I walked over to the window and set the money on the windowsill.

A cloud of blue gray smoke billowed out of his nostrils and into the open air. "I don't usually let customers take my boats out for joyrides. Too much risk."

I expected the man's counter, and produced another hundred. "Then maybe this can mitigate that risk a little."

Tómas held my gaze for a few awkwardly long seconds, then looked down at the money.

I knew what thoughts filled the man's head. I saw it in his eyes. A couple hundred bucks was more than he would make in a week. And while losing one of his boats in... let's call it an accident, would set back his livelihood, this cash would go a long way to replacing the craft.

I'd been on river boats before that friends had rented for the day for this same amount of money. And those were nice vessels—cabin cruisers with a bathroom, galley, speaker system. Brand new in some cases, or at least in like-new condition. The flip side to that comparison was that those boats were insured. Fat chance of that with this two-bit operation.

"Enrique said you were the guy to see," I added, doing my best to leverage the new acquaintance I made on the ride to the village. "But if I need to find someone else, I can. I only came to you because he said to."

I made a show of looking out over the water, then to the ruins of the fort several hundred yards away. There weren't many options for boat rentals, if any, in this area. But I spied another dock between where I stood and the fort, and figured I could convince Tómas with the threat of losing cash in hand.

"You know Enrique?" he asked.

"No, sir," I shook my head. I wasn't going to lie about it. "I just met him today. But he recommended you, and he was honest with me. So, I figure if he trusts you, then I can too."

Tómas chuckled. The sound was mixed with a smoker's cough—a signal of a lifetime of lighting up one after the other. "Perhaps you are too quick to trust people."

"Probably," I agreed. "But like I said, take it or leave it. If anything happens to your boat, I'll replace it."

"Replace it? Heh. How can I trust you?"

"You can't. But I've given you enough money to get you on the way to another boat." Truth was, with that kind of money he could probably upgrade tomorrow.

He considered it for another thirty seconds. The water lapped against the pilings as he thought, and several birds squawked from nearby. The moment felt like the proverbial calm before the storm. I'd already decided I would probably need to replace the old man's boat. With what was coming, it was the more likely outcome than simply returning it safely to the docks.

He scooped up the two bills and shoved them into the right-front pocket of his dingy gray shorts.

"I like you," Tómas said. "Follow me."

Relief drizzled down my chest into my gut.

The man walked to the front of the building, and I followed his track, stopping at the front corner. I stood and waited until he emerged through a creaky, red wooden door that looked like it might fall off at any moment.

Something about the man reminded me of the shaman, though the two looked nothing alike except in terms of their age. Even then, the shaman appeared to be in good health, and in strong physical shape.

Tómas was shorter and carried himself with the frailty brought on by a long, difficult struggle in life.

"Do you have a preference which boat? They're both available." I looked back toward the spot where Enrique dropped me off. *Like there's a line.*

"The blue one is fine," I answered, motioning to the boat that looked like it was in better shape. Talk about a race between two turtles on that assessment.

Both vessels were probably older than me. The paint was chipped and flaked off the hull. The single outboard motor on the back might have been one of the original of its kind. No telling how many times that thing had been repaired through the decades.

"That one is my favorite too," Tómas said, leading the way with a motion of his hand, indicating me to follow.

He ambled along the dock, avoiding a few planks that had broken away. It was a wonder the thing was still standing. Everything about this operation was suspect. I half wondered if the boat's motor would even start. Or if he would charge me extra for that.

When we reached the boat, he hopped up over the gunwale with surprising agility and stepped into the wheelhouse.

I climbed aboard and joined him at the controls, noticing a key with a metal banana key chain dangling from the ignition.

"This one is easy to use," Tómas said. He turned the key, and to my surprise the motor on the back rumbled to life.

It didn't sound like it was in prime condition, but it functioned, and that was all I needed. Unless I would need to make a quick getaway. In that instance, I'd be screwed.

"You shift this to go backward." He pulled a weathered metal lever. "This here is the throttle," He motioned to another lever. "Push this forward when you want to go."

"Anything else I should know?" I asked after the minimal boating lesson.

"If you want to try to catch some fish, there are rods and reels in a cabinet on the front side of the wheelhouse."

"Thanks." I had no intention of doing any fishing.

"Okay. You have a good time. Bring it back in four hours."

The time frame reminded me that I hadn't bothered negotiating that part, but four hours was more than I needed. I knew exactly where I was going thanks to the compass in my pocket. If the coffin of Sir Francis Drake was still out there in the bay, then I would find it.

"Will do," I confirmed.

The old man stepped back over the edge of the boat and onto the dock. He made quick work of unhooking the cleat, moored by a rope that looked as old as him. He tossed it aboard and waved.

I acknowledged his signal with a wave of my own and eased the throttle. I almost felt surprised when the boat actually started moving backward. After clearing enough room to turn around, I shifted the lever into the forward position and gave it a little more power on the throttle.

I didn't notice any No Wake signs, but I wasn't going to gun it. If Gladius Dei was out here in the bay, I needed to be subtle, which would test my patience.

After cruising through the rippling water for a minute or two, I glanced back over my shoulder at Tómas, standing on the dock with his arms crossed, watching me guide his boat out to sea.

A few other fishing vessels of similar make and age bobbed in the water off the starboard side. Those two had nets dangling from cranes. Their captains stood opposite each other, talking about the day's catch or whatever two small village fishing guys discuss.

I turned my attention back to the water ahead. Out beyond the peninsula to the port side, the waves of the ocean built up more than in the bay. They rolled in on three-foot swells and stretched onto a sandy beach before retreating back amid the foam.

A chill shot through my entire body as I looked out beyond the tip of the peninsula. The white sixty-foot yacht sat atop the water about half a kilometer from shore. Maybe farther.

I'd seen no other boats like it since arriving here, and this village seemed to be devoid of the kind of money that could afford such a yacht.

The multimillion-dollar vessel wasn't entirely dissimilar to the one I'd seen off the coast of Delos, with only a few subtle differences in shape and model. "These guys have boats all over the world?" I wondered out loud.

I hadn't expected an answer, but Xolotl finally chimed in after being silent for what I thought must be a record amount of time.

"Yes."

"Like their own navy?"

"No. Not like that. But I don't have to tell you that they are well funded. Anyone could see that."

He was right. Even if he was just guessing. Gladius Dei was being funneled money from somewhere. I doubted they were able to siphon money away from the Catholic Church. So if not from there, from where?

The voice remained silent on the subject.

I kept the speed steady as I watched the yacht, only prying my eyes away to check to the left and right, making sure no other boats were coming my way. After passing the two fishing vessels in the bay, the only other ship I saw was the yacht.

As I drew closer, I noticed people moving around on the deck. A diver emerged at the stern of the boat and climbed up the ladder. I swept my eyes from there toward the bow and quickly ducked down out of sight just behind the controls.

I'd seen a man with binoculars standing on the port side, looking out in my general direction. I was pretty certain he'd been aimed at another angle, but I couldn't be a 100 percent.

I waited another thirty seconds before I risked taking a peek through the window. The guard was looking the other way now, peering out to the northwest.

I found an old straw hat hanging on the port side of the wheel-house, and quickly put it on my head. It wasn't the best disguise, but it would have to do.

Slowing the boat's speed to a crawl, I pretended to make myself busy in case the men on the other ship were getting too curious. As I rummaged around, I continued stealing looks over at the yacht, scanning the windows for any sign of Vero. She wasn't on deck. So, I figured they were keeping her in the quarters somewhere.

A burst of activity distracted me from the questions. The men on the back were waving to someone inside the yacht. I was still a few hundred yards away, but I could hear their excited voices.

They were hovering around a steel crane on the back of the boat, all staring at the cable in the water.

"Not good," the voice in my head commented.

"No," I said. "Not good at all."

29

Every feeble plan I'd managed to scrape together over the last half hour since arriving in Panama flew out the window.

To be fair, the trip had taken seconds through the portal—if that long. The moment I set foot in the warehouse, my primary concern—other than finding Vero—had been getting my bearings and finding a boat.

I checked both those items off the list. But in the short amount of time I'd been given to work with, I hadn't had a second to consider how I would approach this. I felt a little lucky to have caught up with the men who'd taken Vero, especially considering the shape, or lack thereof, they'd left me in on Delos.

"No time like the present," Xolotl said.

"I really wish you would get out of my thoughts."

"Hey, you and me both."

I found myself trying to sympathize with him, which gave me the feeling of needing a warm, cozy jacket—one of those with sleeves that tie in the back.

I half expected some smart-aleck comment regarding that sentiment, but he remained oddly silent.

"Any ideas?" I asked, knowing full well that wasn't how our weird relationship worked.

"I would say if we had time and the equipment, going in underwater would be optimal."

"Okay. I didn't expect you to actually answer that one. You... can't give me some kind of magic air bubble around my head so I can swim over there undetected, can you?"

I thought I heard a laugh. And it was an unnerving sound.

"No. No, I don't think that's a thing."

"I had to ask."

"You had to ask that specific question?"

"Listen, I need ideas, and fast. It looks like they're pulling something up out of the water."

"Astute observation."

"I don't need your sarcasm right now, X. I need to know what to do. I'm not a tactical genius. I'm a historian, an archaeologist."

Nothing.

I slammed my hand on the console and immediately regretted it out of the exaggerated paranoia that this boat couldn't take much of a beating. The thing was probably only worth four or five hundred bucks at most. I'd seen boats better than this one, and at least two decades newer, going for just under a grand online—sure, they didn't have a motor, and needed some work, but that was in the States, where the dollar didn't go as far as it did here.

I could easily pay Tómas if anything happened to his—

The thought stopped right there. And the answer was right under my nose.

"Now you're talkin'."

"I can't do that. He needs this boat. So what if I can afford to buy him a new one."

"More like five new ones, nice ones with updated displays and sensors. He'd be the king of—"

"Not helping. The point is I'm not going to ram them with this boat."

"Why not? It's the only weapon you got. Yes, you could swim over there, but from the looks of it, I'd say by the time you got there they'd have the coffin open."

I looked back to the yacht and saw the water bursting with something bulky. I shifted closer to the window. "You're right. They found it already. I can't believe they were able to get to it so fast."

"They had the map," the voice reminded me. "Might have been even faster if they'd had that compass in your pocket."

I couldn't believe it. Based on an old map, with an X marking a pretty general location, these guys from Gladius Dei were able to get to the exact location of Drake's underwater tomb in less than a day. Experts had spent years, lifetimes even, trying to track down the lead coffin of Sir Francis Drake.

I let out a growl. "Impossible. They couldn't have arrived here more than a few hours ago."

"They did have a twenty-four-hour head start."

"True."

I was wasting time standing there deliberating on how Gladius Dei had managed to locate the coffin so quickly. I didn't have much time until they pulled it from the water and opened it. Once that was done, I had no idea what would happen next.

"I have a question," I said.

"Only one?"

I let the sarcasm slip. "Before, in a dream or a vision—hard to know which—I was able to use the mist to—"

"Kill one of Carrillo's men while he was being interrogated?" Xolotl finished the question for me.

"Yes. And then again, another time when I was conscious, I—"

"Seemed to be able to control it, use it as an ally?"

Again. "Yes."

"I noticed the same."

"Wait. What do you mean you noticed the same?"

I turned the wheel toward the yacht and shifted the throttle. The old boat lurched ahead like a log wagon in water.

"Gideon, I have been with guardians since the time the houses were first created. I have served many. But in the eons I have roamed this planet, and observed the course of history, I have never seen one who is able to control the mist in such a way."

The boat's bow climbed and dove through the swells, the motor groaning from the back. Wind swirled around the wheelhouse and in through the back opening.

"How can that be?" I asked.

"I do not know. It's possible that your connection to it is stronger than anyone else's, perhaps because of how you came about discovering the medallion."

I looked down at the top of my chest, noting the amulet for a moment. The terror of that fateful night returned, and the memory passed before me as if it were happening all over again.

As quickly as it appeared, it vanished once more, leaving me to the sound of the boat engine, the waves smacking against the hull, and the wind whistling around the wheelhouse.

"None of the other guardians had something so intense attached to their discovery of the medallion?" I mumbled the question, the emotions of that night still lingering in my mind.

"No. My only theory is that because of those intense feelings from that night, you have a stronger bond with the mist than any guardian who came before you."

"But I am not always able to control it. I mean, I did once. Maybe twice. The time in the dream, though, I have no idea how I did that."

"It was no dream, Gideon. That actually happened. You remote viewed it—lucidly, I might add."

The term *remote view* reminded me of the Stargate and MK Ultra Projects, a secret operation conducted decades before by the United States government.

"It's possible," the voice went on, "that with some practice you could learn how to develop your control of it."

I peered ahead at the yacht. We were closing in, and I noticed one of the guards on the port side staring right at me. I tipped my head forward a little so the straw hat would conceal the upper part of my face. It wasn't much, but I only needed to buy a fraction of time.

The fishing boat climbed a slightly higher swell than the others, and at the peak, I looked at the yacht's stern where most of the action seemed to be. Crimson fog swirled around the men standing on deck, including the guard watching me.

At a hundred yards away, he started waving at me, clearly trying to get me to steer off course. I pretended to fiddle with the controls again in an attempt to convince the guy that I hadn't seen him, but when my boat was only fifty yards away, there was no chance that ploy would work.

At this range, I saw the AR-15 gripped in his right hand, slung over his shoulder, as he kept waving with his left.

I focused on the mist, thinking about what Xolotl had said about the emotional connection I had with the medallion, and the power it possessed. "That's it," I realized. "The emotions. The feelings."

"What?"

"You said the intensity of feelings that night when I found this thing"—I looked down at it again for a half second—"were stronger than any you'd witnessed before."

"So?"

"So, maybe that's the secret. Emotion."

I narrowed my eyelids and focused on the guard waving his hand around. A few others on the back of the yacht noticed his frantic gestures, then looked out at me as I narrowed the gap to forty yards.

I ignored them as they joined in, attempting to direct me off course.

Then, I closed my eyes and visualized Vero being kept down below deck. In my mind, I saw her bound with zip ties, stuffed in the corner of a bedroom with a sock stuffed in her mouth. She'd been crying, and it looked like someone had hit her.

I had no way of knowing whether or not what I was seeing was real or just my fears presenting themselves in my imagination. But one tangible thing boiled inside of me: pure anger.

I opened my eyes and saw the guard again, the mist spinning around him. In my heart, I blamed him for whatever misery Vero suffered at that moment. I felt something tangible between me and the mist, a connection through the ether, tangled in a web I now found myself able to control.

The boat lurched ahead. Only twenty-five yards to go.

The man raised his gun and took aim. He fired a warning shot. The bullet splashed in the water just off starboard.

I remained focused on the guard, and then in my mind, commanded the mist.

The red fog wrapped around both his legs, slithering up like two serpents until the strands reached his torso, then merged into one and continued squeezing him, constricting his ribcage until his lungs could no longer take in breath. The mist worked its way up to his neck, and when it reached his throat, the man let go of his rifle, allowing it to dangle by his side as he grasped at the invisible force choking the life from him.

He fell to his knees, desperately trying to get someone's attention, but it was already too late. I willed the mist to squeeze a few more seconds, then abruptly commanded it to throw him overboard.

As if on his own volition, the man leaped over the gunwale and into the water, disappearing from view as the mist followed him into the depths.

I only felt the guard's life energy for five more seconds. And then I knew the deed was done.

The other guards on the ship aimed their weapons at me upon hearing the other's gunfire. I knew what would come next.

"Do it," the voice demanded.

"With pleasure," I answered.

I called the power, and shifted into the creature. Fur rippled across my form, blowing in the breeze. The armor unfolded over it, finishing off the transformation with the helmet. I stayed in the wheelhouse, though now it was a significantly tighter fit—but only to guide the boat to my target.

I couldn't aim at the yacht's hull, not with Vero hidden some-where inside. The impact could seriously injure her, or worse. Instead, I twisted the wheel toward the yacht's stern.

Bullets tore through the wheelhouse windshield and pinged off my armor. More rounds struck the hull as the men on the yacht unleashed everything they had.

It wasn't enough to stop the little fishing boat.

The tow cable straight off my bow bubbled in the water, and I saw something black and metallic emerge. It was the first time the coffin of Sir Francis Drake had been seen by human eyes in over four centuries.

I couldn't believe how the onyx casket had no barnacles on it, no signs of the passage of hundreds of years spent at the bottom of the sea.

The gunmen reloaded their weapons and kept firing just before the bow of the fishing boat struck the top of the coffin.

I heard fiberglass snapping from the yacht, then the sound of metal groaning under the strain.

The crane operator pulled on levers, but the machine smoked in protest.

Bullets kept spraying at me, cutting Tómas' humble vessel to splinters of its former self.

"Definitely going to have to buy that guy a new boat," Xolotl said.

I nodded. "Yep. Seems that way."

The yacht's stern dipped low from the additional weight of the fishing boat dragging it down by the cable.

The crane operator knew there was no other option and pressed a button on the control panel. Suddenly, I felt the floor drop out from under me a second before the hull splashed down hard in the water.

The cable unreeled itself quickly, and I knew the coffin was sinking back down to the ocean floor below.

One of the guards got wise and shot at the motor on the back of the boat.

The first round missed, which gave me enough time to slip out of the wheelhouse and onto the starboard side a second before the next shot struck the aged engine.

Tómas' boat erupted in a blast of fire the second after I dove into the dark, greenish water.

30

I paddled through the water as the orange flash seared the rippling daylight above the surface.

I thought it strange the armor didn't seem to weigh me down, and I easily swam under the mangled fishing boat, past the cable, and to the ladder on the back of the yacht. I could see the silhouettes of the men standing on deck. They swept their weapons back and forth, suspecting the monster they'd seen on the other boat might abruptly emerge and pull them under.

They weren't wrong, but I had other plans.

I kicked hard a few more times and swam under the yacht, over to the starboard side, and didn't come up for air until I was beyond the gunmen's vision. I emerged next to the hull and stayed close for a second, waiting as I listened to the gunmen shouting at each other, some barking orders, others arguing.

Time to really scare the crap out of them.

I let my weight pull me back down under the water for a moment, then kicked both my legs as hard as I could.

The water churned under my feet, and the push propelled me up to the surface again, and into the air.

I shot out of the water and over the yacht railing, landing on the deck with a thud so heavy it rocked the vessel back and forth.

Three gunmen were visible—the others blocked by the cabin's corner. They immediately spun around and opened fire. The bullets bounced off my armor and struck the wall to my right, or fell into the water to my left.

I stalked toward the men as their magazines ran dry, and they fumbled with new ones to reload their weapons.

Three others came into view as I rounded the corner.

"Die, devil!" someone shouted from just inside the cabin door.

I turned in time to see a man charging at me with a huge hunting knife, or a combat knife. I didn't know much about knives, but I knew enough that the blade this guy carried was not the best weapon of choice.

He raised the knife as if to stab me in the head, but I quickly side-stepped, grabbed his wrist, snapped it backward with a sickening crack and forced the tip of the blade through his right eye.

His scream of pain at the broken bone lasted a fraction of a second before he died from his own weapon. I then grabbed him by the waist and spun around, launching him into the sea far beyond the burning wreckage of the fishing boat.

Now all six gunmen were shooting at me, and all with no effect.

Crimson mist twisted around them, begging to feed.

I took a menacing step toward the nearest one, who once again ran out of ammunition, dropped his rifle, and reached for a sidearm on his hip, which I found a little funny despite the dire situation.

"Do you really think that's going to do anything if the bigger gun didn't?"

I reached out and grabbed him by the neck as he squeezed the trigger. The round burst from the muzzle and ricocheted off my helmet, striking one of his comrades in the forehead and dropping him onto the deck.

The shooter grimaced as I tightened my grip. His eyes bulged. The rest of the men didn't dare fire after what they'd just seen happen to the other.

"Trouble behind you," Xolotl cautioned.

"Drop him!" a new voice shouted from behind, only a second after the warning.

I twisted my head slowly, deliberately until I was looking over my shoulder. My heart sank at what I saw.

A man in a black suit—minus the tie—stood just outside the cabin door, holding Vero close to him with a pistol pressed against the side of her head. The sinking feeling tightened my gut into knots.

"I said put him down," the man repeated.

His long black hair whipped around the top of his shoulders. He reminded me of a dark wizard from fiction I'd read in my spare time long ago.

I obeyed and lowered the man to the deck. The second his feet touched, I let him go, and he fell to the floor, gasping for air.

"Good doggy," he said. His voice sounded English.

I growled in response.

Then I caught movement off the starboard side. Another yacht, larger than the one I stood on, was cruising toward us.

How many ships do these guys have?

"Not sure on that number," the voice answered. "But there are twenty people on board that one."

"The Cardinal Virdago Bocello," I mused.

"You will not utter his name," the gunman snapped, tightening his grip on Vero. "Demons such as your kind will kneel before a man so holy as the cardinal. And you will beg for forgiveness of your eternal soul."

"Not likely," I growled.

"We will see."

The four gunmen still standing surrounded me, each holding their weapons close to the narrow gaps in my armor.

The one holding Vero hostage sidestepped toward the starboard rail, so whoever was driving the other ship could see him.

"On your knees, demon," the man spat. "Or I kill her."

I wasn't about to bow to this guy, not without cause. But that gave me an idea.

The other yacht over his shoulder cut through the water, speeding toward us. I noticed a helicopter on the back, bouncing along on the landing pad—its rotors bending and rising with every wave.

"Do it," he demanded, spittle spewing from between clenched teeth.

I drew a long breath through my nose, contemplating my next move. I had to be careful, and fast. A wrong move and Vero would die.

"Don't, Gideon. Just kill him." Vero's order fell on deaf ears. No chance I was going to put her in jeopardy. I'd already done that too many times this week. It had to stop.

I raised my animal hands in a display of surrender. "Okay," I relented. "I'll do it. Just take the gun away from her head."

The man shook his head. "No. I don't think so."

"You could accidentally kill her. The boat lists the wrong way from waves, and you put a bullet through her head. If that happens, you will take a very long time to die."

"Don't threaten me, monster. Down on your knees or I kill her."

My eyes ventured over his shoulder again at the approaching vessel. We were running out of time.

With my hands over my shoulders, I bent my right knee and slowly lowered myself to the deck until the metal armor over my kneecap touched the floorboards.

"Get the net," the leader ordered one of the men watching me.

"You can't possibly think a net is going to hold me, do you?" I asked.

The guard did as ordered and disappeared around the corner.

"Oh, we have something special designed for you, demon. The threads of this net are made from an ancient metal. You won't be tearing through it, I can assure you."

A net made of ancient metal?

I'd say I'd heard it all, but I had a feeling the weirdness in my life was just beginning.

I glowered at the leader, watching the red mist spin around his ankles, begging to take him. Then I parted my lips and showed my fangs.

"What are you smiling at, demon? You're about to die. As is your girlfriend."

I shook my head slowly. "No. It's you who's about to die. This is your last chance. Let her go, and I may consider allowing you to live."

The leader spat. His hair whipped around in the wind, draping a few loose strands across his face. He seemed unperturbed.

"You can stop talking now."

I saw the blond guy who disappeared a moment before coming back around the corner, this time holding a silvery web of netting in his hands. It looked like it was barely big enough to envelop a teddy bear, certainly not something or someone as large as me.

"It is imbued with magical properties," Xolotl warned. "I have not seen anything of its kind in…"

He stopped in midsentence and left me wondering where that train of thought was going. Not that I had time to consider it.

"I think you'll find this particular bond is extremely strong," the leader said, enunciating the word particular.

"You're running out of time, Gideon," the voice warned. "You don't want him to throw that thing over you. I don't know if we can escape if he does."

"Understood," I muttered.

The leader puzzled over the word, but I didn't focus on him. Instead, I locked eyes with Vero, and the tears streaming down her face. The same anger I'd mustered before returned, swelling from my gut and up into my heart. Seeing her held by this madman only made those feelings stronger, and I felt my blood heating as the guy with the net drew near.

He stretched out his hands, and somehow the netting expanded.

"Quickly," the leader said. "Cover him with it."

I heard him speak, but my attention remained on my emotions. I felt the webs of energy pulling on my soul, connecting me to the mist.

I watched it as it twisted around the man, wrapping its way up his legs as it had done the guard I threw into the sea.

He felt it. I saw the confused fear in his eyes.

I sensed his finger tensing on the trigger and silently commanded the ethereal fog. A tendril snaked up around his arm and covered his hand like a pulsing, crimson glove.

"I warned you," I said.

Fear streaked the leader's eyes.

"Cover him!" he shouted.

The blond guard took one step closer, ready to toss the net over me.

Suddenly, the leader twisted the gun, and fired.

The bullet zipped through the guard's skull and sprayed out the other side.

"What sorcery is this?" the leader demanded.

He had unwillingly turned the pistol to the guy I'd been choking and fired a bullet into his forehead.

"The net! Throw it over him. He has some kind of control over—"

Another gunshot, this one to a guard's chest. The man tumbled backward over the railing and into the water.

The last one standing to my left raised his weapon and aimed it at the leader. "Put it down, señor," he ordered.

His answer was another muzzle pop.

He fell to his knees next to me and then forward onto his face.

The last guard ducked behind me, thinking he could use me as a human shield.

I sensed him aiming his pistol at the leader, clearly believing him to be the enemy now.

Beyond Vero, the other yacht began to slow as it drew near. They would be on us in moments.

"Put down your weapon," the leader pleaded, as he tried to fight the mist he couldn't see forcing his hand.

I heard the man's breathing behind me. It was a panic-fueled sound of desperation and fear. Then, his muzzle erupted by my ear. The report sounded like a massive explosion so close to my head. It was so loud, so unexpected, it blurred my vision for a second, and I ducked my head down, thinking maybe he'd shot me.

But I felt no impact, no bullet exiting my head. After the last few weeks, I knew exactly what that felt like.

Amid the ringing clouding the hearing in my right ear, I managed to look up to see a streak of pain cross Vero's face.

My concentration on the mist broke in that instant, and the leader regained control of his gun hand.

The damage, however, had already been done.

I followed the tears on Vero's face down to a red carnation, blooming just to the right center of her chest.

"No!" I shouted.

I started to spring forward, but something flew over my head, and instantly forced me down to the bulwark.

The silvery net splayed out over my entire body in a flash, pinning me down like some kind of magical Lilliputian trap.

All I could manage was twisting my head at a painful angle, enough only to see the leader remove his arm from Vero's waist, and let her topple backward over the railing.

I heard the splash through the ringing in my ear. Then I roared. The sound carried across the waves, but it was impotent—nothing more than one last expression of pain.

The leader breathed heavily as he stepped toward me. He stopped, hovering for a moment as if relishing the victory. The red mist was gone. How was it gone?

I thought Xolotl might answer, but all I heard was the sound of the other yacht's motor throttling down as it approached.

My nostrils flared with every furious breath I took. But another emotion wrapped around the anger inside me. It ripped away every shred of hope, and wrapped it in a blanket of utter despondence.

Despair gripped me, and I believed it was the last thing I would ever feel. Now, I didn't care if I died or not.

31

All I could do was lie there on the bulwark, the hot Caribbean Sun beating down on me. I'd transformed back into my human self—I think because of the magical net pinning me to the floor.

I hadn't done it on purpose, so it was either that or the fact that I was done fighting.

Vero was the last thing I had to live for in this world. With her gone, the light had disappeared from my path and left me in a hollow void from which there seemed no escape.

I thought of Jack and Jesse—the former my old friend, and the latter a new acquaintance. They would probably never hear what really happened to me. A trickle of regret snuck its way into my chest at the thought.

Maybe I should have brought them along after all, but Jesse was a crafter, not a warrior. And Jack was more of a scholar and bibliophile than anything else. Still, I found myself missing them, though that sentiment was vastly outweighed by the loss of Vero.

I shook my head, looking at the place where I'd seen her gunned down—where she'd fallen overboard into the sea.

The other yacht slowed to a stop, and several men, all dressed in the same black tactical gear, tied the two ships together.

The gunman who'd thrown the net over me hovered close by. I didn't see his face, but I sensed him, and I knew he was pointing his gun at the one who was in charge of this vessel.

The leader also kept his gun trained on the other. The last remaining guard watched from my left, uncertain which side to take.

"What happened, Doyle?" the one who shot Vero asked from behind me. "Why did you kill your own men? Traitor."

Doyle turned his head slightly in denial, the strands of black hair still blowing in the breeze. "It wasn't me."

"I saw you! You shot them. And you were going to shoot me!"

"It was him!" Doyle retorted, pointing a bony finger in my direction. "The demon... he... somehow took control of my hand. I couldn't stop it."

"I don't believe you."

Hearing the two argue, while slightly humorous, did little to salve the pain in my heart.

"He's a demon," Doyle insisted. "We know this. His kind are capable of such wicked magic."

He looked down at me with disdain.

"Maybe," the guard allowed. "Maybe you're lying. Maybe you wanted the medallion for yourself."

"Don't you dare question my loyalty to the cause, and to the cardinal. I have devoted my life to this holy endeavor."

"Put down your weapons," a new male voice said from the other boat.

I averted my eyes and saw a man appear just behind Doyle, wearing black and red robes like he'd just come from a monastery. They weren't the kind of vestments I'd seen priests wear, though. These were more akin to the kinds of robes worn at a graduation ceremony, but with a sinister flourish to them.

Doyle immediately lowered his gun and stepped aside, bowing dramatically to his leader.

"Cardinal," he said, keeping his eyes on the deck at his feet, unwilling to meet the gaze of the man he so revered.

So that's him.

Cardinal Virdago Bocello's thick curly hair looked like someone had stirred salt and pepper with a spoon and left it a tangled mess on the top of his head. He had a matching beard and dark circles under his eyes, set against pale skin that looked like it had never been touched by the sun. The only pigment, I imagined, came from his obviously Italian background. And I was basing that assumption purely on the man's name.

I angled my head as much as I could to get a better look at the guy. Doyle retreated a step, still bowing low as the cardinal stepped across a gangplank one of the men set atop the railing between the boats.

He lowered himself down to the deck ten feet away from me with a sinister sort of grace. His shiny black leather shoes clicked as he walked deliberately toward me. To me, the man looked more like a deranged sorcerer than a religious figurehead.

When he was only a few feet away, he stopped and peered down at me. "So, you are the one causing so much trouble," he demurred.

I didn't say anything back.

He cocked his head to the side, inspecting me as though I were a wild animal caught in a snare. "I'm sure you must be wondering how a simple device like a net could render such a powerful creature virtually harmless."

Again, I said nothing.

He bent his knees and crouched close to me, his black and red gown spreading out like a liquid around him.

"You see, it looks like metal," he whispered in a voice so low that only he and I could hear. "But this netting is actually woven from the hair of unicorns."

The statement stunned me, catching me completely off guard. *Did he say unicorn hair? As in, the mythical one-horned horse-type creature?*

I had to remind myself that I'd recently fought a sea monster, and witnessed crazier, supposed mythical things in the last two weeks than I ever thought could be real.

"Terribly difficult to catch, from what I understand," the cardinal went on. "Fortunately, this particular net was created long ago. All I had to do was find it."

He reached out his right hand and pinched a thread of the netting, rubbing it between his thumb and index finger, lost for a moment in distant thought.

"Lucky you," I spat.

"When one serves the Lord, one doesn't need luck."

I stretched my neck, and turned slightly to look him in the eyes. They were so dark they almost seemed black, like two pools of oil set against blank oval canvases.

"And what lord is that, Virdago?"

The question tripped him, and his eyebrows twitched down slightly.

"Ahriman in the business of helping men of the cloth now?" I pressed. I saw the fury simmering in his eyes. "You may have the rest of your men fooled, but not me. I know what you are."

He smirked at the insinuation. "My men," he said, "are fully aware of who we serve. We serve the one true God."

I had sort of expected an answer like that. One colossal question remained, but I didn't expect this guy to answer it. Not truthfully, anyway. How did Carrillo and Amy's father, and the late Vernon Wells, all tie into this? Were they all out on their own, trying to locate the medallion around my neck, or was it all part of some greater orchestration, masterminded by this man and his secret society known as Gladius Dei?

"So, you serve the dark side now? A man of the cloth working for the devil himself."

"I once thought as you do, Gideon Wolf. I believed everything the church taught me. I bathed in their doctrines, until I learned the truth. Only when they ostracized me, and turned my order into a relic, relegated to ceremonial pomp alone, did I realize they were hiding something."

"Oh? And what was that?"

His eyelids narrowed as he leered at me. "That only through fire may the world be changed. Those who dwell in sin must be destroyed so that we may live in righteous glory. Not the dulled-down version so many of the flock perpetuate. They all preach the same thing: a soft, antiquated doctrine that has permitted the world to be submerged in darkness. After I have purged it of the weak, the false doctrines, and those who follow them, only then can we reshape the planet and the human race into the form prophesied in the book of Revelation."

This guy has really bought into this nonsense. One thing was becoming irrevocably clear. Cardinal Bocello had either been completely deceived by the darkness, or he'd lost his mind.

On that thought, I puzzled over the madness riddling his words. "The book of Revelation? You think you are going to create the new earth that gospel predicts?"

His silence answered the question.

"You're insane," I said. "All of you. You know that, right?"

"Your vision is short-sighted, Gideon. But it does not matter now. Soon, I will have your head, and the medallion from your neck. Then we will be unstoppable, and we will purge the earth of all suffering."

We?

If the cardinal wasn't seeking the medallion just for himself, then who exactly was he going to give it to? "Do you mean, like, the royal we?"

He didn't seem to get the joke. Or he was just ignoring me.

"Did you retrieve the coffin?" the cardinal asked one of his men, still staring into my eyes.

"We were about to, your Grace, but he hit the cable just as we were pulling it out of the water."

Bocello nodded. "Clever. Did you really think you could stop me with some poor fisherman's boat?"

"Never underestimate the power of a fisherman," I growled. "Some of the greatest of the Creator's servants were humble fisherman."

"Don't you dare mention the Creator to me!" he snapped, his

ghostly skin reddening in anger. "You know nothing of his plan for humanity."

"Is that what you think?"

"I know it. Unfortunately for you, you will not be around to see the glory come to fruition."

He stood abruptly and turned to one of the men on the bigger boat. He held a scabbard with a sword sheathed within.

"The sword," Bocello demanded.

The man with the blade passed it over between the two boats, handle first. Bocello accepted it with a sort of reverence, gently taking it and turning back toward me. The black leather scabbard was overlaid with an emblem of a serpent winding its long, slender body all the way down to the tip. The head near the matching silver handle faced outward, as if about to strike.

Bocello removed the blade from its sheath, and the shiny metal reflected the sun across my face.

"I doubt you recognize this, Gideon, despite your extensive historical knowledge. The sword of God was once believed to be nothing but a myth, a secret kept within the deepest of legends. Ironic, since one with your namesake once wielded it."

I recalled the story of Gideon from the Bible, but this couldn't be the same sword. Could it?

I wondered how he found such a weapon, but I wasn't going to humor him with my intellectual curiosity. Even though I'd lost any desire to keep living, I wished I could do one last thing before I died —kill Cardinal Bocello and all of his men. But for some reason I couldn't shake loose of the net covering me.

I struggled a little, but the netting felt like an elephant sitting on top of me.

"Pull it back. Just to his neck," Bocello ordered the guard standing just behind me.

The gunman obeyed and bent down, grasped the netting, and drew it down to the silver chain around my neck.

I didn't dare look away from my executioner. I wouldn't give him the satisfaction. If I was going to die here, it wouldn't be like some sniveling rat.

"With this blade," Bocello boomed, "I vanquish the House of Claw and Fang, and claim its power for the Order!"

He raised the sword high over his head, ready to bring it down upon me.

Just as his muscles twitched to begin the killing blow, something rumbled from beneath the boat. It sounded like it originated deep in the water. Then the yacht shook from what felt like a whale hitting the underside of it.

Bocello and his men lost their balance. I looked to the other boat and saw the same thing happening there. The man closest to the railing, who'd handed the sword over, nearly fell into the gap between the ships.

The cardinal looked around, panic filling his eyes. "What was that?"

The two guards watching me shook their heads and immediately turned to search the waters for the source of the impact.

A heavy thud hit the hull, and the boat tipped to port, then starboard, rocking back and forth as if suddenly thrust into a storm.

I didn't know what was down there, but whatever it was didn't seem to appreciate the two yachts being here.

"Don't just stand there!" Bocello yelled. "Find out whatever is down there, and kill it!"

The men on both boats raised their weapons. The two with me only held pistols in their hands, but the guys on the other ship braced rifles against their shoulders as they swept the barrels back and forth. It was hard to see what was going on beyond that. I could barely get a view over the gunwale.

The boat swayed back and forth, seeming to settle from whatever impacted its bottom. An eerie silence settled over the scene.

The deck shuddered as if something extremely heavy was making its way toward us. The two gunmen standing close by, looked back over their shoulders toward the bow, but saw nothing. Another thud, this one closer than the first.

Bocello felt it too, and he retreated a step toward the railing. The plank he'd used to cross over had fallen into the water on the initial impact.

He stared ahead down the starboard side of the vessel and the narrow walkway that led to the bow.

A third bump reverberated through the entire ship.

"You two, check the port side," Bocello ordered, even as he moved toward the other yacht.

He knew as well as the other two that something was very wrong. "You four," he said, pointing at the nearest gunmen on the other vessel, "sweep around the starboard side." Even as he issued the command, Bocello swung his right leg over the rail to climb back to the other yacht.

Then he whispered something into another gunman's ear, and the man immediately set about unlashing the ropes.

The four Bocello ordered aboard the yacht where I still lay bound on the bulwark, vaulted onto the ship and immediately moved forward toward the bow.

Another low boom rocked the boat.

This time, the ship tipped hard to port, throwing off the gunmen's balance. They reached their hands out to brace themselves against the cabin, pausing their movement toward the bow.

The two near me steadied, then reluctantly stepped toward the cabin's corner on the port side.

I felt the yacht leaning hard in that direction, as if something extremely heavy was suddenly on board, and making its way back to stern.

With the fifth impact, the boat rocked again, once more throwing off the gunmen's balance. I looked back toward Bocello, and saw his yacht drifting away. Whatever was on board scared the crap out of him. I could see the fear in his eyes as he withdrew toward the stern where one of the guards was busy unhooking the black helicopter from its moorings.

"Where do you think you're going?" I wondered. Seconds before, the guy had been ready to kill me and take the medallion. Now, something had sent him running for his life.

I struggled to free myself, but the net still pinned me down.

Then I heard one of the guards to my left yell something unintelligible. He and the other managed to get off four or five shots before their attacks were cut short by the loudest roar I'd ever heard in my life.

I twisted my head to see what they were shooting at, and what had made the noise—expecting to see some kind of sea monster like the one that had attacked me in Greece.

Instead, to my utter astonishment, I saw a massive brown bear... in shimmering titanium armor, standing upright at the corner.

And around its neck, I saw a medallion shaped like the head of a bear, with two glowing red gems set in the eyes.

32

"Kill it!" one of the guards screamed, but his voice cut short as the monster swiped its left paw out and cut through the man's torso with razor sharp claws. The blow knocked him through the air and into the water as the second gunman fired the remaining rounds of his magazine at the beast.

The bullets ricocheted harmlessly off the creature's armor. He took a step back, desperate to retreat, but the bear snapped out its head and clamped down on his neck, biting through his flesh with impossibly powerful jaws.

The man only managed a gurgled cry for help before the bear whipped its head sideways, tossing him out to sea the same as the first.

The other four gunmen on board hurried back to stern to help in the fight, but they were tightly bunched in single file on the narrow walkway, and the first to see the bear looked like a grown man about to piss his pants.

His eyes widened at the sight of the enormous bear, and he instinctively took a step back, bumping into the man behind him.

The bear roared again, sending a concussion blast of sound across the deck that nearly sent the gunmen sprawling over the railing. Behind them, the other yacht's motors revved, and the ship began pulling away to my right.

The cardinal, it seemed, scared easily.

The guy in the lead of the four shooters opened fired with his rifle, spraying several rounds at the enormous bear. That only seemed to make the monster angrier, and it lunged forward into the line as the other three tried desperately to fend it off with their impotent bullets.

The creature ripped through the first gunman, slashing him across the neck, tossing him overboard, then onto the next.

The men tried to fall back as they continued firing, but there was nowhere to run unless they thought abandoning ship was a good call. The second one had his weapon batted out of his hands, and as he tried to regain his grip on the gun dangling from his shoulder, the bear's right paw mutated into a fur covered hand, grabbed the rifle, turned it on him, and squeezed the trigger until it clicked.

The gunman fell to his knees with multiple gunshot wounds through his chest before collapsing prostrate on the deck at the bear's feet.

Another roar preceded the next attack, as if the beast were somehow enjoying this. It mangled the third gunman as he tried to load a fresh magazine into the well, slicing off his right arm with a single swipe of claws.

The man screamed like a frightened child. His voice cut off when the bear punched him in the chest so hard that I could hear the ribs within cave, then break with a pronounced snapping sound.

The monster stepped over his body, stalking toward the last gunman, who kept backing away as he emptied the new magazine he'd stuffed into the weapon.

When it ran dry and the muzzle ceased spitting rounds, he dropped it and reached for his sidearm.

"Demon!" he shouted and raised the pistol to fire one last desperate volley.

The bear reared up, stretching its body, then lunged down, snapping its powerful jaws, biting the gunman on the collarbone. The creature tore at his flesh, and the man's body went limp after a few seconds of pointless flailing.

Then, clamping down on the dead man with its sharp teeth, the beast flung the man's body over the rail and into the water.

Off to the right, I heard the sound of the helicopter's engine whining, melding with the boat's motors as it sped away.

I looked over the gunwale and saw they were already fifty yards away and speeding up, while the rotors on the chopper began to slowly spin. I also noticed the flowing black and red robes trailing into the right side of the aircraft.

"I really don't like that guy," I spat.

The cardinal looked back, and for a second I thought we made eye contact. Then the moment was gone, and he closed the door as the rotors turned faster and faster.

Frustrated, I looked back to the bear.

It stalked down the narrow walk toward me, moving faster than before. I looked into its eyes, and I saw something familiar in them. I choked back the emotions, and felt a tear form in my right eye.

"Vero?" I breathed.

The beast stopped a foot away from me and nodded. In an instant, the huge bear before me transformed, shrinking back into the woman who'd somehow stolen my heart. Suddenly, the weight of the net disappeared, and it felt as if it were nothing but a feather resting on top of me.

"How come you got armor from day one?" I asked.

The creature shrugged. "I don't know. I'm new at this." As the words reached my ears, she transformed back into the beautiful woman I recognized.

I stood up and it fell at my feet, though I had no idea how, and I rushed to her, wrapping my arms around her and met her lips like I'd waited a thousand years for just that moment, that embrace, that kiss.

As much as I wanted it to last an eternity, I had to let go. I pulled back and looked her up and down.

The blood on her tank top was gone, as was the bullet hole. Around her neck, the medallion hung against her smooth skin.

"They're getting away," Xolotl reminded.

I hadn't thought that I would miss his voice, but in the minutes I'd been trapped under that magic net, I found myself strangely alone without him.

I know.

I looked back to the other yacht and found myself grimly happy to see the red mist again as it swirled around the men on the deck. The helicopter was already in the air, hovering over the pad as it began to take off.

"We have to stop him," I said, turning back to face Vero.

"How? He's in a helicopter. Unless one of your powers is flight, I don't think that's possible."

"We can at least catch up to the other ship and finish off his men. This boat should be faster," I insisted. "It's smaller. I know we can catch them."

Vero sighed and shook her head. "I... accidentally damaged one of the motors when I was coming back to the surface."

"That was the heavy thud we felt on deck," I realized.

She nodded apologetically. "I'm so—"

I shook my head and pulled her close again. "Don't apologize. Okay? You don't ever have to tell me you're sorry. Understand?"

Tears welled in her eyes. "Okay," she managed, then kissed me again.

We tore ourselves away to look back at the helicopter as it climbed into the sky.

"There might be another way," I said, letting my finger slip away from her waist. I turned and stepped to the railing, focusing all of my energy on the fleeing aircraft.

Red vapor trailed after it like a weird sort of exhaust. I reached out with all the emotion I could muster, extending my hand toward the chopper. I felt the faint pull of the power surrounding the two occupants, but it was weak. I breathed harder, clenching the muscles in my arm and torso to draw even more energy to the mist.

I saw the helicopter tilt to the left.

"Almost got 'em," I muttered.

Vero watched from my side, remaining silent.

"Almost got 'em," I repeated.

I felt the mist pulling on the men in the cockpit, but I couldn't get a lock on either one of them. Instead, my power was split between the two. I grimaced, straining as I tried to pull the chopper down to the water.

"Come on," I grunted.

The aircraft tilted to the right, then back to the left, but kept gaining altitude, and distance.

My grip on the mist around the two occupants weakened. I summoned every ounce of rage I could from within, and pulled one last time.

The helicopter jerked downward, and for a moment, I thought I'd done it. Then, as quickly as it came, the bond snapped like cold taffy, and the aircraft surged away, the nose tilting ahead as the pilot pushed the engine to its limit.

I lowered my arm and nearly fell to the deck, suddenly weakened by some kind of exertion I'd never experienced before.

Vero reached out and wrapped her arm under my left armpit to brace me, and I eased back onto the bulwark, sucking in huge gasps of air to catch my breath.

It was like I'd just run four hundred meters.

"Are you all right?" Vero asked, running her finger through my hair.

"I... I couldn't get them. I... I had them. I just... They were too far away. I couldn't... I couldn't focus enough on the pilot. Couldn't see him." I spat out the words between breaths.

"It's okay, Gideon. It's okay. We'll find them."

I kept panting for another minute. Finally, my breathing slowed, and I looked over at her sitting next to me, concern filling her eyes.

"I thought I'd lost you," I managed. "I thought you were dead. I... how?"

She shook her head. "I don't know. I felt the bullet hit me. It hurt, but not as bad as I thought it would. Then I fell over. I hit the water. I felt myself drifting down. I remember thinking, *I don't want to drown.*

Then I saw a strange light and heard a voice calling to me. The voice of a woman. It was soothing, motherly almost. I looked below and saw the coffin cracked open, and the red light spilling out of it. I didn't have the strength to swim to it, but somehow, the light pulled me in. The voice kept telling me to put on the medallion. That's when I saw it, floating in the center of Drake's casket, as if coming to me on its own.

"The next thing I knew, the pain from the bullet was gone, and I felt a powerful energy throughout my body. Then—"

"You became the bear," I finished. "The bear is one of the animals most strongly related to Artemis, and the legends suggest that was the beast she could shift into."

She nodded. "Yes. A voice in my head told me what to do, and somehow, I did it." Vero stopped and looked at me with a confused glimmer in her eyes. "That's the voice you have in your head?"

"Nice not to be alone for a change, isn't it?" Xolotl asked. "You're not the only freak here now, son."

I ignored him. "Yes."

"Except mine is a woman. Is that really Artemis in my head?"

"What does she say?"

Vero blinked for a second, listening. "She said that she's the power of Artemis, sort of like a spirit, but not quite that."

I nodded, understanding.

"I hear other things too," Vero continued, "quieter voices, but more of them. Like I'm in a crowded restaurant."

"What are they saying?" I didn't expect that, and since I didn't hear anything of the sort, my curiosity tugged at me.

"I can't understand them. Too many. It's weird. Wait." She paused, then her face lit up like Rockefeller at Christmas. "They're animals. Artemis said they're animals. Can I speak to animals now?"

"She was a protector of nature and all its creatures. The myth suggests she had a strong connection to deer, in particular. It seems she has passed that on to you."

Vero looked around at the water, peering into it as if listening to the fish speak.

I stared out toward the other boat, frustrated they were getting away. But at least Vero was alive, and that filled me with gratitude.

"We'll find them," I said, full of resolve. "Sooner or later, they'll slip up, and we'll be ready."

She stepped close by my side, and I felt her fingers intertwine with mine as we gazed out to the horizon to the sound of the ocean slapping against the hull.

"Wait a minute." She faced me, interrupting the moment. "How did you get here? I thought... you were dead."

I kept my eyes fixed on the other boat as it continued putting distance between us. "Turns out the old lady we helped on the beach wasn't just some random tourist. She was an oracle."

"Like Myra?"

I answered with a nod. "Seems so."

She didn't say anything else, probably because she was trying to wrap her mind around so many new and crazy things.

"Come on," I said after a minute of squeezing her hand. "I know someone who could use a new boat."

Vero twisted her head and looked at me, questioning me with her stare. I simply smiled back, cradling her head in my hand as I slowly, gently pulled her close and kissed her.

33

I stood on the pavestone driveway that circled around in front of the mansion, staring at the white exterior and terracotta-tiled, two-story home.

Two days before, we'd made a charitable visit to a very different building—the shack that belonged to Tómas. He hadn't believed it when I told him he could keep the nearly new boat, and had been certain he could fix the broken motor. I knew he was right.

This visit to the enormous home before me, however, wasn't for charity.

A palm tree stood on either side of the steps that climbed up to the heavy, oak doors. The wood featured reliefs of fields filled with agave set in a valley between mountains on the edges near the hinges.

It was a pretty impressive design, and mirrored the land surrounding the mansion.

"So, this is the place?" I asked.

Vero stood next to me, glaring at the opulent home. The palm leaves swayed in a breeze that rolled across the valley. The shrubs and flowers that filled the landscaping in front of and around the sides of the building shivered, as if touched by the cool air.

Winter was here, and while it didn't tend to get that cold in this part of the world, the undeniable chill in the air signaled the change of the seasons.

"Yes. This is his house." Indignation overflowed in her words.

I nodded and walked around to the driver's side of her car and pulled on the trunk lever. The lid clicked, and I stepped to the rear and flipped it up. The man in the back struggled to free himself from the zip ties I'd put on him earlier, but he wasn't going anywhere.

Duct tape on his mouth kept him mostly silent, save for the moaning, grunting sounds that escaped his throat.

Red mist spilled from the trunk as I dragged him out, letting his body hit the driveway with a painful thud.

It hadn't taken long to find the man Gonzalez paid to burn down Vero's cantina, and with a little agonizing persuasion, he eventually confessed to the arson—which turned out to be attempted murder.

He spilled his guts about how Eduardo Gonzalez had paid him to kill Vero and destroy the bar, not in that particular order. But we'd left the country, and the killer never had the chance to eliminate his target.

I'd wanted to kill Gonzalez before, but now I had even more reason. To me, the man's fate was sealed.

I shifted into the monster and picked the man up by the back of his neck. Vero mutated into her bear form.

"Shall we?" I asked.

She nodded.

We stalked up the steps that widened at the bottom, funneling visitors to the door at the top. Stone railing stood on either side.

Stopping at the door, I held the assassin up high toward the camera in the right-hand corner above the entrance, showing his face to whatever security watched from within.

"Should we ring the doorbell? Or should we knock?" I asked.

"You're kidding, right?" Xolotl asked.

"Let's knock," Vero answered.

She raised her fur covered paw-hand, balling it into a fist, and then smashed it into the heavy door.

The wood caved in a single blow, splintering as it ripped from its hinges.

Gunshots blasted from inside the mansion. Rounds bounced off our armor, sending sparks raining all around us. Some of the bullets struck the hostage I held aloft, ripping through the man and killing him in seconds.

Through the dust, I saw three men in security outfits, surrounded by crimson vapor, standing inside at the base of two sets of stairs that went up to the second floor.

I threw the body at the guy in the center, hitting him squarely in the chest and knocking him back onto the floor. He slid to a stop between the staircases and struck a decorative wrought iron table that held an expensive-looking vase.

The container wobbled, then fell—crashing to the floor in dozens of pieces as he rolled his head, trying to figure out what just happened.

Vero surged ahead, taking the gunman to the left. The desperate man fired the remnants of his magazine at her, which only seemed to anger her. She skidded to a stop as he tried to back up, grabbed him by the ankles, and swung him high into the air like an ax. At the top of the arc, he screamed, but the sounds cut short when she whipped him down onto the tile floor, killing him the instant his head hit the floor.

I charged at the guy on the right. He retreated as he reloaded his weapon.

"Amazing how these simpletons think their bullets will do anything, isn't it?" Xolotl asked.

"Yeah," I mumbled just before I reached the shooter.

The mist whipped around him in a frenzy. I grabbed him by the wrists, pulled him close, and snapped my sharp teeth onto his neck. I felt warm liquid spill across my lips, and that weird energy that came with the blood of the wicked coursed through me.

I let him fall to the floor, his limbs twitching as life left him to be replaced by the mist that seeped into his nose and mouth.

The gunman by the shattered vase had nowhere to go, but still he tried to back away. His exit was cut short by the table behind him.

Vero and I approached him like two predators in the grass, stalking our next meal.

He fired the last of his rounds at me. I merely shook my head as the two of us stopped on either side of him.

I reached out and picked up the table by the heavy wooden top, and raised it high.

"Stop!" a man shouted from above.

Vero and I looked up to see Gonzalez leaning over the railing on the second floor. Light from the enormous, gaudy chandelier in the center of the ceiling gleamed in his eyes.

I paused for a second, then smashed the table down onto the guard's head, crushing his skull and breaking his neck in one blow.

Vero took a step back, keeping her gaze fixed on Gonzalez. I joined her by her side, exceedingly curious to hear what the man had to say.

"Please," he begged. "Just stop. Whatever you are. You understand me, don't you?"

"Oh, I understand," Vero answered.

She took a few more steps back to the edge of the steps, and shifted into her human self.

"I understand plenty."

Gonzalez's eyes widened in unbelieving fear at the sight. "Vero? How?"

"You destroyed my cantina, Eduardo. And you were going to try to kill me."

He shook his head vehemently. "No. That's not true. I swear. I would never—"

"He already told us," she said, jerking her thumb at the vanishing body of the man who'd taken several bullets in the center of the room.

Gonzalez continued shaking his head. "I will give you anything you want. Please. You want money? Take it. I'll rebuild your cantina."

She ascended the first step, then the second, moving deliberately.

I circled around the other side, transforming back into my human self as I climbed opposite of her.

Gonzalez looked at me, astonished to see two shapeshifters in his home.

"It's you?" he said. "What are you?"

I shrugged. "You wouldn't believe me if I told you."

Vero reached the top of the stairs on the other side. I saw the over-size pistol in Gonzalez's hand—a Desert Eagle. I didn't know much about guns, but I'd seen them in the movies. Impractical weapons, I didn't know anyone who owned one.

He raised the gun and pointed it at her. "Don't move another step. Or—"

"Or you'll what?" Vero cut him off. "Shoot me? Go ahead, Eduardo."

He aimed the pistol. "Don't take another step."

She did. And he fired.

The bullet hit her in the chest, and she winced at the pain I knew all too well.

She stumbled back a step, and Gonzalez grinned a devilish, satisfied smile.

He turned toward me and aimed. "You're next, monster."

The mist swirled around him, dancing and churning—eager to consume its next victim.

His trigger finger tensed, but he never got off the shot.

Behind him, the armored bear hovered over him, and roared so loud the foundation of the building shook.

Gonzalez spun around and faced the beast. He fired another shot, but the round glanced off Vero's helmet.

She grabbed him by the throat and raised him high. His feet dangled at her chest, kicking around as if that could free him from her grip.

He gurgled, gasping for air as she squeezed. He tried to beg for his life, but the words were muted, unintelligible sounds.

Vero squeezed harder.

His face darkened, and his eyes bulged.

Then, the kicking lessened second by second, until the body went limp.

She tossed him over the railing to the bottom floor where he hit headfirst, snapping his neck at an awkward angle to add insult to injury.

I stared at the body for a second, watching the mist flow into it. Then I turned and faced Vero.

She changed into her human self again and glared at the dead man. "So strange," she said.

I nodded. "Yes. But extremely convenient," I said. "No bodies to hide." I took a breath and sighed. "You okay?"

She nodded, and winced. "Yeah. But getting shot really hurts."

I chuckled. "I know. All the more reason to be grateful for the armor. Best upgrade ever."

Vero smiled at me. "Thank you. For coming to find me. For everything."

I appreciated the sentiment, though guilt pummeled at my heart. "I feel like I didn't give you a choice in all this," I admitted. "And I should have. I should have asked you. Should have told you."

She shook her head and stepped close to me. I could still smell that sweet scent on her, mingling with a hint of sweat.

"This is our path," she said. "I wouldn't change anything."

I wrapped my arms around her waist and pulled her near.

"What's next for us?" she asked. "Off on another adventure?"

I nodded with a hint of resignation drawing across my face. "Yes. There are five more medallions to find. And the cardinal is still out there."

He was only one of several loose ends, and I kept wondering who the man in the lab coat was I'd seen in my vision, and how he played into all this. For now, I'd take this victory and savor it.

"Let's get out of here," I suggested. "I want to kiss you, but it's kind of a weird place for that sort of thing here. What with all the carnage and all."

She laughed and nodded. "My place is fine."

As we walked down the stairs, clasping each other's hands, I still had more questions than answers.

I wondered how the magical net the cardinal's men used on me had felt so heavy, then suddenly as light as paper.

"Oh, that," the voice in my head answered. "Simple, really. Unicorns are creatures of the purest emotion. It ripples through every fiber of their being, including their hair. Incredibly strong stuff, by the way. But that net reflects your emotions. When it was weighing you down, what were you feeling?"

Anger. Rage. A thirst for revenge.

"Those are not pure thoughts," he said. "They are the opposite of everything that makes up what a unicorn is."

So, those negative feelings make it heavier.

"Exactly."

We reached the bottom of the stairs and walked outside into the cool, evening air.

"Where to next?" Vero asked as we looked out through the valley.

I took a long breath and exhaled. "After your place?" I joked.

She grinned and squeezed my hand tighter.

"Tennessee. We need to find a clue that leads to the next medallion. And I have a few friends who might just be able to help."

THANK YOU

I just wanted to say thank you for reading this story. You chose to spend your time and money on something I created, and that means more to me than you may know. But I appreciate it, and am truly honored.

Be sure to swing by ernestdempsey.net to grab free stories, and dive deeper into the universe I've created for you.

I hope you enjoyed the story, and will stick with this series as it continues through the years. Know that I'll be working hard to keep bringing you exciting new stories to help you escape from the real world.

I'll see you in the next one.

Your friendly neighborhood author,

Ernest

OTHER BOOKS BY ERNEST DEMPSEY

Sean Wyatt Adventures:

The Secret of the Stones

The Cleric's Vault

The Last Chamber

The Grecian Manifesto

The Norse Directive

Game of Shadows

The Jerusalem Creed

The Samurai Cipher

The Cairo Vendetta

The Uluru Code

The Excalibur Key

The Denali Deception

The Sahara Legacy

The Fourth Prophecy

The Templar Curse

The Forbidden Temple

The Omega Project

The Napoleon Affair

The Second Sign

The Milestone Protocol

Where Horizons End

Poseidon's Fury

Adriana Villa Adventures:

War of Thieves Box Set

When Shadows Call

Shadows Rising

Shadow Hour

The Relic Runner - A Dak Harper Series:

The Relic Runner Origin Story

The Courier

Two Nights In Mumbai

Country Roads

Heavy Lies the Crown

Moscow Sky

The Adventure Guild (ALL AGES):

The Caesar Secret: Books 1-3

The Carolina Caper

Beta Force:

Operation Zulu

London Calling

Paranormal Archaeology Division:

Hell's Gate

Guardians of Earth:

Emergence: Gideon Wolf Book 1

Righteous Dawn: Gideon Wolf Book 2

Crimson Winter: Gideon Wolf Book 3

ACKNOWLEDGMENTS

As always, I would like to thank my terrific editors, Anne and Jason, for their hard work. What they do makes my stories so much better for readers all over the world. Anne Storer and Jason Whited are the best editorial team a writer could hope for and I appreciate everything they do.

I also want to thank Elena at Li Graphics for her tremendous work on my book covers and for always overdelivering. Elena definitely rocks.

A big thank you has to go out to my friend James Slater for his proofing work. James has added another layer of quality control to these stories, and I can't thank him enough.

Last but not least, I need to thank all my wonderful fans and especially the advance reader team. Their feedback and reviews are always so helpful and I can't say enough good things about all of them.

Made in the USA
Middletown, DE
27 April 2023

29541757R00172